THE BEAST IS AN ANIMAL

THE
BEAST
IS AN
ANIMAL

Peternelle van Arsdale

Margaret K. McElderry Books

New York London Toronto Sydney New Delhi

Photo credits:
When it's dark: copyright © Thinkstock/john north
You'd better lock the gate: copyright © Thinkstock/Gudella
Hear it scratch: copyright © Thinkstock/yuriz
It sucks your soul: copyright © Thinkstock/ehrlif
The beast is an animal: copyright © Thinkstock/swkunst

MARGARET K. McELDERRY BOOKS
An imprint of Simon & Schuster Children's Publishing Division
1230 Avenue of the Americas, New York, New York 10020
For information about special discounts for bulk purchases, please contact Simon & Schuster Special Sales at 1-866-506-1949 or business@simonandschuster.com.
The Simon & Schuster Speakers Bureau can bring authors to your live event. For more information or to book an event, contact the Simon & Schuster Speakers Bureau at 1-866-248-3049 or visit our website at www.simonspeakers.com.
Jacket design by Sonia Chaghatzbanian
Book design by Sonia Chaghatzbanian and Irene Metaxatos
The text for this book was set in Clois OldStyle.
Manufactured in the United States of America
First Edition
10 9 8 7 6 5 4 3 2 1
CIP data for this book is available from the Library of Congress.
ISBN 978-1-4814-8841-9 (hardcover)
ISBN 978-1-4814-8843-3 (eBook)

For Galen

The Beast is an animal
You'd better lock the Gate
Or when it's dark, It comes for you
Then it will be too late

The Beast is an animal
Hear It scratch upon your door
It sucks your soul then licks the bowl
And sniffs around for more

The Beast is an animal
It has a pointy chin
It eats you while you sleep at night
Leaves nothing but your skin

—Old Byd Nursery Rhyme

THIS IS
WHERE
THE
STORY
STARTS.

ay back in the beginning, there were two sisters. They were born minutes apart, each with a velvet coat of black hair on the top of her perfect head. The mother had labored for two full days, and it was a miracle she survived. At least hourly the midwife feared she'd lose the mother and the babies with her. But the girls were born with lusty cries, and the mother wept with relief. The midwife laid each girl in the crook of the mother's spent arms. When one of the girls rolled from the mother's grip, the midwife caught her not a second before she crashed to the floor. At the time, the midwife thought it was a stroke of luck. Before too many months had passed, she would wish she had let the evil thing drop.

But that was later. In the meantime, there were other reasons for feeling dismay at the new arrivals. Two healthy babies might seem like a blessing, but in this village of half-empty larders and dry fields, the birth of two girls was more a cause for condolence than for celebration. The villagers shook their heads and hoped that such ill fortune wasn't contagious.

The father was pitied. He must surely have been hoping for a son—another set of strong hands to plant and harvest. A farmer needed a capable boy to mend the fences, and to keep his goats and sheep from being preyed upon by wolves.

The mother was regarded as something worse than pitiable. It would have been better not to have any babies at all than to give birth to two girls. Some even said it was an act of spite on the mother's part. Only a truly disobedient woman would do such a thing.

The mother had always been the quiet sort, keeping to herself and her kitchen garden. The farm where she and her husband lived was the farthest from the center of town. No one passed by their door on the way to anywhere else. No one popped in for a chat. If you were to visit you'd have to do so on purpose. And no one ever did.

From the start, the mother noticed something interesting about her girls. But she said nothing about it, not even to her husband. The girls were identical matches—the same black hair, the same round, gray eyes. They even had the same birthmark, a vaguely star-shaped blotch on the back of one calf. But there was one difference between the twins. The two-minutes-older girl always reached for things with her left hand, and the two-minutes-younger girl with her right. The older had the birthmark on her left calf, and the younger on her right. The black hair on their heads curled in exactly the same way, but in opposite directions. The girls were mirror images of each other—identical, but not identical.

Such things might not worry a mother when times were prosperous, when crops were healthy and there was plenty to eat. But when rains refused to come and harsh winter was followed by parched summer, any little thing could become a cause for fear. And there was something just strange enough about her twin daughters to give the mother an uneasiness that fluttered in her chest.

The girls grew, and still the rains didn't come. Clouds would gather, and the town's hopes along with them, but not a drop would ever fall. As summer neared its end, and the prospect of another long, hungry winter settled in the villagers' minds, their dread turned into fear, which transformed into suspicion. What had changed, they asked themselves, since that short time ago before the drought, when they'd all had enough to eat?

A healthy, self-preserving instinct told the mother to keep her girls away from those narrowed eyes. And for a long time they were safe. But one day a neighbor came visiting with a basket of eggs she'd had trouble selling in town. The mother's chickens rarely laid enough, and her husband did love eggs, so she invited the woman into her kitchen to settle on a price.

The neighbor sat at the mother's table, looking around with curious eyes. She noted with a spark of envy the clean floors, the mother's white apron, and the little girls' chubby cheeks. The children were barely a year old but already walking and babbling nonsense. The neighbor watched while the older girl reached out with her left hand, and the younger girl reached out with her right. Then she noticed the funny star-shaped birthmarks on their smooth, round calves. A tickle of recognition started at the nape of the neighbor's neck and licked across her forehead. This was something different—very different indeed.

The neighbor didn't return home straightaway. Instead she went to the blacksmith, who was chatting over the fence with the innkeeper. The High Elder's wife passed not a few minutes later, and she couldn't help overhearing what they were discussing. Normally she wasn't much for gossip, but this was important news: One of her neighbors had discovered what was different in the village since last year. It was two mirror-image babies, both given a star-shaped birthmark by The Beast. The Evil One. The One Who Kept the Rain Away.

The father had only just returned from the fields for the day and sat down to supper with the mother when their meal was interrupted by a firm knock on the door. In truth, the mother and father had heard the dozen or so villagers approaching their farmhouse long before the knock. He had raised his eyebrows to his wife, and then looked through the front window, out into the summer twilight. There was a low murmur of voices through the crickets. The mother moved to the door but the father reached for her shoulder and held her back. Together they waited for the knock.

The mother and father heard the shuffling of feet on the path to their front step. Then one set of feet emerged from the others, followed by the rap of knuckles on wood. The father went to the door and listened to what the villagers had to say.

The villagers were quite reasonable. They didn't blame him, they said. The drought was obviously the work of a witch, and they were willing to believe that he was an innocent victim. After all, they knew it wouldn't have been his choice to have a daughter, much less two daughters, much less two daughters with the mark of The Beast. Clearly, they said, his wife was a witch, and those mirror twins were the witch's evil offspring from her unholy mating with It—The Beast. The father was given two choices: He could banish the witch and her children, or he could banish himself along with them. The villagers said they would come back at first light to hear the father's decision.

The father was momentarily relieved. The villagers hadn't even mentioned burning his wife and daughters, or crushing them to death, or drowning them. His next thought was a less happy calculation. If he and his wife and children were banished, they would all starve. No other village would take his family in, and the father would have no means to feed them all through the winter—not without his farm. It would be a slower death than burning, but more painful in its own way.

After the villagers left, the father told his wife that there was only one thing to do. She and the girls should leave. They should make for the fforest, which was said to be haunted by old, unholy things. The father didn't believe in such nonsense, but his neighbors did. Which meant that no angry villagers would dare follow his wife and girls. The father reassured the mother that in a few short days he would come find his family. Then he would build them a shelter, and he would visit them regularly after that, bringing them food and firewood until it was safe for his wife and children to come back home. With luck, he said to her, the rain would arrive long before the first frost. The villagers would realize their mistake, and all would be forgotten.

At dawn the next morning, the villagers watched as the father led his wife and daughters to the edge of the great wilderness. The mother's shoulders were bent, strapped down with as much food and clothing as she could carry, along with a sharp knife and an axe. She had to leave all her chickens behind, but she led one she-goat by a long rope. The father dared not kiss his wife or embrace his children. He turned his back when the mother and girls entered the fforest. A villager gasped and swore later that the mother, twins, and goat had vanished before her very eyes.

The fforest was very dark.

The mother spent those first few days and nights in a quiet state of panic. The girls were remarkably solemn and compliant for toddlers and seemed to sense that now wasn't the time for crying or pleading. The mother found a dry cave, and she built a fire, and she never closed her eyes while the sun was down. The girls slept through the howling of the wolves. The goat did not.

On the fifth day the father came, just when the mother had given up hope. He found them by the smoke of their fire. Weighed down with nails and supplies, he built them a drafty shack at the mouth of the cave. Then he told his wife that he had to return to the farm.

The mother kept the goat inside the little shack with her

and her daughters for fear the wolves might get to it otherwise. The goat gave them milk and kept the girls warm at night while their mother stared at the door waiting for her husband to come take them home.

At first the father came once a week. Then he came once a month. Each time he visited, the mother asked, "When can we come home?" But even after the first rains came and the drought was over, the father said it wasn't safe, that the villagers hadn't forgotten, that he'd heard of a witch being burned in the next village. When the mother said, "But I'm not a witch," the father nodded and looked away.

The girls had seen their fifth winter when their father stopped coming for good. They lived on sinewy game and goat's milk, and their mother muttered aloud that she feared what would happen to them if they couldn't feed the goat. She had a measuring look on her face when she said it. The girls held tight to the goat. They would starve sooner than eat their goat, they said.

The mother had long since stopped staring at the door waiting for her husband to come. For some time now when he did come it had been only to leave them supplies. He didn't touch his wife or look at the children. When he stopped coming altogether, the mother wondered if he were dead. But she thought not.

One cold morning, under a steel gray sky, the mother closed the goat up in the shack and led her daughters wordlessly through the fforest. None of them had walked this way in years, but they knew the path by heart. It was late afternoon, the sky already darkening, when they arrived at the back door of the farm that had been their home. The mother knocked, and a stout, ruddy-faced woman answered the door and sucked in her breath. Then the father came to the door. Surprise, then shame registered on his face. He placed his hand on the ruddy woman's shoulder. This told the mother all she had suspected. She was no longer a wife, and her husband was no longer her husband.

The girls had grown wild over the years, and they felt nothing more than curiosity as they stood in the warm, fire-lit doorway of their father's home. Then a scent of stewing meat met their noses and their mouths watered. The memory of that smell followed them all the way back to their cold shack, and food never tasted the same to them again. The warm goat's milk, the trout they caught in a cold silver stream, the stringy rabbit they cooked over the fire until it was crusty black in some spots and blood red in others—none of it filled their bellies. A gnawing, unsatisfied sensation curled and slithered in their stomachs even when they were full, even once the memory of that stew faded and they could no longer conjure the scent of food cooked in a real kitchen.

As the girls grew tall and strong and restless, their mother diminished. Each year they spent in the fforest bent her shoulders and clouded her eyes. While the girls skittered across mountainsides, climbed trees, and caught fish in their bare hands, their mother sat in the dark, damp shack. Then she started to cough. Then she no longer sat, but lay on her side. Her breath rattled in her throat, and her skin thinned to transparency.

Over the years the girls had less and less to do with their mother and more to do with each other and the fforest, but still it came as a shock to them when they returned to the shack one evening to find their mother dead. The goat lay beside her, and looked up when the girls entered, their black hair brown with mud. The girls looked at each other uncertainly, and some vague memory of civilization told them they needed to bury their mother. Long into the night, they dug a hole deep. The wolves howled and the sisters heard the rustling of leaves. The older sister hissed between her teeth and they both heard the rumble of a low growl in response. But the wolves came no closer.

The girls lived on alone. The goat curled up next to them at night as always, and sometimes when it nudged their faces in the morning, it brought back memories of their mother, and how she'd stroked their hair and kissed them. The vague dissatisfaction in their bellies soured into bitterness.

One day the girls found themselves walking toward the village. They were past needing to speak to each other. When the older sister set foot in the direction of their father's farm, the younger sister followed without question. They waited until dark, until long after their father had made his final check on the animals, and was fast asleep beside his wife in their warm house. Then the girls crept in and opened the barn doors wide and unlocked the chicken coop. They let the wolves do the rest. Soon there was nothing left of their father's livestock, just feathers and bones.

But that wasn't enough to satisfy the girls' bitterness. So

they turned to the other villagers' farms, and in one night of creeping and crawling, they unlatched all of their barn doors, and opened all of their coops. Then the girls perched themselves in the trees and listened to the feasting of the wolves.

When the village grew quiet again, the girls withdrew to their fforest home. In the hours before dawn, they lay wakeful, eyes unwilling to close. Something happened in the girls in those hours. It was an opening up of one thing, and a closing of another.

The next morning, the girls smelled a whiff of fear in the air. It filled their bellies and made them feel warm in a way they couldn't remember since some dim, fairy-tale time when they'd been toddlers who slept in beds. They decided it was time to visit their father.

The sun was just about to dip below the horizon when they moved through their father's fields looking for him. Dirt and leaves had become as much a part of them as their own skin and hair, and they were near enough to touch their father before his eyes widened in alarm, and he saw them standing there, two women made of earth. At the moment he gasped, open-mouthed, the older sister breathed in his terror, and the hair on her arms lifted with the pleasure of it. The father's hands scrabbled across his chest as if urgently looking for something he'd lost, and then he fell backward, dead, into his own field.

The younger sister touched her right hand to her sister's face. The older sister's eyes had gone black for just a moment. Then they paled to gray again.

The older sister reached for the younger sister's hand and

together they went to see the ruddy-faced woman. The younger sister knocked, and the ruddy-faced woman answered the door. Her fear gave off a sharp odor, like spoiled milk. The younger sister saw the woman's simple mind and her meager soul spread out before her as if on a table, just inviting her to eat it up. So the younger sister did. She inhaled the woman's fearful soul like it was a warm supper. The woman did as her husband had—her hands clutched her chest as if something precious had been yanked from it, and then she fell dead onto her kitchen floor. The girl glanced down at the ruddy-faced woman's body, and she felt a barely satisfied hunger. The sisters returned home and their hunger grew.

The next day, the sisters waited until night fell thick and black, and then they returned.

As they neared the village, the girls were surprised to find another girl—a child, really—standing in a field of darkness as if she were waiting for them. This girl wasn't like their father or the ruddy-faced woman. There was no fear in this child when she looked upon the sisters. She looked at them only with interest. Curiosity. The girl aroused a memory in the sisters, a memory of being a child in this village once. And so the sisters decided to leave this child unclaimed—to leave all the children. It was the frightened adults—the ones who accused, the ones who banished, anyone older than the sisters were themselves— that the sisters would seek out. They were the ones whose fear the sisters could smell like smoke in the air. In a way, the sisters would ease their fear. They would take it all away.

The sisters continued on, visiting every home in the village.

Leaving the children sleeping in their beds, and the adults dead and hollowed out in their own. And so the sisters stole what should not have been stolen, and left only a hole, an absence, in the place of what had been ripped away. It was a dark little hole at first, one that would spread in the coming years. Soul by soul it would grow. But the sisters knew nothing of this.

Finally, they were satisfied. The moon sank low in the sky, the stars dimmed, and they walked home to their shack in the wilderness through silver leaves, their feet grazing the fforest floor as if they were being held just aloft.

As they neared the shack, the sisters smelled blood, and pain and fear as well, but this wasn't pleasant to their noses and their footsteps quickened. The door to the shack was agape. Perhaps the old goat had nudged it open in the night. The goat's blood pooled thickly just in the spot where she had often lain on sunny days. The wolves had dragged the rest of her away.

The older sister felt nothing. The younger sister had the glimmer of a memory of something called sadness, but it floated just out of her reach. They were girls no longer, nor were they women. They had become something else. They found that they had little need of food and water anymore. There were so many frightened, uncertain souls in the world just waiting to be eaten up. And all the girls had to do was breathe them in.

Their names were Angelica and Benedicta. And they were the soul eaters.

PART

1

*When
it's
dark*

ONE

Nights were long for Alys.
And they were always the same. Her mother washed her and dropped her flannel nightshift over her head. She tucked Alys between linen sheets and under wool blankets that felt heavy on Alys's restless limbs. Then came Alys's night-long entrapment by darkness and quiet and the absence of sleep.

Alys looked longingly after Mam as she left the room. Mam turned back once and smiled at Alys, then closed the door behind her, snuffing the glow of light from the warm kitchen. Alys imagined her father sitting out there, pipe in mouth, toes near the fire. Then she lay in bed listening to the sounds of the house fall around her—the low murmur of her parents, the clattering of a dish, the footsteps on wood floors.

Then silence.

She could hear them breathing. Mam's soft sighs, Dad's snores, a moan.

Alys was seven now, and she'd been this way for as long as she could remember. She dreaded the night.

If only she were allowed to get out of bed. It was the knowing that she couldn't get out, that was what made sleeping so impossible for her. Told to lie still and sleep, Alys felt the strongest urge to do exactly otherwise. Her eyes instead flew open and stayed that way. She had no siblings so she couldn't know this for sure, but she'd been told that she was an odd child this way, that most children knew to give in to sleep when the time came. Alys could not do this.

Alys decided that this night would be different. This night, when the sighs and the snoring rose in the air, she would declare an end to her nights of entrapment. She would make the night her own.

She waited long after silence fell, just to be sure. Then she dropped her feet to the cold wood floor. It was end of summer, near harvest, and although the days were still warm, already she sniffed autumn in the air. She found her woolen stockings and boots, a wool overdress. She was not a child who needed to be told what to wear. Mam always told Alys that she was sensible that way.

Alys wasn't being sensible now. This wasn't the wisest night for her to wander. She knew this, and yet she couldn't stop herself. She'd made a plan, and after so much waiting, after such a long imprisonment, she refused to wait another night. She couldn't wait. She wouldn't. Not even after what had happened last night with the farmer and his wife, nor the night before that, when the wolves came and ate up all the chickens, and goats, and horses in the entire village of Gwenith. Alys was sad about Mam's chickens. They were so sweet and warm in her lap, and they laid such nice eggs.

Alys had heard her parents talk about the farmer and his wife, the ones who were dead. They lived way out on the edge of the village, nearly to the fforest. Mam had said the only reason they were found at all is that someone thought the farmer might know what had happened to all the animals. Mam said that surely all that bloodshed was the work of a witch, and that was where the other witch and her twin girls had lived. And then Dad said that just because you had married one witch, didn't mean you had married another. Mam disagreed, and said she supposed it did mean that very thing, because then why else was the farmer dead? And weren't Mam's own dead chickens proof they were all being punished for that man's sins and whatever he and his wife had been getting up to out there where no one could see them? Then Dad had given Mam a look, and Mam realized that Alys was listening, and well . . . that was the end of that.

Alys should have been afraid of the wolves and the idea of a witch being married to a farmer, but she wasn't. Alys, in fact, had never been afraid. Her favorite nursery rhymes were the scary ones. The ones about The Beast sucking out your soul and leaving behind nothing but gristle and skin. Those were the ones Alys liked best. When her friend Gaenor squealed and shut her eyes and clapped her hands over her ears, Alys just laughed and kept singing. Sometimes she'd promise Gaenor she'd stop, and just at the moment Gaenor trusted Alys enough to drop her hands from her ears and open her eyes again, Alys would continue:

> The Beast, It will peek in on you
> When you're fast asleep
> Open up
> Invite It in
> And oh your Mam will weep

Alys stepped out of her room, listened again for Mam and Dad's breathing. Then she was through the kitchen and out the kitchen door before she could think twice or change her mind.

The air was chill and moist and open around her. And the sky, oh the sky. It was awash in stars.

Alys looked up at the sky, felt lifted up by it. She turned to see how it might look different, to catch parts of it that she couldn't bend her head back far enough to see. It was lovely to be so free, everyone in the village asleep, and Alys not even trying to sleep. If she could spend every night this way, Alys thought to herself, she'd have no reason to dread it anymore.

Standing in Mam and Dad's kitchen yard, Alys began to feel hemmed in again. She could sense the house rising up behind her, the coop and the barn on either side of her. And she knew that through the darkness rose their neighbors' houses. What Alys wanted was a fallow field—a stretch of tall grass that she could feel spreading out all around her as far as her eye could see through the dark. And Alys knew where just such a field lay. She only had to get herself to the road, follow it out of the village, and there it was, big and wide and bordered only by fforest that was even bigger and wider than the field.

Her legs carried her through the dark. She held her arms out to either side, felt the night air float over and around her. She was alone but not lonely.

Then the field. In she walked, feeling the long grass brush her skirts, scratch and tickle even through her stockings. No longer could she feel any kind of structure around her. When she reached the center of the field, she looked up again at the stars. The sky was an endless bowl tipped over, the stars pouring down on her like grains of light. She opened her eyes wide to take them in.

She felt them before she saw them—the women.

It wasn't that they made a sound. It was more the way they didn't make a sound that attracted Alys's notice, the sense of a presence without bodies attached. But they did have bodies, she saw. These women. These women made of mud and leaves. They floated through the grass and they saw Alys with their wide gray eyes that glowed even in the night, as if they were lit from within.

And still Alys wasn't afraid. Curious, yes. Alys had never seen women like these before. They weren't village women—at least not from any village that Alys had ever heard of. They didn't even look like travelers. Travelers were odd-looking sorts, but these women were odder. They looked, it occurred to Alys, more like trees than women.

And then they were near her, next to her, standing either side of her and each resting a hand of mud and clay on her shoulders. They were slim, and although they were much taller than she, Alys realized that they weren't women at all. They were still girls. Older than Alys, but maybe not so much older. Not mothers, certainly.

"What is your name?" Only one of the girls said it, and yet it seemed like both of them did. Alys felt a kind of energy pass through her shoulders, a shivery thread connecting their hands.

"I'm Alys."

"Alys, go to sleep," the other said.

When the other said it, Alys felt an instant tug in her eyes, like a curtain being pulled. But no, Alys thought, that wasn't what she wanted. She sent the curtain flying up again, opened her eyes wider. "But I don't want to sleep," Alys said.

"There is no fear in this one, Benedicta." The girl sniffed the air around Alys. She had been sniffed by Gaenor's dog just like that.

"No, there is no fear, Angelica."

Benedicta. Angelica. Alys had never heard those names before. She thought they were beautiful. And there was something beautiful about these owl-eyed girls, their long dark hair tangled with branches and leaves.

Then they left her. Just as quickly as they came, the girls floated on. Out of the field and into the dark, disappearing at a point off in the distance that told Alys nothing about where they were going.

TWO

Alys woke up in the grassy field, her hair and clothes damp with dew. The sky was a bright, clear blue overhead. She often dozed in the early morning. It was when her parents rose, the sky just barely more blue than black, that Alys found she could easily fall to sleep, knowing that the world was waking up around her. But she'd never slept this late before, and she sat up with a start, knowing that her parents must have been looking for her.

She got to her feet and ran to the road. It hadn't seemed nearly so far when she walked it the night before, but now home was far, very far. Her breathing was heavy and hurtful in her chest. Her own heart and breath were all she could hear, and then it struck her how strange that was. The village was always a bustle at this time. There should have been the sounds of wagons and iron pounding iron, women calling to children, men calling to each other. But there was none of that. There wasn't even the call of birds. This was a silence fuller and bigger than anything that had fallen around Alys during her long nights awake.

She stopped running, couldn't run any farther, and then she did hear something—wagon wheels behind her, headed toward Gwenith from somewhere beyond. She turned and saw a traveler's caravan coming toward her. A covered wagon driven by a man and pulled by two gray horses.

The man wore a wide-brimmed hat tugged low on his forehead, and his long red hair lifted over his shoulders like flapping wings. At the sight of her, he pulled up on the reins and came to a stop.

"Hey there, little one," he said. "You're far from home."

"Ay," Alys said. "But I'm going there now."

"Well no sense running anymore. Climb in and I'll take you there. You just point me the way."

Alys walked up to the wagon, looked up at the man. His eyes were dark green like moss and his hair was red but his beard was shot through with threads of white. He smiled at her. It was a kind face. A face she liked looking at. "Ay, all right," Alys said.

He held a hand out for her and she settled herself on the seat next to him. "I'm Alys," she said.

The man tipped his hat. "And I'm Pawl, fair Alys."

She smiled then. He was a nice man. And she liked being called fair. It was like something out of a story. "My house is just up that way, the third on the left, past the blacksmith. Mam and Dad are going to be awful upset with me so I'd like to get there fast if you don't mind."

Pawl nodded and winked as if they held a secret between them.

As they drew closer to the village, Alys grew uneasier. She wasn't sure which she found more frightful—the prospect of her parents' anger, or the strange spell of quiet that seemed to have fallen over the village.

"It's awful odd, ain't it," Pawl said. "How quiet it is."

"Ay," Alys said. "Maybe it's because of all the animals being dead and all."

Pawl raised two red eyebrows in the air. "What's that about dead animals?"

"Ay, the wolves came and ate them all."

Pawl whistled. "Well now. No wonder it's so quiet then." He shook his head. "I never heard of such a thing. Weren't the barn doors closed? And the coops?"

"Ay, they were," Alys said.

"Well then how would the wolves have gotten into them, do you suppose?"

"High Elder said it was the work of The Beast," Alys said.

Pawl looked at her thoughtfully. "I never did meet a wolf who took orders, did you?"

Alys shook her head. "I never met any wolves at all."

"No? Well I'll tell you something. I never met a wolf could open a barn door." Then Pawl clucked his tongue. "Oh, my Beti is not going to be happy with me." He looked at Alys. "Beti's my wife."

"Why's she going to be mad at you?"

"No livestock in Gwenith means a bunch of unhappy people who aren't going to be so interested in trading with me. I'm a traveler, fair lass, and so I need to trade with your people. That's how I make my living. And if I go back to where I come from in the Lakes empty-handed . . . well, like I said, my Beti will have a few words to say about that."

"Oh," Alys said. None of this meant very much to her. She knew the Lakes were far away, and that the travelers were strange folks who came from there. They dressed funny and didn't comb their hair and she'd heard some other things said about them, the kinds of things adults spoke low under their breath when they thought you weren't listening. Things Alys didn't really understand. Right now, Alys just wanted to get home. She needed to pee something awful, and the more afraid she grew of what Mam and Dad would say to her, the more she feared she might lose her water right there in the wagon.

"It's there," Alys said. "Right there."

Pawl drew up in front, but suddenly Alys didn't want to get out of the wagon. Something told her she shouldn't go inside. A fierce intuition deep in her belly kept her attached good and tight to the wagon seat.

"Did you want me to go in with you, child? Maybe ease the way with your folks?"

"Ay," Alys said. "Maybe." But that wasn't what Alys wanted. Alys wanted to stop everything right here and not go in there at all. Then Pawl was out of the wagon and lifting her down, and then Pawl was knocking on her parents' front door.

And there was no answer.

He knocked again, this time harder. Harder than you'd ever knock if you thought someone was home and they might hear you. And still there was no answer.

"Why don't we just go in," he said. He pressed the latch and then they were inside. The house was so quiet. And cold. Alys shivered. The kitchen was empty, no fire in the hearth. The sunlight coming through the windows was bright and strange. Nothing here was right. Alys sensed that Pawl was as unnerved as she. He looked at her with an odd sort of smile and said, "Well lass, why don't you wait right here while I go see."

"See what?" Alys said.

Pawl opened his mouth, then closed it. Then opened it again. "See what's what."

Alys sat in her chair at the kitchen table to wait for him. She stared down at the wood, at the ghostly rings of tea mugs and long knife grooves.

She heard Pawl's steps, slow and steady. She heard a door open, more steps and a pause, and then a single note hung in the air—half cry, half intake of breath. She rose to her feet and followed the sound.

Pawl stood by her parents' bed, and Alys could see Mam and Dad both lying there, still as anything. And Alys knew they were dead. She knew they were dead the same way she'd known Gaenor's old dog was dead when they'd found him under the back porch. There was just something about dead that was different from alive.

Alys made no noise but Pawl jerked his head toward her anyway. "Oh no, child. No, no. You mustn't."

Alys ran past him to Mam's side, and picked up Mam's cold hand. But it wasn't Mam's hand anymore, and that wasn't Mam. Mam was gone and what was left was a body from which everything important had been taken. There was just a shell and nothingness, and the song in Alys's head came fast and loud and she swore she'd never sing it again.

The Beast is an animal
It has a pointy chin
It eats you while you sleep at night
Leaves nothing but your skin

THREE

Pawl tried to convince Alys to stay in the wagon while he went in search of help, but Alys refused. She held fast to his hand, and once she did so he held fast to hers as well. And they stayed that way.

Pawl pounded on the first door they came to. He pounded and pounded again, and Alys didn't know what to feel in herself, but she felt panic rising in him. Inside Alys only felt cold, and she shook with it. Her teeth clattered.

Then they heard the shuffling of feet on the other side of the door and Alys felt Pawl's relief right through the skin of his hand.

Enid opened the door. She was fifteen, almost a grown-up to Alys. Her hair was undone and she wore her nightclothes, and she rubbed her eyes like a child. "I'm sorry," she said. Then she looked confused as if she weren't sure what she was sorry for, but sensed the awkwardness of the situation.

"Your parents," Pawl said. "Where are they?"

"They're . . ." Enid trailed off and looked behind her, then looked back to Alys and Pawl.

"Child," Pawl said, his voice too loud, "is there something wrong? Are you all quite well in this house?"

Enid looked so strange and Alys couldn't at first think why. Then it struck her. Enid's eyes were her prettiest feature, a watery blue like dawn sky. But this morning they were swallowed by black, the blue of her irises just the thinnest border around bottomless pupils. Enid stared at Pawl, saying nothing, until Pawl moved past her, tugging Alys behind him.

Once in the kitchen he stopped and turned to Alys. "Child, you must listen to me this time. Stay here. Let me go see."

Alys didn't argue, had no desire to. She looked back at Enid, who stood in her own kitchen and yet seemed as if she didn't know where she was. Then Alys thought of Enid's sisters and brother. She looked up at the ceiling of the kitchen as if she might see them through it.

She walked over to Enid, held both of her chilled hands in her own. Enid was such a big girl, and Alys was such a little girl. And Alys could no longer bear to be the only person other than Pawl who was awake in this village. So she did the only thing she could think to do. She went searching for the jug of water that you could find in every kitchen, and she tossed it over Enid.

The girl squealed and shook, and when Alys looked at her

again her eyes were blue and not black and suddenly Alys felt less alone.

Once Enid had wiped her eyes, she looked back at Alys as if she hadn't seen her before. "My parents," she said. "Where are they?"

Enid's parents were dead, same as Alys's. And on and on it went, from house to house and all the same. No longer did Pawl bother knocking, he just walked through front doors and found them all. Children fifteen and younger all alive and sleeping deep. Parents, older siblings, aunts, uncles, grandmothers, grandfathers . . . dead. Emptied out. In one night, Gwenith had become a town of orphans and hollow shells.

Enid left her sisters and brother sleeping and told Pawl that they must wake Madog. He was fifteen also and her intended. Once he was awakened, Madog left his own two sisters sleeping, and followed Pawl, Alys, and Enid to Alys's kitchen. Pawl was quiet and so were they. Enid and Madog held hands, hard and frightened, the same way that Alys held Pawl's.

Alys finally knew real fear. She hadn't thought she could be more frightened than when she'd seen Mam and Dad lying in their bed cold and gone. But she had grown more frightened as the morning wore on and the sun straight overhead made everything stark and bright. It was a comfort at first to have Enid awake, and then Madog, but now it disturbed her all the more how terrified they were. And Pawl, too.

After Pawl sat them all down in Alys's kitchen, he paced the room. He stomped across, stopped, looked up at the ceiling.

Stomped back, shook his head. Finally he looked at them. "There's only one thing for it. You must take care of each other while I go for help."

"Help?" Madog said. "Nearest help is Defaid, and that's two days away." Before today, Madog had looked like such a man to Alys, his chin already bristled with golden beard, and his arms and back were strong from farming. But he had a child's eyes now. Round.

"Ay, I know," Pawl said. "But I've got just the one wagon and I can't drag you lot of children on foot all the way there. I'd lose half of you. There must be fifty of you in this town, ay?"

Madog didn't answer, only nodded.

"But what about the babies?" Enid said. "How will we take care of all of them? We've at least ten children under the age of two in town. And that's not counting the little ones three, four, and five who'll be running wild and scared without their parents."

Pawl scratched his red and white beard. "Ay, you've a point." Then he brightened. "Don't wake them."

"Don't wake them?" Enid said. "But what if they wake on their own? And what if their first words are to ask where their mams and dads are? Or what if they're crying for their milk and I have none?"

"Child, I have none of the answers you're looking for, but I will tell you this. You kids have been bewitched. I don't think those babes are going to be waking up on their own. You just leave them be and hope for the best. This whole town"—he waved his hand in a circle in the air—"has had something evil happen to it. And the faster I can get you all out of here, the safer you'll be. And the fastest way I can see to do that is me riding alone to Defaid and bringing back as many riders as I can for this lot of sleeping children."

Madog spoke up then. "What about the . . . the bodies." He said it flatly, as if trying to pull away from his own words and what they meant.

"Close the doors and leave them be," Pawl said. "And hope the weather stays cool." Then he found something to stare at on the floor.

Alys looked back and forth between round-eyed Madog and white-faced Enid.

Then she looked up at Pawl and made a quick calculation. "I'm going with you."

FOUR

Pawl tried to talk her into staying with Enid and Madog, but Alys clung to him tightly, and she knew he didn't have the heart to peel her away. So he told her to pack her clothes and be quick about it.

It was early afternoon by the time they were off, and Pawl said he'd only stop to rest the horses as much as he had to, that they wouldn't be lingering any longer than necessary. He said this while he looked into the deep fforest on either side of the road. Alys followed his eyes between and among the trees. She pulled herself tighter into Mam's coat, which she'd grabbed from a hook in the kitchen at the very last moment. It smelled a bit like Mam, and a bit like breakfast.

After a few hours he stopped to water the horses in a stream near the road. He dug into a sack and handed Alys some dried meat, cheese, and an apple. She sat on a rock and he sat on a stump, but soon he was up again, looking at her, looking into the fforest, looking back at her.

He was frightened. Alys had forgotten about her own fear once they'd left the dead village behind them. It had been replaced with a heavy sort of something in her chest, like a rock she had to carry that was so dense it made her slow. But Pawl's fear pricked her own, and she felt a tickle along her spine like the light stroke of a fingernail.

Alys finished eating and rose from the rock and Pawl was already at the wagon waiting to lift her up. Then they were off again, and as the sun dimmed toward late afternoon, Pawl's constant scanning, left and right and left again, gave him the look of a nervous bird. As if sensing how she looked at him, Pawl shook himself and smiled. "Nothing to fear, fair Alys. We'll have you to Defaid soon enough, and safe and sound we'll be."

Alys was old enough to know when an adult was trying to convince her of something he didn't quite believe himself. "What's out there in the fforest," she said, "that you keep looking for?"

Pawl regarded her, then lifted his eyes skyward, as if seeking help from a passing crow. Then he laughed, but without much mirth to it. "What do you think I'm looking for, child?" There was no sharpness to his question, just soft surrender. "I've never had a child of my own and like as not you're too young to be telling this to, but your parents are dead and what I'm looking for out in those woods is what killed them. And I think you know that, Alys, because you're a watchful little thing, always taking things in. You'll do just fine in Defaid if you hold onto that and don't let go. Just keep your eyes open and your mouth mostly shut, child. And no more talk of what's in the fforest. That's my best advice to you." He nodded at her, then looked back at the horses and the road in front of them, as if all had been settled.

"What's in the fforest?"

Pawl rolled his eyes up again. "And didn't I just get done telling you, child, how there's no good to come from talking about that?"

"Ay, but we're not in Defaid yet."

Pawl laughed in a short, shocked burst. "You are a cunning lass if ever I met one." Then his face grew serious again. "Well I suppose I'd want to know myself if it were my parents." He glanced at her as if measuring her for a new set of clothes. "Now mind you I don't know for sure, because I've only heard tell. Stories, really, that's all I've heard. But what I think done that to your parents and all the others . . . well, I think what done it to them is soul eaters."

Alys felt something clench inside of her when he spoke the last two words. *Soul eaters.* Because isn't that how her parents had looked, as if their very souls had been eaten out of them? As if all that was left was all that you didn't need? "What are they?" she said.

Pawl shook his head. "There are so many stories. Stories older than me. The kind of stories you tell to keep young ones tucked in bed at night. My own mam and dad told them to me, and I expect their mams and dads did the same. Some say the soul eaters are demons. That The Beast made them out of mud and evil intent. That they snatch people's souls and then bring them back to The Beast to suffer for all eternity."

Alys thought of her dear mam and dad and the hollow shells that were left of them. She thought about all the good parts of them gone off somewhere terrible. Somewhere frightening and painful. She shivered in Mam's coat. She wondered if Mam was cold without it. Were spirits cold? "You think that's what happened to my parents? That soul eaters took them to The Beast?"

Pawl jerked his head back toward her, opened his mouth and crunched up his face in a wince. "No, no, child. No such of a thing. Your parents are dead. Their suffering is over. I don't believe in that nonsense. No more than I believe wolves opened up your barn doors."

"Well, what do you believe?"

"Child, I believe in the ground under my feet and the sky over my head and that I get hungry before suppertime and sleepy before bed. All else are tales and nothing more."

Alys narrowed her eyes at Pawl. She'd never met an adult who claimed to know so little about so much. "But you believe in soul eaters. You said so."

Pawl paused, pondered his next words. "I'll tell you the truth, Alys. Before today I doubted. But what happened to all those poor folks back in your village . . . well. That's not natural. It weren't illness nor wolves nor cold nor hunger that took them away in their beds."

For the first time since the night before, the memory of the girls that looked like trees came to Alys. She didn't know how she could have forgotten them, and yet she had. She thought of what Pawl had said, that the soul eaters were demons made of mud and evil. She thought of the girls. Their mud-caked skin. Their leafy hair. And she wondered if she, like all the sleeping children back in Gwenith, had been bewitched somehow. "I think I saw them last night," she said to Pawl. "The soul eaters." Then Alys told Pawl about the girls, and what they'd said to her, and their beautiful names. *Angelica. Benedicta.*

Pawl's mouth dropped open as she talked, and then he pulled up on the reins so suddenly that Alys nearly fell to the floor of the wagon. He grasped her by the shoulders. "You must never, never tell anyone that story. You must promise me this, Alys. No one in Defaid must ever hear it. Do you understand me?"

He looked so angry with her that Alys thought she might finally cry. She hadn't cried yet, and as young as she was she knew that must be odd. Enid had cried. Even Madog had wiped tears from his eyes. But Alys hadn't, not once. Now she thought she could, though. Because Mam and Dad were dead and she was with this strange man going to a strange town and he was suddenly mad at her for seeing something. And maybe this meant that Mam and Dad being dead was somehow her fault. Should she have known those women were bad? Should she have screamed? "I'm sorry" was all that Alys could say now. And then she burst into tears. She sobbed until her stomach hurt just as much as her heart.

All the while she cried, Pawl held her to him, pulling her head to his chest and petting her hair, making soft shushing noises. Finally she quieted. "It's I who should be sorry," he said. "I'm not mad at you, child, and you've nothing to be sorry for. A terrible thing has happened to you, and I'm going to see that you're taken care of. And in all of Byd, I don't think there's a better place for you than Defaid. At least you'll have Enid and Madog and others that are familiar to you there. And them Defaiders. Well, they'll be decent to you. But the thing you need to know about a Defaider is that they don't like what's different, and they don't like what they don't understand. And if they think . . . well, how do I put this? If they think you had some sort of contact with the soul eaters, they might turn it around on you somehow. See a taint on you. And I don't want that to happen to you, child. So you must trust me, and keep your story between us. I'll take it to my grave and you do the same. Agreed?"

Alys nodded into his chest. She was only seven, but she knew what Pawl meant by a taint. She remembered well enough the High Elder's sermons about The Beast and how It found those given to temptation, and how It led them astray. And once you had the mark of The Beast on you, there was no erasing it. You were claimed. She wondered what the mark of The Beast looked like.

Pawl let her go, and Alys immediately missed his arms around her. She straightened up on the seat next to him, and they rode quietly on.

They rode all night. Pawl urged Alys to sleep in the caravan but she refused, insisted she could stay awake with him. Yet sleep she did, and when she woke up she was curled at his feet like a dog, and the sky was pink and dawning.

Pawl told Alys that he would take her to the High Elder of Defaid, tell him all that had happened, and then the High Elder would surely send riders and wagons out for the rest of the children. As they passed through the outlying farms of Defaid, Alys noticed their neatness and their sameness. Their whitewashes and stone fences. This was the farthest she'd ever been from home, but she found it looked no different. The only difference was that these folks still had their animals. And the children had parents. And there was noise, so much sound compared to the sudden silence of Gwenith.

The houses were close together now, which meant they were in the main part of the village, where the tradespeople and craftsmen had their homes and shops. There was a school-house, bigger than the one in Gwenith, and a large whitewashed meetinghouse with broad double doors. Alys took these things in, but what she mostly noticed were all the eyes on her. Every villager seemed to follow her and Pawl with their gaze—man or woman or child, they all stared, unsmiling. Alys felt sick. The sour remains of her last meal rose in the back of her throat.

She tugged on Pawl's sleeve as he stopped in front of the meetinghouse. "Maybe," she said, her voice dry and whispery in her mouth, "I could go with you to the Lakes?"

But Pawl didn't hear her. He was already down from the wagon and tying up the horses. And Alys couldn't bear to repeat the question for fear he'd say no. He reached up to her and lifted her down, and Alys felt unsteady on her feet, unused to solid ground after so long swaying with the wagon.

Alys became even more conscious of eyes all around them, and then men gathering, big men in black robes with white collars and hats. They were Elders, just like the Elders back in Gwenith, only somehow bigger and blacker and whiter. And then Pawl was telling them what had happened and voices were raised and she and Pawl were swept through the doors of the meetinghouse. Then a woman came in wearing a black dress and a starched white apron and she took Alys by the hand and drew her away from Pawl. Alys reached out for him, but he smiled at her, and said, "Go with Mistress Ffagan, child, and I'll come find you later."

So Alys did. She went with the strange woman who held her by the hand and took her to another strange woman who lived on the far side of town, in a stone house that bordered a wide field and had the biggest tree that Alys had ever seen behind it.

Alys was seated at the strange woman's kitchen table and given a glass of milk, and bread with butter and honey. The sight of it made Alys sick again, but she tried to sip and eat, because Mam had always told her to eat what she was given.

While Alys chewed and swallowed, the women went through a doorway into a small adjoining room, and there they whispered and looked back at Alys every so often. Then they came out again.

Mistress Ffagan had a round face dotted with two round brown eyes, a snub nose, and a mouth that seemed too small. Alys did not like her. The other woman, the woman who lived there, was thin and sharp-nosed with dark brown hair pulled flat against her head. She had no soft parts, not like Mam.

"I'm Mistress Argyll," the sharp-nosed woman said to her. "And this is where you'll be living from now on." She looked Alys over, as if she were expecting to find something that wasn't there. "Have you brought no clothes with you?"

"Ay, I have," she said. "They're with Pawl."

Mistress Argyll looked at Mistress Ffagan. "The traveler who brought her here," Mistress Ffagan said. "That's who she means." Then Mistress Ffagan looked at Alys. "He'll bring them here before he leaves. I'll go see to that now."

Alys followed Mistress Ffagan with her eyes, and thought about correcting her mistake. Alys might have informed her that in fact Alys was not staying here, that she was going with Pawl to the Lakes. But there was no point in that, Alys knew. She could see that Mistress Ffagan was not a woman who would let a child tell her what she wanted. So instead Alys waited for Pawl to come for her.

Mistress Argyll sat down across from Alys. "Your color's good," she said.

"My color?"

"Your skin, child. You don't look sick. That's why you were brought to me, especially. I'm a healer, a midwife. You have them in Gwenith, don't you?"

Alys nodded. "I'm not sick."

"I know you're not, I can see that well enough." The woman looked off to the side, and Alys sensed she didn't like looking at Alys straight on. "You should eat then. Since you're not sick."

"I'm sorry," Alys said. "I don't much feel like eating."

"No," Mistress Argyll said, glancing back at Alys. This time her eyes made it all the way to Alys's face. "I expect not." Alys felt relief the moment the woman turned away from her again.

The kitchen was quiet while Alys sat there with Mistress Argyll, but the sounds of the village of Defaid rose all around them outside. Through all the other noises, Alys made out the tread and roll of Pawl's wagon wheels. She stood up from the table, pushed back her chair. "Thank you for the food, Mistress Argyll." Then she turned and left through the front door.

Pawl came to a stop and hopped down. He reached into the wagon and dropped Alys's bags at her feet. He lifted his hat and tipped it at Mistress Argyll, who had walked up behind Alys. "May I bring these inside for you, Mistress?"

"No need," she said. "My husband will do it. He's in the wood shop now, but when he comes home he'll see to them."

Pawl dropped his hat back on his head, smiled, and reached for the bags anyway. "Oh but it's no trouble, let me just do this one thing for you and the lass."

"No need," Mistress Argyll said, and with a tone that caused Pawl to drop the bags again.

Alys walked up to Pawl then, tugged on his sleeve, pulling him down so she could talk into his ear. She felt his red hair brush her cheeks, and her lips touched his red and white beard, which was so much softer than she'd thought it would be. "Take me with you to the Lakes, Pawl. Please." Alys said it louder this time, making sure that he heard her, and the strength it took her to say the words stung her eyes and she realized she was crying again.

"Oh child," Pawl said, and he stood back up, dropped a gentle hand on her shoulder. He looked around him then, and Alys did too, and she wondered why he didn't pick her up and put her in the wagon, why they didn't leave. He'd told the Defaiders about the other children. And now they could go, couldn't they? Because Alys couldn't stay here. She wouldn't.

Suddenly the black and white men were back, and the black and white ladies, and Mistress Argyll's hand was on her other shoulder and Alys was farther away from Pawl than she had been before. She cried out to him, and she saw him talking to the High Elder, looking at Alys, talking to the High Elder some more. She saw the High Elder shaking his head, and then they were all around Pawl, and Pawl was looking around him but it was as if all that black and white were swallowing him whole and then he was in his wagon. And then Pawl's wagon was moving away, and Pawl was looking back at her and he looked so sad but hopeless and why was he so hopeless and why couldn't he take her, and Alys cried out to him one more time.

She heard Mistress Argyll's voice above her. "Crying won't help, so no more tears now, child."

And so she stopped crying, and that was the first lesson Alys learned in Defaid. The first of many.

In the hours that followed, this is what happened: Mistress Argyll introduced Alys to a steel-haired man named Brother Argyll. Mistress Argyll told Alys that she was to call them Mother and Father. Mother told Alys to eat her dinner. Father showed Alys where to put her clothes. Mother told Alys to wash and to put on her nightdress. Father pointed Alys to the bed where she was to slide herself between linen sheets. And then Alys lay in the dark, the door closed between her and these strange parents, the silence of night falling around her and this village full of strange people.

Alys felt chilled and alone. Exposed and afraid. It was only in that still, black moment that she remembered: She'd left Mam's coat in Pawl's wagon.

The night was good.

The sisters left their mountain shack. They didn't need it any-more, its straw that smelled of goat. Its hearth where meals had been cooked. When they ate such things.

That was long ago. When they had a mother. Before.

They felt The Beast looking at them. Observing. They dared It to interfere with them. It did not. They looked back at It, unafraid. It bared Its long fangs at them. They hissed back.

They nested in the trees. They were comfortable there, perched like owls. There would be no more hearths or homes for them. And where there were hearths and homes—and moth-ers and fathers, and people who feared what lay beyond their doors in the dark, dark fforest—that is where the sisters would watch. And wait.

And they would float, and they would hide. They would

climb and they would crawl. They would slip in the shadows and beckon in dreams.

The sisters wouldn't be caught. Never that. They would be careful now. The villages would be on guard against them. The sisters would have to be like the wolves. Like The Beast. Keep to the fforest. Hunt only at night.

The night was good. It was where the fear grew. And the sisters would feed on the fear, and they would never, never be hungry.

PART

2

*You'd
better
lock the
Gate*

FIVE

Alys moved through the following days doing what she knew she was supposed to do, but alternated between feeling nothing and feeling too much. She wanted to sleep and yet she hated to sleep. Each time she opened her eyes to the as yet unfamiliar walls around her, it wasn't so much a shock as a reminder that her home was gone. That Mam and Dad were gone. That Mam's hands would no longer smooth her hair or drop her nightshift over her head or set her milky tea in front of her in the morning.

Enid, Madog, and the other Gwenith children arrived in Defaid just as Alys had last seen them—Enid and Madog awake, and all the rest sleeping. The sleeping children were laid out in wagon after wagon. It had taken some time for the Defaid men to return with them, and Mother had told Alys it was because the men had to dig graves and bury all the bodies first. Mother was blunt that way. Mother said there were so many bodies that they buried families together, instead of digging a separate hole for each person. Alys wanted to be comforted by this. She wanted to imagine Mam and Dad asleep together. But all she could picture were the shells she'd last seen of them. The image came back to her over and over. Unbidden and unwanted. She'd be peeling carrots for Mother and would remember peeling carrots for Mam. But instead of picturing Mam's face alive, she pictured it as she'd last seen it. She'd have to shake herself to make it go away. Mother looked at Alys at those times, eyes fixed and curious, and Alys couldn't bear to look back. There was something about the way Mother looked at her—it wasn't like other people. Alys felt Mother's eyes like fingers on her skin. Under her skin.

When the Gwenith children first arrived, Mother and some of the other village women were asked how best to wake them, as if any of them had seen such a thing before. Then Enid told the women how Alys had done it with her, swift and harsh, but effective. So that's what the women did—from oldest teenagers to youngest babies, the children were all doused with cold water and woke up sputtering to a town they'd never seen before.

The Gwenith children with siblings did best adjusting to the strangeness and new orphanhood of their lives. The children with no brothers or sisters walked around a bit like ghosts. Alys was an only child herself, and she wondered if that was how she appeared to the others. She didn't think so, though. Because Alys had made a decision for herself. She promised herself that someday, she wouldn't live in this village anymore. It wasn't her home and no amount of telling her it was could make it so. Someday, she'd find her way to the Lakes and she'd live in a caravan, and that would be her home. In a caravan there would be no reminders of what she'd lost. There would be no house that wasn't really her house. No parents who weren't really her parents.

For the first few weeks, the older Gwenith children were kept in the meetinghouse and the schoolhouse. The babies and the youngest children were divided among the families in town. Some of the families wished to keep the children they were given, and those children were told the same that Alys had been told—to call these new people Mother and Father, Sister and Brother. Others of the children were told that this arrangement was only temporary.

Defaid had no intention of keeping all these children—fifty new mouths to feed was more than even such a prosperous farm and shepherding town could be expected to take in. So they sent fast riders to the villages of Pysgod, which hugged the river to the north, and Tarren, which clung to the base of the mountains in the northwest, telling them what had transpired and asking them to take on some of the burden of caring for these orphans. But there were no takers, and the explanation for that was obvious to all. If a village didn't *have* to take in a load of orphans who'd been exposed to something awful, well then why on Byd would they want to?

It was then that the Gwenith children were permanently divided up among the Defaiders, siblings mostly kept together.

Alys learned all of this from Mother, with whom she spent most of her time. Alys had hoped to see more of her friend Gaenor, but Gaenor and her sisters and brother had been sent off with a family clear on the other side of town. And they had each other, after all, whereas Alys had only herself.

Except for the discomfiting way that Mother looked at her, Mother wasn't such bad company. Alys had grown to appreciate how she didn't seem to have other adults' way of talking differently around children. She talked to Alys the same as she talked to anyone. And Alys had grown used to Mother's long silences and seeming coldness, too. At first Alys had thought Mother was angry with her all the time, but then it struck her that this was simply Mother's way. Father was quiet, too, but not unkind. He was a carpenter and gone most of the day, but when he returned for dinner and then evening supper he nodded to Alys in a way that made Alys feel that he was happy to see her, even though his face never betrayed it.

Still, Alys did not grow so used to Mother and Father that she was ever tempted to break her promise to Pawl. She spoke not a word about the soul eaters, not even when the village women gathered around Mother's table with their tea and oat cakes and talked about the soul eaters as if they actually knew what they were and what they'd done. That was one thing that Pawl was wrong about. He'd made it seem as if the Defaiders were too fine and holy to talk about evil things such as soul eaters. But there was a kind of glee that they took in it, Alys noticed. Their faces glowed, they warmed to the task. *Wolves and soul eaters,* they said to each other around Mother's table. *All descending on one town like that? It was the work of The Beast.* And then they all shuddered and patted their hearts with laundry-chapped hands.

"What do you think them Gwenithers had been up to?" one of the women asked. Some only clucked and shook their heads.

Mother said, "Going about their business, just like us, I expect."

The High Elder's wife, Mistress Ffagan, said, "The Good Shepherd wouldn't have abandoned the Gwenithers that way if they'd been following Him like good sheep are supposed to do." She cut her little round eyes at all of them. "There must have been some straying going on to attract The Beast's notice that way. Someone in Gwenith was cavorting with The Beast. Someone. Or more than one. Out there in the fforest, doing Shepherd knows what. You mark my words."

And the women did, with nods and more chest pats.

Alys's cheeks burned and she felt a sizzle of anger like a hot little coal in her belly. But just as quickly that anger was replaced by shame. For if anyone had been attracting The Beast's notice, hadn't it been Alys herself? Wandering in the middle of the night, touched by soul eaters. She could conjure the exact sensation of their hands on her shoulders, the sense of connection that passed from one hand to the other—through her. She'd thought them beautiful. And she thought it still. And yet they were the creatures who had killed her parents. Creatures who had touched her and let her live.

"What do you suppose they got up to out in the fforest?" one of the women said. "The cavorting with The Beast, I mean."

Silence fell over the table like a blanket. "Mistress Hardy,"

Mistress Ffagan said, her round brown eyes gone stony, "we righteous followers of the Good Shepherd cannot know, can we?"

Murmurs of assent followed, and their attention turned to tea and cakes.

While the women talked on, Alys stayed quiet with eyes and ears wide open, just as Pawl had taught her. She fixed her gaze on Mother, whose face was as unmoved as it ever was. Alys was learning that Mother was no fool. But if Mother knew what Alys had done, or hadn't done, the night the soul eaters came . . . well, Alys shoved that thought aside. Alys would be a Laker soon—eventually—she told herself. And then she would be no concern to these holy folk.

It wasn't long after the dispersal of all the Gwenith children among the Defaiders that Father came home early one afternoon and announced to Mother and Alys that the High Elder wished to speak with Alys. Father took her to the High Elder's home, the biggest in the center of town, with a wide, whitewashed front porch and an apple tree right in the front yard. The High Elder answered the door himself, and for the first time Alys found herself looking directly up at him. His hawk-beak nose was extraordinarily large, and the first thing Alys noticed about him as she raised her eyes to his face was the blackness of his nostrils.

The High Elder led Father and Alys into a front hallway and then directly left into a spotless room with a massive and shiny wooden table, a large book on top of it, and a broad chair behind it. There was no other furniture in the room.

"Child," the High Elder said, "do you know why you are here?"

Alys didn't know if he thought her quite young and dumb and unsure of why she was in Defaid at all, or if he meant something simpler than that. She decided to answer the easier question. "Father said you wished to see me."

"And why?" The High Elder said.

Alys lifted her eyes to Father, but he kept his own on the floorboards. "I . . . I don't know," Alys said.

"Because, child, you were the one awake, were you not? This is what the traveler told us when he brought you here. That he found you wandering, when all the rest of Gwenith was either dead or asleep. Is that true, or did the traveler lie?"

Alys tried to work out in her head what Pawl would want her to say. He'd want her to say as little as possible, she concluded. "Ay, I was awake."

"And why was that?"

"Because I don't sleep. I've always been like that."

"And your parents allowed you to wander at night?"

Alys thought about the women around the table, how they wondered what the people of Gwenith had done to cause their trouble. Alys felt the hard little seed of shame in her gut bloom and unfurl. She couldn't bear for this big black and white man with his big black nostrils to think ill of Mam and Dad. "No," Alys said. Her voice was too loud, she realized, and the High Elder's black horizontal eyebrows descended in a line. She tried to steady her heart. "They didn't let me, but I did anyway. Just that once."

"You are a disobedient child," the High Elder said. "We must train this out of you. You hear this, Brother Argyll? You and Mistress Argyll must keep a close watch on this child."

"Ay," Father said. "We will."

"And what did you see when you were out wandering, Alys?" The High Elder looked down at her and Alys found her own eyes drawn to the floorboards.

"Nothing," Alys said. Alys had told them all this, many times before. She'd told Mistress Ffagan that first day she'd arrived. And she'd told them the same every time they had asked since. "Just the stars." Alys refused to look up, but she felt his eyes on the crown of her head.

"Brother Argyll, a word." The High Elder turned and left the room and Father followed him, hat in hand.

Alys was alone in the room. Her eyes traveled to the massive wooden table, and the large book. They'd had no books at home in Gwenith, save for the Shepherd's Word, a small black leather volume with the teachings of the Shepherd handwritten in Mam's long, thin script. Alys went to the big book and she struggled to open it. She stuck both hands in the middle of its pages, and she lifted.

Inside the book was a beautiful picture. It was full of color, with shiny yellow paint like sunlight around the edges. It was actually three pictures in one, Alys realized—one at the top, one in the middle, and one at the bottom—and each was very different.

The topmost picture was all bright blue and green and snowy white. Blue sky, rolling green pastures, and at the center a man in white robes with a long white beard holding the staff of a shepherd. Happy, chubby children all dressed in white gathered around him, and one perched in his lap.

The middle picture was painted in earthy shades of soil and grain. There were brown fields of wheat and barley, and sturdy farmers plowing behind big-rumped horses. There was a serious-faced Elder standing on the steps of a meetinghouse, his hands pressed together in prayer.

Alys's eyes glossed over the top two pictures. They didn't hold her gaze the way the one at the bottom did. It was all red, and black, and yellow, full of smoke and bursts of bright flame. At the center was a long funnel that led up to the earth above. Tiny human figures fell like floating ash through the funnel's long expanse, and at its base was The Beast. Alys had never seen a picture of The Beast before, but she didn't have to be told that's what this creature was. She knew. The Beast perched at the bottom of the funnel, Its mouth wide open to catch the falling people. It crouched on two thin, bird-like legs. Its arms were inhumanly long, and attached to Its body by featherless wings of skin and bone. Its body was covered with black hair, thick between Its legs and covering Its chest. Two ears ended in peaks like horns over Its head. A black tongue jutted out between Its long fangs, waiting to catch those little falling bodies.

Alys reached out a finger to the picture in the book. She traced the doomed figures, stroked the beastly wings.

She didn't hear Father and the High Elder enter the room, she was so transfixed by those wings. So she cried out with surprise when the High Elder's hand came down on her own, then with pain when he squeezed her hand until she felt bones pulling together.

Then this is what happened:

Father stared, white-faced. The High Elder told Alys to push up her sleeves. He handed a long stick to Father, and then the stick came down on the white flesh of Alys's arms over and over and over again. And all the while the stick came down, the High Elder preached. He told her about The Beast that perched in Its fiery hole. How It tore the flesh from sinners' bones while they screamed, how It plucked out their eyes with Its long black claws, and how the agony never ended. Because once their bones were picked clean, and their eyes were gouged, it all grew back again and the torture began anew. And *that* was the fate of little girls who didn't learn obedience. They would be embraced by The Beast forever and forever and forever.

SIX

All the way home from the High Elder's house, Father had been silent while Alys cradled her sore arms in her lap and rethought everything she'd begun to believe about Father and Mother. She remembered what Pawl had told her about Defaiders. She wished she had a brother or a sister, someone who was all hers and truly hers. Not these fake parents to whom she'd been given. She wanted her mam and dad. Tears stung her eyes and she willed them back inside. *Crying won't help,* Mother had said.

Just as they arrived at Mother and Father's house—Alys had already decided it was her house no longer, if she'd ever thought it was—Father turned to her. "Child, I'm more sorry for that than I can say. But someday I'm hoping you'll realize that punishing you was for your own good. The sooner you learn not to follow your whims, the better for you. I'm not saying it's right. I'm saying it's the way it is. Do you understand me, Alys?"

"Ay," Alys said. Once inside, Father told Mother what had happened, and Mother offered to put a salve on Alys's arms. Alys refused.

Father protested as Alys turned to go into her room and closed the door behind her. Mother only said, "Leave her be."

Alys sat in her room for a while. There was nothing in there but her narrow bed, a table beside it, and some hooks on the wall for her few articles of clothing. She'd had no plan when she came in here, and now she felt bored and closed up. This was where she'd have to spend all night alone, and she didn't want to be stuck in here now. But she also hadn't wanted to be out there. With them. Alys could run out easily enough, leave Mother and Father calling behind her. But Alys had learned a great deal about getting along in the short time since she'd been in Defaid, and she knew the best way to have some unhindered time to herself was to offer to do a chore that took her away from home. She got up and went into the kitchen.

Mother was shelling peas, and Father looked up from his tea.

"Mother, is there anything you need from the fforest edge? I'll go gather it for you."

Mother turned, and she looked Alys full in the face in a searching, examining way. Alys looked away. "Ay child," Mother said. "There is. I could use some horsetail and slippery elm. Take a basket and your sharp knife."

And with that, Alys was out and free.

She walked first to the nearest stand of elms. This took her away from the village eyes—the shepherds with their flocks and the women in their gardens and the children at their play. Alys pulled out her knife and sliced a neat stack of strips. Slippery elm, Mother had taught her, was for colds and sore throats. Alys felt capable using the knife, comfortable carrying it. This was something Mam would never have let her do.

Thinking that, Alys felt guilty for a moment. Instead of the terrible image that so often came to her, she remembered instead Mam's soft curves and the way she kissed Alys on the forehead before bed. Then she forced herself to think about something else. In its own way that memory was just as painful as the other.

Horsetail grew nearer to the fforest, so Alys walked on to where the woods began. As Alys drew closer to the green wall of trees, the air cooled and dampened. In the shade along the fforest's edges, the sounds of scythes slicing through grain and horses' hooves off in the distance grew muffled, and with her back to the fields, Alys could almost believe that she was alone in all of Byd.

The fforest was deep and old. Trees grew tall and thick, their branches intertwining far overhead. Moss and fern carpeted the exposed roots, mounds of rock, rotting stumps, and fallen trees. The air was fog, and moisture dripped and trickled from fronds and leaves. Alys heard scurrying and slithering, fluttering and clacking.

All this Alys noticed from the fforest's edge. Beyond this border, she was forbidden to go without Mother. Whatever foraging she did had to be done right here, in full view of the cultivated fields. She could walk along the fforest's edge, farther and farther away from the village as she did now. But Mother had told her that she should never step both feet inside when she was alone.

Except that Alys did. She always did when Mother sent her foraging. Although Alys was far from the village now and hadn't seen anyone for some time, she glanced to her right every now and then, to be sure that no one was near, that no one noticed the mouse-gray girl blending in with the tree trunks.

Then into the fforest she went.

She dug her fingers into the mossy crevices of trees as she passed deeper and deeper into the fforest, stepping over branches and trickling springs. Mist veiled her hair and face and her clothes grew damp and heavy. She walked this way for some time, longer than she should have. There was no sun overhead to point her in the right direction, only the green and gray cover of leaves and fog. She could wander a bit to the right or left and find herself hopelessly turned around. But Alys wasn't afraid of getting lost.

Alys felt only relief. Relief to be away from the black-and-white Elders and their black-and-white wives. And relief to be away from the eyes—all the eyes staring at her, the girl who was awake when everyone else lay dead or sleeping. The adults tried to be secretive about it. But the Defaid children didn't try—when they caught sight of Alys they pointed and gaped openly until their parents dragged them away. She'd heard the town gossips whisper behind her back: *There she is, the one who was awake when the soul eaters came. The one who says she never saw anything. I don't believe her. Do you?*

Alys wasn't sure which made her more uncomfortable—the pointing of the Defaiders, or the weird sort of awe shown her by the Gwenith children. They looked at her like she was special. Like she knew something they didn't—something important that might help them understand what had happened to their parents. It made Alys angry at the children sometimes, because she was just like them, wasn't she? She'd lost her parents the same as they had. And she was only seven. What did she know? But then, of course, that was all a lie she told herself and them, just to help her carry on the pretense of being good. Because she did know something about that terrible night, and all the time—waking, eating, washing, working—she felt this difference weighing on her. All the time she regretted having gotten out of bed that night. If she hadn't been so disobedient, then she would be just like the other children of Gwenith. Just as orphaned as they were, but at least not wicked. *If I'm special at all,* Alys told herself, *it's because there's something terribly wrong with me.*

Alys kept walking.

The Elders said the fforest was full of evil things, creatures of The Beast. Having the trees all around her, their branches like arms, Alys could think only of the tree girls—the soul eaters—who'd spoken to her and glided past her that night. She looked around her. It occurred to her suddenly that they could be nearby, or just a little deeper, a little farther. Maybe today they would find her again—or she would find them. This should have made Alys quake and run. And yet Alys was drawn to them with a fascination that frightened her. Perhaps that was proof enough she was bad. But she felt seeing them again might tell her what kind of a child she was once and for all. Mam had told her about the dunking test for witches. If the accused drowned, then she was good. If she floated, then she was a witch. Alys thought it might be the same for her. If she met the soul eaters again and they killed her, then she'd know she was good like Mam and Dad. If they didn't kill her, then she was bad. It would be terrible to be bad. But at least she'd know. If she was bad, she couldn't go live with the travelers, even if they'd have her. Which they wouldn't. Not if they knew. So maybe instead of living in the Lakes, she'd find a cave in the mountains. Build herself fires at night and live on berries and mushrooms. She pictured herself looking like the tree women, living in her cave. Maybe her eyes would grow large and bright like theirs.

At this thought, a tickle of apprehension made her scalp tingle. Perhaps she wasn't ready to live in a cave. Not quite yet.

Alys's heart beat just a bit faster. It was time to turn back, she told herself. Another day she would return here. Yes. Some other day.

Her feet slowed almost to a pause, then, just ahead, she saw a pale clump amid all the mossy green—a bloom of fat mushrooms, enough to fill her basket to the top. They looked so homey and welcoming. So much like something a good girl would pick. And though she was still angry with Mother and Father, she knew they would like the mushrooms. Alys hopped over branches and sank to her knees, snipping off the mushrooms with her knife.

What are you?

Alys sat straight up, then scrambled to her feet. A voice was in her head, but it wasn't her voice.

What are you?

She turned around, dizzy. The voice was in her chest now, too. There was no one speaking to her though, nothing but green and trees all around her. Then she glimpsed a flash of movement. Alys could have run, but she no longer remembered which way to go. And the thing moving out there in the fforest was everywhere at once—first it was in front of her, then to her right, then behind her.

"What are *you*?" Alys said to the air, to the fforest, to the thing moving among the trees.

The moment the words left Alys's lips, the thing stopped moving, and Alys realized she knew exactly where it was. Straight ahead of her there was a tree, and ten black claws wrapped around it like vines. As if sensing it had been spotted, the creature retracted its claws in a flash.

Alys's ears closed up to all but the sound of her own breathing.

I'm looking for the girl. Are you the girl?

"What girl?" Alys said.

You're her. You're the girl.

Then the creature came out. A creature she'd seen only once before—in the High Elder's book. The Beast. There It stood on Its long, bird-like legs, Its featherless wings pulled in close to Its body. It was half again the height of the tallest grown man that Alys had ever seen. Its eyes—tiny, black, shiny, and sharp—were pinpoints above a short snout with gaping, sniffing nostrils. Pink lips pulled back over fangs, long and thin, the two longest extending well past Its chin. A black tongue jutted out between Its teeth, tasting the air.

Alys resisted the urge to fall backward. She felt a clenching in her heart like a muscle that had been worked too hard and too long.

The creature stepped toward her, lifting Its long bird legs over roots and fallen limbs, Its black-clawed feet clacking against rocks. When It was close enough to touch, It bent forward at the waist and pushed Its face directly into Alys's own, so close that she could stare straight into the shiny black of Its eyes. She smelled earth and fur. The Beast's nostrils dilated and contracted, sniffing her. Then Its long black tongue slipped between Its fangs and Alys felt It graze her left cheek.

You're the girl. Give me something. Give me that.

It hinged backward at the waist, and then down again, now staring at the small, sharp knife that Alys held in her hand. It reached out one claw and tapped the knife on the blade. Tap, tap.

Yes, that. Give me that.

"Why do you want my knife?"

It hinged up again, looked Alys in the eyes. Alys looked back, blinked. The creature blinked.

To hold. To remember you by.

Alys's heart unclenched, the pain in her chest now gone. The hair on her arms lifted, and she felt warm blood flow to her skin. Hardly knowing why, but feeling that it was exactly the right thing to do, Alys gave the knife to The Beast, handle first.

The creature grasped it fully. Then It tilted Its head, sniffed.

Show me your arms.

Again, hardly knowing what she was doing, but not at all hesitating, Alys rolled up her sleeves and showed The Beast her forearms, striped with red welts from the High Elder's stick. Then It licked her.

The moment The Beast's tongue touched her skin, Alys was lost to herself. Or rather, she became—for a moment— something else. She became storm and weather. She wasn't she or he. She was dirt and tree and root. She smelled the mineral wetness of rain on rock. No, she didn't smell it. It wasn't sensation. It was being. She was the rock. She was the rain.

Then Alys came back to herself. She felt a chill across her skin as The Beast's tongue ran up one arm and down the other. Its tongue felt like a thousand feathers softly landing on her. And like that, the stripes were gone.

"Thank you," Alys said. She was no longer the weather, but she sensed the weather in The Beast. She smelled the rain.

You've seen them. The soul eaters.

"Ay," Alys said. "I have seen them."

You will see them again.

Alys thought of what The Beast had first said to her—It had asked *what* she was. Not *who* she was. And The Beast had said that It was looking for her. "Why were you looking for me?" Alys said. "Why me?"

The Beast cocked Its head. *You are like them.*

This was her answer, then. The answer to the question that had buried deep inside of her the night the soul eaters passed her by. The question that had grown ever since, roots as deep as its branches were wide—that was now as big as the tree in back of Mother and Father's house. Alys felt again the shiver that had passed through her when the soul eaters had touched her shoulders. She felt the thread connecting them, connecting her. The likeness to those creatures that had killed her parents.

"Am I . . . am I evil then?"

The Beast regarded her closely. Then It opened Its mouth as if to roar, but instead Alys felt wind. It blew through her and Alys felt stream and canyon and blade of grass and petal. Then The Beast crouched low and leapt. Alys heard scrambling and scraping and leaves slapping. She thought she saw a flash of movement in the trees overhead, but The Beast was gone.

SEVEN

That evening, Alys refused to let Mother look at her arms. There could be no explaining their smooth, unmarked whiteness.

Mother shrugged. "Suit yourself." She gave Alys some salve and let her go to bed without helping with the dishes.

As Alys lay sleepless in her bed, she thought of nothing but The Beast. She recalled the sensation of weather. Of being weather. Was that evil? Was it unnatural? But what could be more natural than wind? Alys felt it blowing through her, felt herself spin with it.

Hours had passed but she was no closer to sleep when she heard a light tap at her door. Mother opened it, holding an oil lamp. "Wake up, child. I need your help."

Alys dressed quickly and emerged to find Mother already

wrapped in her shawl and standing by the door with the lamp in one hand and a basket in the other. "Come."

The village was dark and quiet, and Alys knew without being told which house they were headed toward. It would be the only one with lamps lit, the only one where sickness kept everyone awake. As a midwife, Mother was often called away in the middle of the night. Alys would know this had happened because Mother looked grayer the following morning, the circles beneath her eyes more purple than lavender. This was the first time Mother had awakened Alys to come with her.

The lit-up house belonged to the Pryces. Mary Pryce had given birth to a baby boy the day before. Mother hadn't attended the birth. Mary's mother had called the town's other midwife instead. But now they wanted Mother. Mistress Pryce must be in a bad way. The villagers had their friendly loyalties to one midwife or another for routine complaints, but Father had said that when things looked grim, they always called Mother.

The night was mild, but when Mother and Alys entered, the house was stifling. A fire blazed in the hearth and all the windows were shut tight. Alys began to sweat under her wool. Mother blew out her lamp and set it on the kitchen table where Brother Pryce was sitting. He was a plain-faced man with thin blond hair. He looked pale and frightened. Mary's sister, who looked to be about Enid's age, stood rocking the baby. He mewled and fretted.

Mother took in the room with her sharp eyes. "Where's Mary?"

"Upstairs," Brother Pryce said. His voice came out choked.

"Our mother is with her," the girl said.

"The baby needs his mother. Sarah, give the baby to Alys. Then I want you to tamp down that fire and open a window."

Sarah hesitated, but Alys took the baby from her. He was small and heavy. Alys stared into his open brown-gray eyes and his tiny open mouth. She felt his confusion at this place he was thrust into. How hard and bright it was.

"Mother said the windows must stay shut to keep the demons out," Sarah said. She wrung her hands and looked at Brother Pryce. He looked at Mother, but said nothing. Alys sensed an empty space where his body was. As if he'd left a wax figure of himself sitting here and the real him had gone elsewhere.

Mother shook her head. "There are no demons here, child. Just do as I say. Alys, come with me."

Upstairs, there were two rooms and Mother led Alys toward the lamplit one. Here, too, a fire blazed and the windows were closed tight. Mother set down her basket and took the baby from Alys. She gave Alys a wordless look, which Alys understood without question. Alys tamped down the fire and opened a window. The fresh air was bliss in her face.

Mother had told Alys there was a particular smell to death. Alys had been around enough dead and dying animals to know what she meant. There was a sweetness to the rot of death, like meat gone bad. But the smell in this room wasn't death. It was stale breath and unwashed bodies.

Mary lay against pillows, sweaty and flushed. Mother held the baby in one arm and pulled back Mary's blankets with the other. She petted her like a child, making soothing noises in the back of her throat, almost like singing. "Sit up now, child. You're going to feed this baby boy. She unlaced the top of Mary's nightgown and felt her breast. "Ay, your milk's come in, child. And your boy needs it. Come now." The baby seemed to sense the nearness of milk and had grown frantic in his mewling. Then, as soon as Mother pressed the baby to Mary's breast, there was silence. Mary weakly stroked her baby's small head, and Alys tried not to stare. She wondered if Mary would live. Mother had told Alys that fever after birth was a bad sign. She hoped Mary wouldn't die. It would be a shame for that baby not to have a mam. Often enough when the mam went, the babe soon followed.

Mother turned to Mistress Jones, Mary's mother. "Sister, you look spent. You leave this to me now. Go lie down. I won't leave your daughter. Rest now."

Mistress Jones looked fit to fall over. But still she protested. Mary said to her mother, "It's all right, Mam. I'm feeling better." Alys didn't believe Mary, but Mistress Jones wanted to, so she kissed her daughter's forehead and ran a hand over her grandson. Then she left the room like a passing shadow.

"Now Mary, " Mother said, "you must listen to me. You're sick, and I can help you, but you have to do as I say. You're going to feed your boy good and full, and then Alys here is going to take him. You and I have work to do."

After the baby was sated and asleep, Alys sat with him on a stool in the corner and watched Mother. She stripped Mary out of her sweat-damp nightshift and passed careful hands over her belly, still large from pregnancy. Alys stopped trying not to stare. Mother didn't need her here to help, Alys realized. She'd done all these things alone many times before. Mother had brought Alys along because she wanted her to learn. Alys obliged by remaining quiet and watchful.

Mother took something from her basket, something small, wrapped in linen and tied with string. She patted Mary's shoulder. "I'm going to make you some tea, and you're going to drink it down." Then she left the room.

Mary looked over at Alys then, and Alys smiled at her. Mary had a sweet, round face. She looked barely older than her sister.

Alys stood up. "Would you like to see your boy?" Mary nodded and Alys brought the baby over to his mother, nestled him in her arms. As Alys rested him there, she felt heat rising off Mary. Not a raging heat, a small flame. Alys touched her hand to Mary's belly, just as Mother had done. Alys felt the flame inside of Mary, she felt the blood in Mary's veins and the air in her lungs. And something else. Something that didn't belong. It was a spot of sick, right under Alys's fingers, and Alys had the strangest feeling that she could reach right in and pull it out and then Mary would be well.

"Alys?" Mother was looking at her, and Alys didn't know how long she'd been standing there, her palm flat against Mary's belly.

"It's all right, Mistress Argyll. The child has a gentle touch." Mary patted Alys's hand.

"Ay," Mother said. "She does. Alys, take the babe."

Alys did as she was told. Mother held a cup of tea to Mary's lips and told her to drink it down. The tea smelled like leaves gone to slime and it turned Alys's stomach. Mary made faces but took it all.

"Now, Mary," Mother said, "let's get you up."

"But Mistress, I can't," Mary said. "I can barely sit."

"Ay, you can and you will. And when those contractions start, you're going to want to be up. We're going to walk around this room until you pass what you didn't pass before." Mother looked at Alys. "The afterbirth, child. It all needs to come out, or it rots inside. And that's what brings the fever. You don't want that, Mary. So let's get you up and make sure you're here to feed that baby boy when he wakes up crying for you."

It was over within an hour. Mary bit her lips and bore down and walked, and sometimes she crouched down. Soon her legs were streaked with blood, and Mother was gathering a mess of something in linens. Mary wept in Mother's arms. "It's all right now, child. It'll be all right now." Mother beckoned Alys with her eyes, and Alys went to her. Mother lifted the baby from Alys's arms and gave him to his mam. Then Mother wrapped her arms around mam and child as if to make sure Mary wouldn't drop the babe.

Alys rested her hand on Mary's belly, so lightly she barely touched the muslin of her nightshift. She felt the warmth of blood and breath inside of Mary. Nothing out of place. Everything put to right. She looked up at Mother and saw that Mother's eyes were already on her. Then Mother placed her own hand over Alys's.

"Now," Mother said, "if anyone asks either of you what that

tea was, you say it was chamomile. Nought else but that. Just a soothing cup of chamomile tea."

Alys slept fitfully that night and when she awoke to help Mother with breakfast she couldn't remember exactly what she'd dreamed. But she knew she had. Images came to her in flashes. Crying babies, blood-streaked legs, and the gnashing of The Beast's fangs. But also wind and rain and leaves in her hair. The sensation of climbing a tree—so strong and vivid that she thought it must be a memory even as she realized it couldn't be. When in her life had she ever climbed anything? Never. Girls didn't climb. Least of all trees.

After their breakfast of oatmeal, cream, and honey, Father went off to his carpentry shop as usual. Mother set Alys to mending one of Father's shirts. "After you finish that, Alys, we're going for a walk in the fforest. Bring your sharp knife." Alys held her needle over the rough linen of Father's shirt, frozen.

"I don't have it," Alys said. Her knife. She'd loved it. More than she'd loved the doll she'd left behind in Gwenith, if she were honest about it. She loved the way the knife felt in her hand. The perfect weight and size. Father had carved the handle himself.

Mother looked at her with her dark and searching eyes. "What do you mean, you don't have it?"

"I must have left it behind yesterday." It was a lie that wasn't a lie. Alys was getting good at those.

"Well, we'll just go find it then," Mother said.

Alys looked up at Mother, about to say that she'd go look for it herself, anything to avoid Mother's close observation, but the door opened and Father appeared. His black, sawdusted outline was sharp against the midmorning sun. "We've been summoned to the meetinghouse," he said. "Everyone." As they walked there, Father told Mother and Alys that the Elders had come to a decision about the village's future and how they could save themselves from what had happened to Gwenith.

The villagers packed themselves into the meetinghouse, men and boys on one side, and women, girls, and babies on the other. They sat crammed on long, backless wooden benches. The High Elder sat in a wide seat at the front, with the other Elders lined up to his left and right. The High Elder was the tallest and most broad-shouldered of all of them, and Alys wondered if you became High Elder by being the biggest.

When the villagers had all settled in, two brawny boys who looked the spitting image of the High Elder closed the doors of the meetinghouse. Then the High Elder rose. "We Elders have asked ourselves," he said, "what did the people of Gwenith do to lose the protection of the Good Shepherd above? Why did He forsake them, and allow The Beast to send Its wolf children and the soul eaters among His flock? Who brought this evil upon them?"

There was a murmuring among the villagers, and Alys heard *witch* muttered and hissed over and over around the room. And *soul eaters* as well. She felt narrowed eyes staring at her and the other Gwenith children. She thought of Pawl and his warning never to speak of the soul eaters. What would he say to her now, if she told him about The Beast? He'd probably run from her. Even Pawl would be frightened of her then. Alys felt despair. She'd learned to lie without lying, but she'd never be able to pretend so well as she needed to, she'd never be able to hide from what she'd done. What she'd seen and allowed to happen. It would rise up from her like a stink. It would burst and seep out of her like fruit gone bad from the inside out.

The High Elder raised one hand, palm facing out, and the villagers quieted. "The answer, my friends, is that we cannot know. We cannot know what happened to the village of Gwenith. But we can remain vigilant within ourselves. Vigilant to the temptations of vanity, adultery, sloth, and gluttony."

Alys's mind began to wander when the words grew long and meaningless to her ears. She knew that gluttony had something to do with eating too much. She'd heard Dad refer to the Gwenith High Elder as a glutton more than once, and he had been a big, round man who always seemed to show up at the door after Mam had baked one of her pies.

Mam's pies . . . there wouldn't be any more blackberry pies this year. But there'd be apple. Or, there would have been. Alys came back to the present with a thud. She had no idea if Mother baked pies. No idea at all.

The High Elder was still talking. "We can give thanks that the evil that took the poor folk of Gwenith has passed us over. The Shepherd found us worthy of His care. He judged the wicked and spared the rest of us."

Alys felt a sharp, familiar curl of anger in her belly. These folk thought that her Mam and Dad were dead because they were bad. But she knew Mam and Dad weren't bad. Alys was the bad one. She was the girl who wandered and let soul eaters brush past her in the night, who thought they were beautiful. And who handed her knife to The Beast, handle first—instead of burying it in The Beast up to the hilt, the way any of these good people of Defaid would surely have done. Instead of being confused by Its scent of rain, she was lulled by it, and soothed by the tickle of Its tongue on her forearms.

"But we cannot only trust in the Shepherd's protection," The High Elder said. "We must show Him that we are worthy of His care. And we shall keep The Beast's vile creatures from us by building a great wooden Gate around our village."

There was a hubbub of talk and whisper in response.

The High Elder held up his hand again. "I know, brothers and sisters, I know. You wonder how this can be done. We have already begun the designs, and every man and boy in this village will lend his back to the task. Elder Miles has drawn a map of the new Gated village of Defaid. All you folk who live outside of the perimeter of the Gate will be moved inside. Yes, you will have to leave your homes and build new ones within the village Gate. But in exchange for this minor sacrifice, you will be safe in the loving bosom of the Shepherd. You must consider the grief that befell Gwenith as a warning to us all. They harbored The Beast among them, in some form that we cannot know. They lost their way. We must not lose ours."

The High Elder's sermon now over, the villagers all stood and the adults gathered in groups asking each other questions none of them could answer. Alys looked up at Mother and Father. "We'll have to move, won't we?"

"Ay," Father said. "We shall."

"Can they make us?" Mother said. "Can't we just tell the High Elder that our faith is strong enough as it is, that we don't have to leave our home and run and hide behind some Gate?"

"Heledd," Father said. This was Mother's given name. "You know the answer to that question as well as I. The High Elder has told us what to do, now there's nought else but to do it."

Alys felt sorry for Mother. She did so love her house, and Alys had even grown fond of some parts of it. That huge tree in the back, especially, the one that grew taller and wider than any tree Alys had ever seen.

But she couldn't quite make it all the way to truly pitying Father. Because there was the problem of the stripes on her forearms. The Beast had healed them, but Alys could still recall their sting. And though Father would say that he had no choice in the matter, and it had occurred to Alys that he hadn't hit her nearly so hard as he no doubt could have . . . still, he did it just because he'd been told to do so by the High Elder. So no, Alys couldn't feel too sorry for him. And she also swore that when she was a grown-up, she'd never do anything that she didn't want to do. Certainly not just because some man in black and white told her to.

EIGHT

Alys lagged behind Mother, hoping—unreasonably—that the slower she walked the more likely it might be that Mother would forget about the knife. But Mother never forgot anything. As occupied as she was by the Gate and her horror at leaving her home—not even that could distract her from the knife.

"Where were you when you last had it, Alys?" She and Alys stood along the fforest's edge, and she looked at Alys inquiringly. Alys remembered the first time she'd met Mother she hadn't looked at Alys straight on. Now Alys thought it might have been a kindness when Mother did that. Mother knew the power of her own eyes. Knew how Alys wiggled when she felt pinned by that gaze. Now, Alys knew, Mother wanted her to wiggle. She wanted Alys to know she wasn't fooled.

One twitch of Alys's eyes was all it took. Just one glance

into the moist depth of the fforest. Alys looked straight back at Mother, but it was too late. Mother saw. Mother always saw.

"You went into the fforest alone, didn't you?" Mother said, flat and certain.

"Ay, I did."

"Well then, let's go find it." Mother turned on her heels and into the fforest she went, without a backward glance. She stepped over rocks and branches with a practiced step, like there was no part of this fforest she didn't already have memorized. They walked in silence, Mother in the lead, and Alys realized she wasn't looking for the knife at all. Finally Mother stopped and looked at Alys. "We're going to have to be careful. Much more careful."

Alys felt herself cocking her head like Gaenor's old dog.

"The wandering, Alys. I know the urge. I know why you do it. But if you think you're watched now . . . child, you have no idea. They're not building a Gate to keep folks out. They're building a Gate to keep folks in. Especially folks like us." Mother grabbed Alys's wrist. "Tell me, Alys. Tell me that you know."

With a jolt, Alys felt it. The sense of walls closing in around her. Stifled, as if the breath were being squeezed from her lungs, she felt a desperation to crawl out of her own skin. Mother released her wrist. Alys's stomach rose to her throat and it was all she could do not to retch at Mother's feet.

"I've been careful, so careful," Mother said. "But now no amount of care is going to be enough. They'd burn us for witches if they knew what we can do. Don't look at me like that, child. I know you know. I know you felt what I did in Mary's belly. I know you felt what I did when I held your wrist just now. I knew it from the very first time you sat at my kitchen table. Don't ask me how. But I knew."

There were too many questions Alys wanted to ask, and she was afraid at any moment Mother would stop talking. She'd recede again into silence. "Why are we like this? Are we bad?"

"We're not bad, child. How can it be bad to be able to lay hands on someone and know what's wrong inside?"

"Then why would they burn us for witches?"

"Because they're afraid," Mother said. She shrugged. There was no more to be said about that.

Alys thought about how Mother had lied about the tea. "The tea you gave to Mary. Was that magic?"

Mother made a noise in the back of her throat. "Alys, you're smarter than that. There was nothing magic about it. Nature was doing what nature does. My mother taught me what roots will bring on labor or help a woman pass the afterbirth, just like her mother taught her. But the Elders don't want us interfering in things that way. They think we should give ourselves over to the Shepherd, and that's that. If we live, we live. If we die, we die." Mother made that noise again. "You're no fool, Alys, and neither am I. So I'm going to leave my root cellar behind when we move inside the Gate, and we'll not speak of this again. You keep yourself safe, you hear? Because once we go behind that Gate, we've cast our lot with the Elders. And they'll not let us change our minds. Do you understand, child?"

Alys nodded, although she was not at all certain that she did. There was so little time. Too little time to ask all the questions she had. Mother never talked as much as she did right now, in this dim and dripping fforest. "What about soul eaters?"

Mother narrowed her eyes at Alys. "What about them?"

"Aren't you afraid of them?"

Mother breathed out. Her face softened. "I suppose I should be. After what they did to your mam and dad and the rest of those poor Gwenithers. But I'm more afraid of a cough that won't go away, and a fever that gets hotter and hotter no matter what I do. That's what wakes me up in the middle of the night, child." Then Mother turned for home. "Come, Alys. Father will be wondering about supper."

Alys wasn't at all sure what came over her, but she said, "What about my knife?"

Mother looked back at Alys. Rolled her eyes. "Child, you know we'll never find that."

Just as the High Elder had ordered, farms and outlying homes were abandoned, and the village collapsed in on itself. The people shrank together in a tight bunch, and Alys felt the constriction like a noose. The Gate, the High Elder told them all, would be locked up at sunset and opened only at dawn. In this way, they would be safe from The Beast and Its followers.

The construction of the Gate began immediately, and the air was filled with the racket of sawing wood. The balding of the fforest around Defaid was something terrible to behold, tree after tree crackling and falling. In the central part of town, where once there had been airy spaces between sturdy stone houses, now wooden houses filled in every gap. Mother and

Father's new house would be small compared to their old one. Just one floor and a root cellar, and two bedrooms off the main room that contained kitchen, hearth, and table. One afternoon, cutting potatoes in her old kitchen that she'd soon have to leave, Mother said to Father, "Hot in the summer and cold in the winter, that's what a wooden house is." She shook her knife in the air. "Of course the High Elder doesn't have to move. Oh no. Not him in his stone house."

The rush to build new homes as well as the Gate itself was fevered and desperate. It was full autumn now, and once the weather snapped cold and the ground froze there would be no more sinking pillars into the ground, or digging cellars. So it seemed that every day, the village of Defaid grew more crowded with structures, and the Gate rose and lifted around all those structures like something looming and alive.

The Gate was shaped in a triangle, with covered watchtowers perched on top of the three corners. From the roof of each watchtower there was hung a strong iron hook for suspending a single lantern. In the floor of each watchtower, there was a trapdoor and a ladder, and these were the only routes up or down the Gate, a climb of twenty feet. The entire perimeter of the Gate was connected by a long, perilously narrow walkway, attached to the gate three feet below the top. Finally, there was one set of doors through the Gate. The doors opened twenty feet wide and fastened shut with a piece of wood so large and heavy that it would take eight men to close the doors each evening.

While the town's builders and craftspeople engineered the Gate, the Elders discussed how best to guard it. The daytime guarding was no concern. There were plenty of strong men around to stand at the Gate and check the travelers who came in for trade, and then make sure they left again before the Gate closed at sunset. It was the nighttime guarding that worried the Defaiders. Who among them would risk that? How could they keep themselves safe, especially out in the fields, guarding their flocks? They thought of wolves and soul eaters and shuddered.

Then one day, all the children of Gwenith seven years of age and older were summoned to the meetinghouse, and this is what they were told:

The Elders had conferred, and they agreed it was only right and proper that the children of Gwenith should be the ones to guard the Gate every night. They would also be responsible for leaving the Gate at night to watch the flocks. The children of Gwenith had been passed over, after all. The Beast posed no more danger to them. Therefore, who better than the children to guard the Gate each night? Who better than the children to go out into the pastures at sunset and watch over the sheep until daybreak? Of course this responsibility wouldn't be expected of the youngest—those under the age of seven. But all the others would be divided evenly among posts on the Gate and sent out into the fields with the sheep. Just as the sheepdogs left their scent to warn away wolves and foxes, so the children of Gwenith would be lanterns in the night, warning away any creatures of The Beast who might be tempted to visit ill upon the village.

It was additionally agreed that one man of Defaid should stay up with the children each night, to make sure the Gate stayed closed. That man would remain in the guardhouse, safe inside the Gate. Then they gave all the Gwenith orphans a reed whistle to wear on a leather cord around their necks. At first sign of danger, the orphans were to blow on their whistles, warning the villagers from sleep so they could seal themselves up in their root cellars, safe from soul eaters and other Beastly things.

And thus the orphans of Gwenith became the watchers of Defaid. And thus Alys learned exactly how much she'd do just because a man in black and white told her to.

NINE

Alys had once thought she loved to be awake at night, but that was the notion of a stupid child who lay in bed and had the luxury to decide if she was tired or not.

Now, Alys was tired all the time. She felt sick all the time, too, day and night. More than once she had fallen asleep with her chin on the Gate, and awakened seconds later with angry splinters buried deep. A few splinters were the least of her worries, though. One misstep on the narrow walkway that circled the Gate and down you went—a fall of twenty feet that nothing softened. It had been a few months since the children began watching, and already there had been broken bones. It was only a matter of time, Madog muttered to Enid, before one of them broke their neck. And then, Madog said, maybe the Defaiders would see reason. They'd have to admit that this was no job for children.

Then one of the children did break his neck. It was Bergam, an only child like Alys, and also just seven years old. Alys was out in the pasture that night, so it was Enid who told her the next day how she'd heard his cry in the dark and then the sound of his body making contact with the ground, and how she didn't think she'd ever forget that terrible bump in the night.

Madog was wrong. Bergam's falling changed no minds in the village. The Elders only told the Gwenith children to be more careful.

Alys had almost fallen to her death once herself. It was during the first freeze that it happened. The walkway was slick with ice, and Alys's eyes hadn't yet grown accustomed to the night. Now, Alys could walk the entire perimeter of the Gate with her eyes pressed closed and her hands tied behind her back. But at the beginning, every night was a terror—a fight against sleep and falling.

The children were meant to keep their distance from each other. They weren't to talk or huddle together. They were to disperse themselves evenly and watch. So when Alys lost her footing on the icy walkway, when her hands clawed against the side of the Gate and found no purchase, she should have fallen to her death with no one to catch her. Instead, someone lunged after her—a quiet little boy named Delwyn, who'd stuck close behind her because he hated to be alone. And somehow, together, Alys and Delwyn managed to pull themselves upright again instead of breaking their necks. Alys and Delwyn clung to each other in the moments after, their two hearts beating so fast. Then she whispered a quick thanks to him, and they each found their footing again.

Now, every day that passed in Defaid was the same for Alys. Mother woke her at noon for dinner and chores and a few simple lessons, fed her supper before sunset, and then sent her off to her post on the Gate or to guard the sheep outside the Gate. When sunrise ended her watch, Alys returned home again to breakfast and sleep, just as the rest of the village was awaking.

It might have been companionable, spending every night with the other children of Gwenith. But they were all too tired to talk or feel even an urge to play. Alys's friend Gaenor was fading under the strain, as if she were growing invisible before Alys's eyes. In Gwenith, Gaenor had been pink-cheeked and always laughing. Now she was a sallow-skinned shadow of herself with ribbons of purple under each eye.

Alys supposed that she must look much the same. All the children of Gwenith did. Whether each of them was dark-haired or light, tall or short, with eyes of stone or moss, there was never any confusing a child of Gwenith with a true child of Defaid. The Gwenith children had a hollow-eyed look to them. The circles under their eyes ranged only in their depth of color, from green to gray to plum. And there were no stout children of Gwenith. Most looked as if a strong wind might blow them off the Gate at night. And of course, occasionally, one did.

The children of Defaid, on the other hand, were apple-cheeked and careless. They laughed easily, played in the sunlight, and slept soundly in the dark.

Alys didn't much like the children of Defaid. Them or their stupid rhymes. She had come to hate all of the old songs, despite the fact that she'd sung many of them herself, back in her Gwenith days. Now, though, she felt different about them. Those rhymes stuck in her ears and she wished she could shake them loose, but they hooked themselves in and wouldn't let go.

> *If you think It cannot see you*
> *You are surely wrong*
> *Hide beneath your bedroom covers*
> *Try to sing a song*
>
> *While It creeps up ever closer*
> *It will softly coo*
> *Sorry dearie, you're in trouble*
> *Beast has come for you!*

She thought back to all the times she'd frightened Gaenor with such rhymes and she felt that must be some other child—not her—who'd done that. And in some other life. Ever since Mam and Dad had been taken by the soul eaters, and The Beast had come to Alys in the fforest, those old songs had brought Alys's stomach up to her throat. She felt her heart harden and darken when she heard some thoughtless child of Defaid singing one. She wanted to grab one of them by the hair—maybe precious Cerys, one of the prettiest little girls in the village—and tell her exactly what The Beast looked like when It came for you. How

It didn't coo, It spoke to you from the inside. Made you feel the wind. She wanted to watch Cerys's eyes grow wide with fear. Wanted to make her cry.

Alys scared herself sometimes. When she got angry like that she was certain that no other child of Gwenith had such nasty thoughts. The other Gwenith children were tired. Weary. Sad, often. But not angry. Not bitter. Alys's bitterness had a sharp taste. It sucked her mouth dry. Outwardly, though, Alys was just like any other child of Gwenith, and she found that the others had stopped looking at her as if she had the answer to some mystery they couldn't fathom. She was as tired as they were. She moved through her days with the same resignation they did. Their lot was the same.

Alys had thought she dreaded the night when she was little, but now the night was a monster that perched big and dark before her every day of her life. And that monster's home was the Gate, a mountain made of wood that Alys was coming to know better than her own bedroom. She was losing the ability to imagine a time when it hadn't existed, when her days and nights hadn't been patterned by it. It was bad enough in the summer, when days were long. But in winter, it seemed they'd barely finished their chores when the light had begun to shift, and the Gate called to them.

Each evening, the children of Gwenith climbed up the Gate, or walked off into the darkening fields with sheepdogs trotting by their sides. Meanwhile, the villagers of Defaid gathered around for their last glimpse of the purpling horizon while the men locked the doors to the Gate good and tight. Then they all sang a hymn:

Shepherd watching,
Watching over
We your flock
Of humble sheep

Thank you for your
Tender caring
We your flock
Now go to sleep

Alys had always refused to sing along with the villagers' sunset hymn. And eventually, all of the children of Gwenith stopped singing. For many of them the moment of resistance came with their first snowfall—or rainstorm—spent slipping along the walkway, or huddled under the leaky roof of one of the watchtowers, or shivering out in the fields. Not that it mattered, Alys reckoned, whether the children of Gwenith sang along or not. The children of Defaid sang loudly enough for all of them.

And so years passed this way, and Alys grew from a small, hollow-eyed child into a taller one. She looked back on her first days in Defaid now, and wondered how she had ever survived. The things she knew as a twelve-year-old dwarfed the things she thought she knew at seven. Though some things, of course, had remained the same. Alys still loathed the Elders and gave their mistress wives as wide a berth as she possibly could.

This wasn't always possible, however, because Mother was often sending Alys on some chore, usually outside the Gate.

Mother probably meant this as a kindness—a way of giving Alys some air. But to gain that sliver of freedom, Alys first needed to visit Elder Miles or his wife to ask for permission. After the Gate arose, the High Elder had divided the town into wedges, like a pie. Each wedge belonged to one of the Elders. Elder Miles was their Elder, and Alys thought of him as the High Elder's own personal shadow. He stuck so close to the High Elder, in fact, that Alys had a private nickname for him. She called him Shoulder. Wherever the High Elder was, there was Shoulder Miles, leaning in, whispering into his ear.

Ordinary Defaiders could travel in and out of the Gate as they wished, on just three conditions. One, they had to check in and out at the guardhouse. Two, they must return before sunset. And three, they could never, not ever, return to the old abandoned homesteads. The punishment for trespassing in those parts was banishment from Defaid forever. Alys figured the Elders knew that if the villagers got a taste of their old places, of the fresh air that could be breathed out there, they'd never return to this dusty, overcrowded town.

Children of Gwenith were given even stricter instructions than the ordinary Defaiders when they wished to leave the Gate. They were required to visit their Elder and have their names signed into a big book. Then they were given a numbered iron bracelet to wear while out, and to return when they were back. The wearing wasn't the important part—it was the returning. Each Elder knew that if a bracelet didn't come back to him at the end of the day, then a child of Gwenith had wandered.

The Elders of Defaid feared wandering more than anything

else. Alys would have liked to see the High Elder's face if ever he woke up one day to find all the Gwenith children gone. But that would never happen. The children knew the bargain they'd made. They gave Defaid their eyes and ears, their bodies and youth, and in exchange Defaid gave them shelter, food, clothing—and some illusion of safety. There was more than cold and hunger to fear on the long road between here and anywhere else. Stories had begun to circulate among the children about visions in the night pastures—visions of women like trees, whispering and singing, promising sleep and rest. It was only the older children—sixteen and older—who'd seen the tree women so far. And none had followed those lulling voices. But it was a matter of time, Alys thought, before one of them did. *To sleep.* Who among them wouldn't sacrifice anything for that?

None of the children of Gwenith had to be told to keep these visions to themselves. Confessing such a thing to a Defaider would get you lashed—or worse, banished. So the children of Gwenith never spoke of the singing except to each other, and in the hushest tones as they walked out to the fields.

Alys wondered sometimes if any of the people of Defaid ever heard the singing, ever saw the soul eaters. She thought not, though. Defaiders were snug within their Gate at night. No singing would reach their ears there. Inside their great wooden walls, the Defaiders were protected. Nothing came through the Gate that the Defaiders didn't expressly invite. Travelers were allowed in for trade, but they had to be out before sunset. The guards made sure of that.

Alys could never glimpse a traveler without thinking of Pawl.

She had seen him many times over the years. He and his wife, Beti, always had a smile for Alys. And every time he saw her, Pawl said the same thing. "There she is, the lass I found. Isn't she a pretty one?" He'd told her how the Elders wouldn't let him take her back to the Lakes with him, though he'd tried mightily to convince them. And there was only so hard he could push, he insisted, or they might never let him sell there again. Besides, he'd thought she was better off with her own kind, in a safe, stable home, not a drafty caravan. He hadn't known then—couldn't have known—what the Defaiders would make the children do. Alys heard his excuses and she saw that he meant every one of them. But even at age twelve, old enough to know how this world worked, she wanted him to be braver than his excuses. She wanted him to pick her up and take her back to the Lakes with him, with no thought to consequences. But she would never again ask him to save her from her circumstances. And they never again spoke of that day that he had left her in Defaid, and of how she'd cried for him.

That was still the last time she'd cried.

Alys had just finished washing the last supper dish when Mother said they must go to the Gate. It was a late summer day and already night seemed to be falling faster than it had just the day before. Alys went to her room to put on her extra nighttime layers of wool and looped her whistle around her neck.

Tonight she was to be out in the pastures with the sheep. A night like this the pastures could be pleasant. She could walk through the tall grass all night, and the sheepdogs were a sort of comfort, even if they weren't at all interested in people. They were working dogs whose only focus was keeping the sheep safe from foxes and wolves.

But walking through fields of grass never failed to remind Alys of the night in Gwenith when the soul eaters had come. Ever since she had first heard about the singing and the tree-women visions of the older children, she'd kept her ears pricked for their music. Sometimes she thought she heard it, heard someone calling to her, a gentle shushing, and then she realized it was just the wind in the leaves, the rustling of branches. She wondered how long she would have to wait to see the soul eaters again, and what would happen when she did. She felt drawn to them and frightened of them at the same time, and it was agony to her. The other children may have stopped looking at Alys as if she were different, but Alys knew better. Every day she felt like a monster walking among the innocent, felt as if she were trapped on the other side of a locked door. This feeling that Alys's true self was hidden created a distance between Alys and everyone around her, even the other children of Gwenith. She had no real friends among them. Not anymore. Her closest friend, Gaenor, had died of fever when they were both ten. Gaenor had been fading since the first day she'd arrived in Defaid, and in one week of sweat and coughing she had faded fully away. Not even Mother could save her.

Alys thought about all of this while the Defaiders sang their evening hymn, and then none too soon she was walking through the Gate with a black, tan, and white sheepdog by her side. Ahead of her on the path toward the pastures was Delwyn, whom she'd clung to on the Gate back when she was just a wee child of seven. He walked with his two brothers, Albon and Aron, who were both sixteen years old and identical twins. Delwyn was twelve now, the same age as Alys, but she was a good head taller than he was, and broader, too. He was just a slip of a thing, with hair so fair as to shine white in the moonlight. He was so quick and quiet on his feet that his brothers had nicknamed him Rabbit.

Delwyn wasn't so quick today, though. Alys could tell he wasn't well by the way he dragged his feet. And she saw that once Aron was sure the doors to the Gate were closed behind them, he knelt down and pulled Rabbit onto his back to carry him. It occurred to Alys that Delwyn was too old to be carried— she couldn't imagine anyone carrying her. But Delwyn looked more like a child of eight than twelve. As if he had decided to stop growing in this place.

Alys caught up with them. "Is Delwyn not well?"

Albon looked at Alys, a worried expression on his face. "Fever," he said.

Alys was silent. All the children knew what fever meant. It meant that you could wake up in a few days' time feeling better, or you could sink ever deeper and in a week's time you'd be dead. Like Gaenor.

Aron said, "We're going to bed him down under a tree, and leave a dog with him. Then we'll watch his pasture for him. Our Rabbit needs sleep if he's to get better."

They weren't supposed to do this. If the Elders found out, Albon and Aron would be punished severely—maybe even banished. But the Elders wouldn't find out. Who would tell them?

And no Defaider was ever brave enough to leave the Gate at night and check on them.

Alys's pasture, bound on all sides by dense hedges to keep the sheep from wandering too far, was beyond Delwyn's. She waved goodnight to the boys and walked on with her dog.

Hours passed while Alys walked her pasture. The moon arched overhead, then dipped westward, and that, finally, was Alys's signal that she could pause. She had grown chilled in the night air and needed to eat something to stay awake. She sank to the base of a tree and pulled out the food she'd wrapped for herself before she left home. She ate a hunk of sharp cheese with brown bread, then sank her teeth into an apple, and after she gnawed it down to seeds and stem, she sighed. Clenching her legs beneath her, she rose to a crouch and heard a mew.

Two yellow, moonlit eyes met hers and a small, striped wildcat emerged from the grass, tentative and questioning. Cats weren't allowed in Defaid. The Elders preached that they were outcasts of the Good Shepherd—untrainable, sneaky, and selfish at heart—unlike the dogs who worked their sheep. The High Elder said that wolves and wildcats were to The Beast what dogs and men were to the Good Shepherd.

Alys had often seen wildcats hunting in the pastures, but always from a distance, never so close. She froze in her crouch and caught her breath. The cat froze as well. Then, after several slow seconds, the animal approached, one cautious step at a time. Finally, when it was just a breath more than an armspan away, Alys reached out, palm up, and waited. She wondered what the cat's fur felt like. She felt a cold dot of moisture on one fingertip as the cat touched her with its nose, then the edge of a few teeth as it nudged her hand, rubbing her with its cheek, then looking up at her, half welcoming, half challenging. Alys scratched its cheek and chin the way she'd seen villagers do with the friendlier dogs. A rumbling began in the animal's throat, and then spread to the rest of its body. Alys found herself mesmerized. She felt the rumbling in her own body. She felt warm and furred. She felt cat.

Then she felt pain. The animal had sliced her palm with one of its claws, then hissed and sprang backward, its fur standing on end, its eyes narrow and teeth exposed in jagged spikes. Blood bubbled from a long welt that sizzled and throbbed across Alys's palm. *Evil thing,* she thought to herself. Alys grasped a rock to throw, but the cat had already raced off into the long grass. Alys threw the stone anyway, knowing full well it would never find its mark. Then she licked the blood from her hand and stood, trembling. She was cold again.

She shivered, and then she thought about Delwyn, asleep in his pasture all alone. Maybe, Alys thought, she could check on him. Alys could give Delwyn some of the mint tea she'd brought with her. That was one thing Mother had always said, that fever sucked folks dry so you had to keep filling them back up again. Decided, Alys stood up, pulled on her pack, and walked toward Delwyn's pasture.

She saw him, curled asleep under a tree, just a lump beneath wool blankets with a white-blond head poking out of the top.

And then she saw them. The girls who looked like trees,

the girls who were really soul eaters. They were floating toward Delwyn, across the field.

And then the girls who looked like trees saw Alys. And they floated toward her.

And they were near again, and so beautiful with their wide gray owl eyes. Still taller than Alys was, but not so much taller anymore. Their hair was long and black and wild, stitched through with leaves and sticks. Their clothes seemed made of leaves and sticks as well . . . or soil, if cloth could be made of soil.

Now they were near enough to her to speak, and Alys was never quite sure if they had come to her or if Alys had gone to them.

They rested hands on Alys's shoulders, one on either side of her, just as they'd done to her years before. Once again Alys felt the invisible thread that stretched from one girl's hand to the other, running through her.

"It's the girl. You remember her, Sister?"

"I do, Angelica. I remember the girl."

"Do you wish to come with us, girl? You could rest with us a while."

That word *rest*. It settled in Alys and it was all she could do not to give in to it, not to let her eyes droop, then close. It would be so sweet, to sleep. To rest. She thought of Delwyn and she forced her eyes to remain open.

"But it's not her time, Sister. It's not her time."

"Ay but it will be, Benedicta. Before too long."

And then they withdrew their hands from her and the invisible thread was broken, and they floated away and away from Alys until they were gone.

TEN

Alys knelt down next to Delwyn and put her hand on his head. She felt his heat inside of her own body, and a sudden rush of ache in her head and joints, a weakness that weighed her down like a yoke dropped onto her shoulders. She pulled her hand away from him and the feeling drained away. She opened her sack and pulled out the jug of tea, then she shook Delwyn awake. He looked up at her confused and wide-eyed for a moment, as if he weren't seeing her. Then his eyes cleared. But the sheepdog that lay next to him was seeing nothing. It was as still as stone. Alys reached out a hand to touch its thick pelt and she felt its slow breath, and her own breath slowed, her own eyes drooped. She'd seen sleep like that once before, in Gwenith. It was a bewitched sort of sleep. She yanked her hand away.

"Delwyn," Alys whispered, afraid to startle him. "Here, you

must drink some tea." She held the jug to his lips with one hand and helped him sit up with the other.

"Alys," he said, "I had the strangest dream."

"What was it?"

"I saw two slim trees floating through the field right there." He pointed a thin finger straight ahead of him into the pasture. "But instead of branches, these trees had arms and legs, and then I realized they weren't trees at all—they were women. And they just . . . floated toward me. They never did speak a word, but I felt like they were calling to me by name, like I could hear them in my head sort of singing to me. And it was beautiful, Alys."

"And then what happened?"

"Just when I thought I might get up and go to them, they stopped . . . and that's all I remember."

Alys sat all the way down next to Delwyn, and though she'd never done anything like it before, she pulled Delwyn close to her, and set his head to rest in her lap. Then she pulled his blanket over both of them, and she softly stroked his hair while telling him to go to sleep.

Alys stayed like that for hours, and she felt the heat rise out of Delwyn. As dawn was just beginning to blue the sky, Delwyn's fever broke, and his sweat-damp hair stuck to his head. It was time for them to be getting back to the Gates, so Alys shook him awake. They both crawled out from under the blankets, and the sheepdog roused itself from sleep as well. Then they both went looking for Albon and Aron.

At first they couldn't find the twins, but then Alys's eyes

were drawn to a center of unrest among the sheep out in the field—a hollow space that the sheep circled but refused to enter. When she and Delwyn waded among the flock, they found both brothers at the center of that circle. They were flat on their backs, mouths and eyes wide open.

Alys had seen those looks before. The look not just of death, but of soul death. Delwyn screamed and he gripped his whistle, ready to blow.

Alys yanked the whistle from his hand, gripped him hard by the shoulders. "You listen to me, Delwyn. Look at me. Just look at me, not at them." Delwyn's eyes kept traveling back to his brothers and their horrible expressions, so Alys dragged him out of the field. Then she turned to him again. "We'll get help, Delwyn. But you must listen to me for a moment. That dream you had, you must never, ever breathe a word of it to the Elders. Or to any other Defaider. Do you understand me?"

Delwyn looked back at her, white and terrified, but he nodded.

"And you also won't tell any of them that you slept under a tree all night. You will tell them that you walked your pasture, the way you always do, and in the morning you came here to find your brothers. And that is all you will say. You must promise me this, Delwyn."

Delwyn nodded again, looking like such a child. No, not a child, Alys corrected herself. Like one of the village girls' rag-dolls. Something made to look like a child but with no life in it.

She blew her whistle then, and she screamed, tugging Delwyn behind her. Madog came running first, and she told him what they'd found. And about the tree women that Delwyn had seen. "Tell no one," Madog said. "You know this, yes?" He was looking at Alys, not at Delwyn. Delwyn had gone someplace else inside, where there was no hearing or making sense of words.

Alys nodded.

"Now go wait in the pasture while I fetch the Elders. All I'll tell them is that you were walking back to the Gate from your separate pastures, and that's how you found them. Ay?" He looked at Delwyn now. "Ay, Delwyn? Say it."

Delwyn raised his eyes. They looked like glasses of clear, still water. He was so far away, Alys thought to herself. Right here by her, but not here anymore. Still, Delwyn nodded finally. "Ay," he said in a small voice.

Alys and Delwyn waited for the Elders at the edge of the pasture, unwilling to see again what they wished they hadn't seen at all. But once the Elders arrived, the children were forced to lead the way to the boys' bodies.

The Elders stood staring at the lifeless boys. The High Elder asked Delwyn what had happened and the boy went silent. His mouth dropped open and nothing came out, and Alys watched him in horror. This was no good, she thought to herself, no good at all. The Elders could not know about the tree women, how they called to him. Any child of Gwenith who admitted to seeing a soul eater—and who lived to tell the tale—would be banished. Or worse, burned as a witch. A creature of The Beast.

"We were on our way back to the Gate from our separate pastures," Alys said. "And we didn't see Albon and Aron on the road ahead of us, so we decided to look for them. And then we found them here, just so. We haven't touched them."

"I asked the *boy* what happened. Not you, Alys," the High Elder said to her, lowering his black brows so they met the top of his awful hawk nose.

The other Elders remained silent.

"This is the work of soul eaters," the High Elder said. "Creatures of The Beast."

The other Elders nodded.

The High Elder went on. "Evil seeks evil," he told them. "Like seeks like. The boys were disobedient. The proof is here before us. Why weren't they in their own pastures, instead of here together? How many times before have they deceived us, these two wayward children? The Good Shepherd can only guard the sheep who follow Him."

"It is as you say, High Elder." This was Shoulder Miles speaking. He folded his arms over his belly. "These boys invited The Beast into their midst. Worse, they have led The Beast's demons nearly to our doors."

There were a few intakes of breath at this. And not for the first time, Alys wondered at the fear of men who huddled behind a big wooden Gate at night.

"The boys brought this evil upon themselves," the High Elder said. "Thus nothing has changed for the Good Shepherd's loyal flock in Defaid. Life shall return to the way it was, and we shall once again learn the lesson that the Good Shepherd can only protect those who follow Him."

Alys bit her lip so hard she tasted blood. There were too

many things she wanted to say and the words crowded in her mouth and it was all she could do to keep them inside. She looked at Delwyn, and she saw a boy who only resembled the child she'd spent the night stroking. This child was just a mirror image of that boy—thin and cold, and nothing behind it.

ELEVEN

That afternoon, when Alys emerged from a restless few hours of fitful, dream-filled sleep, she begged Mother to send her on a chore.

"You've that look in your eye, Alys," Mother said. "That restless look. I know there's no sense trying to keep you here. But do you really think Elder Miles is going to let you out of the Gate to go foraging after what happened to those poor boys last night?"

Alys looked up at Mother. "Ay, he will if we give him something for it."

Mother straightened, hands on hips. "And what would you have me bribe him with?"

"Honey, Mother. You know how he likes it. Him and that fat belly of his."

Mother shushed Alys, quick and sharp, as if someone might overhear. "I've told you time and again, Alys, not to be saying such things."

"You've said the same about him yourself," Alys said.

"Ay, well, and that's my mistake." Mother shook her head and reached up onto a shelf for a jar of honey so dark brown it looked almost black. "If you're going to bribe him, it might as well be a good one."

Alys almost smiled, but then remembered there was nothing whatsoever to be smiling about today.

Then Mother handed Alys the basket. "Mushrooms," she said. "We can always use mushrooms. And you can tell Mistress Miles that you'll give her half of what you forage. That should please her. Though how on Byd you'd tell when that woman was pleased, I'll never know." She glanced in Alys's direction. "Now go."

Alys and Mother were quite practiced at lying to Mistress Miles and her husband the Elder. Usually it wasn't that they lied outright, it was that they just left something out. So maybe they'd tell Mistress Miles they were foraging for berries. And maybe they were doing that. But maybe they were also gathering the herbs needed to stop a woman's cycle or to ease the pain of a difficult birth. These were the kinds of herbs that the Elders strictly forbade. Anything to do with the monthlies and the trials of birthing were for the Good Shepherd to decide, they said. And to that, Mother said what the Elders didn't know about those two things was surely quite a lot. Mother was cautious, though. She kept her remedies to herself and she never again mentioned the tea she'd given Mary that night.

Mother and Alys certainly weren't the only ones in the village keeping secrets from the Elders. All of the villagers cut such corners—and sweetened their requests for permission with a hunk of cheese here, or a jar of preserves there. Alys could only imagine how full Mistress Miles's larders must be, thanks to all that sweetening.

Alys squinted painfully when she stepped out into the full sun, blinded for a moment. She stood there, her hand shielding her eyes, until the sun through her eyelids didn't stab needles into her brain, then slowly cracked her eyes open bit by bit, until she could make out the world around her. It had been dry for a week, and dust rose up from feet, wagons, and hooves that passed by. If Alys turned right, she'd be at the Gate doors in less than five minutes. If she didn't need permission to leave, she could walk straight through those doors and make her way to the fforest. Instead, she turned left, toward Elder Miles.

The Elders lived in the nicest homes in the village. Their homes weren't grand, that wouldn't have been seemly. But their whitewash was always fresh, their shutters in the best repair.

Mistress Miles must have been right on the other side of her kitchen door when Alys knocked, because instantly she filled the doorway in her black dress and starched white apron. She was a formidable woman, tall and broad with dark eyebrows that made straight black lines across her face and charcoal hair pulled in a tight bun. "Be quick with what you want, child, it's been a constant flow today and it's keeping me from my work."

Alys handed her the basket with the honey. "Mother wants me to forage for mushrooms. And to give you half."

"I'll ask the Elder." Mistress Miles always called her husband the Elder. She closed the door and left Alys to wait outside.

The door opened again. "The Elder gives you his permission. He's noted it in the ledger. Mind the time, though. He'll know if you tarry." Mistress Miles handed Alys the basket, now empty of the honey, and gave her a heavy iron bracelet with the number nine engraved on the inside.

Alys slipped the bracelet onto her wrist, nodded, and left Mistress Miles's broad skirts behind her.

As Alys walked toward the fforest she thought about the dreams she'd had after her watch had ended. She hadn't dreamed of Albon and Aron, dead in the field. That's probably what a good child would have dreamed about. A child who was more a stranger to such things. She hadn't even dreamed of the soul eaters. Instead she'd dreamed of The Beast. It had been five years since she saw It last, five years of wondering if she'd ever see It again. But in her dream she felt as if no time had passed at all. The weather that was the essence of It was as powerful to her as ever. The sensation of being part of It, and of It being part of everything else—rock and stream, mountain and tree—was so strong that Alys could feel the wind inside of her.

All the time since she'd last seen The Beast, she had spent wondering. Was she good, like Mother, or was she bad, like the soul eaters? There was a part of Alys that wanted to be good. And yet there was another part of her—so insistent and noisy in her head—that wondered why she should wish for that. What would goodness get her? A starched apron? A life spent watching for creatures in the night?

She thought of the way she'd felt when she was with the tree women, how she had been on the verge of surrendering to sleep, and how she would have exchanged anything for a bit of rest. How she might have gone with them if only they'd asked a second time. She also thought of how she'd felt—not herself anymore—when she touched The Beast, the furred cat, and Delwyn's fevered head. It was different from the way she'd felt when she touched Mary's belly. With Mary, Alys had been able to stand apart from the sickness she sensed inside. With the others, there was no separation. Maybe one day she'd touch something—or someone—and lose herself altogether. Is that how it began for the soul eaters? Alys wanted to ask Mother these questions, but if she took one step in that direction, Alys knew Mother would find out everything. She would see through all of Alys's lies and half-truths, and she'd know what Alys had done. Alys wouldn't be able to keep it from her any longer. Mother would know that Alys had let those creatures take her parents. And then Mother would look at Alys differently. Or maybe she would stop looking at her at all. Alys couldn't bear that.

Alys entered the fforest and was enclosed by green and moist earth. It was cool relief after the dry, dusty village. Alys felt something in her back and shoulders unknot as she stepped farther and farther into its damp moss and musty, rotting leaves. This was where she belonged, she thought to herself. Not in that village, or up on that Gate, or in those pastures. It was only here that Alys ever felt that she was going toward something, and not just beating a circular path around a truth about herself that she could never quite get to.

She walked on, deeper and deeper into the fforest. No direction, just deep.

When she heard Its now-familiar voice in her head—the voice that was inside of her but didn't belong to her—she felt a thrill of excitement. This was wrong, she knew, very wrong. And yet this was why she had come to the fforest. This was always why she came to the fforest. To find It.

You saw them again, and they saw you.

"Ay," said Alys. "Both." She looked all around her and then she caught sight of The Beast, stepping with long, knee-bent strides around trees. Alys regarded Its leathery wings and wondered what It must look like flying through the air.

It came closer, ever closer. And then It was sniffing the air around her, nostrils flaring over fangs and black tongue. Alys smelled Its breath in her face. Like fallen leaves.

It tapped the iron bracelet on her wrist with one long claw.

Give me that. Give me that.

Alys pulled it off and handed it over. The Beast hooked it with a long claw. Held it.

Did you see what they did? Did you see them take what should not have been taken?

"No," Alys said. "Not until after."

Like before.

Like before. Like when her mam and dad were killed. Of course. It was the same. They had left her and taken others. And she had let them. She hadn't raised a hand to stop them.

Hadn't spoken a word of warning or threat. It hadn't even occurred to her to do so. She truly was an evil girl. Maybe this was why she was safe from the soul eaters. They only ate good souls. "Why? Why didn't they take my soul, too?"

They don't take children.

"Why not?"

They don't hate children. Yet.

"Yet?"

The Beast didn't answer. It cocked Its head at her.

Alys looked into Its wet, black eyes and the fforest around her dissolved and she felt herself falling. It was as if a great hole had opened in the earth, and she were falling in and down. There was nothing in this hole. The hole itself was nothing. There was no more weather and wind. There was no scent of mud and water. The hole was all around Alys. There was no sound, not even the sound of her own scream, muffled and trapped in her lungs.

Then Alys was back again, the fforest growing up around her, the sound of water dripping off leaves, the scent of moss.

You felt the hole. It grows wider and deeper and bigger and blacker with every soul they take.

Alys shook her head, tried to shed the image—the feeling—of that awful black hole. It brought a terrible memory to mind. "I saw a picture once," Alys said. "A picture of you. And you were sitting at the bottom of a big, black hole catching doomed souls in your mouth."

I do not do that.

"No," Alys said, and she realized that of course she didn't

believe The Beast did that. This creature in front of her might look like the picture in the book, but It wasn't the same thing at all. Alys thought back to what Pawl had told her on the way to Defaid long ago: The stories the Elders told about The Beast and soul eaters were stuff and nonsense they used to scare their people. The High Elder's book was a story, wasn't it? A story the High Elder told himself and his people to keep them on the righteous path. To keep them in line. Keep them from wandering deep into the fforest where there were no starched aprons and white collars. No meetinghouses. No rules. No bracelets and ledgers.

Alys looked at The Beast. "What are you?"

I am The Beast. That is all I am. That is all I have ever been.

"Is the hole a threat to you?" Alys said.

The hole is a threat to all of us, to everything.

"Can't you close it? Can't you stop the soul eaters? You're The Beast. Can't you do anything?"

The Beast was silent, so Alys did the only thing she could think to do. She touched It. She placed her hand right on the center of Its furred chest. Her first thought was how fragile It felt, like touching a bird that was more feather than flesh.

Then she was flying. She was growing. She was swimming. She was sprouting leaves, and losing leaves. Animals were nesting in her, beetles and worms crawled through her, eggs hatched in her. She was becoming earth and water and air.

Then she knew. The Beast could no more stop the soul eaters than the wind could stop them. Or the rain. Or a leaf.

You're the girl. The one like them. You must close it.

Alys had wanted an end to the wondering about The Beast and why It showed Itself only to her. Now that she knew, she felt panic rising inside of her like a flock of startled birds. "You want me to close the hole," she said. "When? How?"

When you are ready, then you will know how.

The Beast crouched, and leapt, and It was gone.

It was where the fear grew.

The sisters looked down at the bodies of the boys who would be tired no longer, who would never again have anything to fear. Angelica sniffed the air around them. Nothing. She and Benedicta had taken everything away.

And out of nothing would grow more fear. That would be a rich meal for the sisters. In time.

Benedicta reached for her sister's hand. "Sister," she said, "next time we should leave no bodies. We should lead them far away into the fforest before we give them their rest."

"Why, Sister?"

"Think of the others. Never knowing what became of the wanderers. Waiting and watching. Can you taste their worry?"

Angelica touched her sister's face, saw her own face in her sister's eyes. "Ay, Sister. Ay."

The sheep stared on, chewing. Blank eyes in blank faces. The sisters floated through them. The sheep drifted away from the sisters like flakes of snow in the wind.

The sisters would return to the fforest now. They would visit the mountains. The Lakes. They would float through some other village's pastures, beckon to a sleepy traveler. The thought of so many souls made the sisters hungry again.

Then they spotted another boy. A smaller one than the twin brothers they'd taken, much smaller. This boy lay beneath a tree, a dog beside him. The child didn't stir, but the dog did. Ears pricked.

"Sleep, dog," Benedicta said. And it did.

"Wake, boy," Angelica said. And he did.

The boy's eyes were open and his heart was welcoming.

"Sister," Benedicta said. "This one is just a child. It's not his time yet."

Angelica sniffed the air. "No, not his time. Do you smell him, Sister? He smells like rain. Those other boys smelled sour. This one is fresh. Clean."

Benedicta sniffed the air. Agreed.

"Shall we take him, Benedicta? Take him for our own, never let him turn sour and afraid?"

Before Benedicta could answer, there was another child. A girl. The girl. The girl who was like them but not like them. They floated to her, and touched her, and flowed through her. The sisters caught her scent of green wood.

They offered her rest, but she hesitated and so did they. It wasn't her time, either. She would be a meager meal yet. The sisters looked into the night and they left the girl and the boy where they found them, the boy asleep now and dreaming of women like trees. Dreaming of the sisters.

The sisters left him there, but not for long. There was a yearning in that boy, the boy with the welcoming heart. The sisters would not have to come for that boy. He would come to them. And soon.

The yearning would bring him.

PART

3

*Hear
It scratch
upon
your
door*

TWELVE

Mother took the blame on herself for the missing bracelet with the number nine. She told Mistress Miles that it was her fault for sending Alys out so early in the day, before she'd had her sleep. No wonder the child had lost it, she said. And then Mother gave Mistress Miles her last jar of blackberry preserves.

The day after Alys and Delwyn found Albon's and Aron's bodies, Delwyn disappeared. The Elders said he'd run away, but the guards on duty insisted they hadn't seen him. Alys pictured tiny Delwyn, a hat pulled down over his white-blond hair, tucking himself into the back of a farmer's wagon. Slipping out unnoticed. And of course he'd leave in the day. He'd leave when none of the other children would think to look for him or stop him. He'd leave while they were sleeping.

In time, the loss of the three brothers became a cautionary

tale—a story told to the children of Defaid at bedtime. "The wages of disobedience," they were all told, "are steep." Minus three children of Gwenith, everything in Defaid went back to the way it was. Except not quite. Because Delwyn was just the first of the wanderers—since his departure, eight more children of Gwenith had run away. Unlike Delwyn, all of the runaways who left after him had been sixteen. They went out to guard the sheep one night, the same as always, and they never came back.

After the first sixteen-year-old left, the villagers tutted and looked down their noses at the rest of the children of Gwenith. The villagers reminded themselves of what the High Elder had always said: *Like seeks like. Those Gwenith children surely had a taint on them*, they murmured to each other.

Then another sixteen-year-old ran away. And another. The villagers' tutting turned inward. They never spoke their concern aloud, but Alys felt it nonetheless. Fear rose off the village. The scent of it caught in the breeze, tickled Alys's nose. She knew exactly what the villagers were thinking. *Who will guard our Gate if all the children of Gwenith run away?*

While the villagers of Defaid whispered and worried, the children of Gwenith kept their mouths tightly sealed. It was only when they walked to the pastures at sunset that talk sometimes drifted to the wanderers. Some of the children hoped the runaways were safe and sound in another village. Those who suspected otherwise kept it to themselves, especially if they were talking to a child whose brother or sister had wandered. They were careful not to speak of the wanderers and the tree women in the same breath. Enid had given them all tight balls of wool and told them to stop up their ears at night should they ever hear the singing. Alys had noticed the older children roll their eyes at this, and toss the wool away. As if, they said, a little plug of wool would have saved Albon and Aron. And so it came to be that when a child of Gwenith turned sixteen it was as if a great hourglass were turned over, and the waiting began.

For months after Delwyn disappeared, when Alys should have been watching for something evil on the horizon or lurking among the sheep, she watched for the glow of Delwyn's white-blond hair instead. From her perch on the Gate, or her watch in the fields, she looked for him every night. And when the doors of the Gate opened in the morning, she always hoped to see him slip through, pale and silent, quick and sly. But he never did.

After he ran away, Alys began keeping careful track of all the children of Gwenith, plumbing her brain to recall the names of each and every one, even the babies who'd died before they could speak more than a few words. On one of her underskirts that no one but she would ever see, Alys sewed the name of each child of Gwenith, grouping them together, brothers and sisters. The names of those who died, she stitched a thin line of thread through. The names of those who wandered, she stitched a thin line underneath.

Over the three years since Delwyn's wandering, Alys had outgrown the underskirt, but she'd cut a neat square of linen out of it, just big enough to contain the names. She kept it tucked away in a pocket in her dress. Sometimes, in the still cold of the night, she parsed the thread ridges of each name with the pad of one finger. She sought out Delwyn's name most often.

Now, fifteen years old and standing on the Gate, her keen eyes scanning a dark landscape she'd memorized long ago, Alys allowed her fingers to search out his name yet again. If by some chance Delwyn were still alive, then he wasn't a little boy anymore. He was the same age as Alys. Nearly a man. Alys wondered if she'd know him again. The night chill wrapped around her. He was dead, surely.

She felt it in some deep part of herself—a connection broken. A fine thread that had tied her to Delwyn ever since he'd saved her life on the Gate. That thread hung loose now, floating and frayed. Her friend was gone. The soul eaters had gotten him, the same way they would get all of them eventually. Alys sensed Angelica and Benedicta out there, biding their time, taking the children one by one, robbing Defaid of its guardians. And sowing pungent fear among the Defaiders with each one they took. She could imagine them sniffing the air, taking it in.

Alys often thought of what the soul eaters had said of her when she saw them last—*it's not her time, but it will be, before too long.* Alys had only months left until her sixteenth birthday. Her hourglass was about to tip over. It had been three years since she'd last seen The Beast, since It had told her about the hole she needed to close. Time—for everything—was running out.

A low hoot, barely loud enough to reach her ears, rose up from the nearest watchtower, and Alys turned toward the sound of Elidir signaling the sunrise. It was the boy's special talent, to know just moments before the first ray would lick over the horizon. Elidir's only sister, Glenys, had run away two years ago. Perhaps that's what made him especially watchful.

Alys made her way to the watchtower, and Elidir nodded to her before she descended. Mirrors were forbidden in Defaid—they were invitations to The Beast, the High Elder said—but Alys didn't need a mirror to know what she looked like. Her face—long, lean, shadowed—was just like Elidir's.

"Wake up, child."

Alys was already awake. She'd heard Mother's footsteps. But she waited for Mother to speak before she opened her eyes to the rough wooden ceiling of her bedroom. Unlike her restless sleep of childhood, now Alys slept flat on her back, unmoving as death the moment she lay down. She woke up as quickly.

Mother hovered outside her bedroom door, pausing long enough to be sure Alys wouldn't fall to sleep again. Not that Alys ever would. Alys got out of bed, pulling smooth the woolen blanket that covered her narrow bed. She dressed in knit stockings, sturdy lace-up boots, and a dove-gray dress that used to fall to her shoes but now just barely grazed her ankles. She would need a new one soon. She had a brown dress, too, and that one was longer but she hated it. The skirt was cut too narrow and it tripped her up when she took a broad stride. She also had a blue dress, and that one was fine, but this wasn't a blue dress day. It was a gray dress day. Alys took the wooden comb from the small table by her bedside, flattened her hair to the nape, then braided and tied it with a thin strip of leather. Last, she pulled on her whistle.

The day was cold and clear. Through the closed shutters she could hear the sound of children laughing in the town square.

Defaid children. The younger ones had spent their morning in lessons and soon their mothers would be calling them home to dinner. The older ones—fourteen and over—would have spent those same hours learning trades, caring for animals, sewing and laundering clothes with their mothers, harvesting or shepherding with their fathers.

The Gwenith children were just beginning their day. In houses all around the village, they were getting dressed in layers of wool. After dinner they'd do their chores. Those of school age would get an hour or so of lessons. Not as much instruction as the children of Defaid received—there wasn't time for that—but enough to teach them their letters and simple sums. Then it would be time for supper. Then watching. Last night was the Gate for Alys. Tonight would be guarding the sheep.

Alys sat down to the table that Mother had already set for dinner. Father was there, hands in his lap. His flat-brimmed hat hung on a hook on the wall, and his steel-gray hair was wet and raked back from his head. Alys could see the lines from his comb. His shirt was clean. He always changed it before dinner. By supper he'd once again be sprinkled with a layer of sawdust. It would catch in every crease in his face, collect in his ears.

"Good day, Father."

"Alys," he said.

Mother set heavy plates before both of them, then brought her own. Mutton in gravy, potatoes, a pile of stewed greens, brown bread and butter.

Father closed his eyes. Alys and Mother joined him. "Good

Shepherd, we thank you for this bounty." He opened his eyes and picked up his fork.

"Elder Miles stopped by looking for you," Mother said.

"Oh," Father said.

"Looked for you in the wood shop. Couldn't find you."

"Wasn't there."

Mother looked at him, waiting. Alys knew she wouldn't be able to wait long. Mother had a restless, impatient streak that she worked hard to tamp down. Perhaps that was why she and Alys got along so well. It was something else they shared. "I know that. Don't know where you were, though. Folks like to know where folks are."

"Ay. Folks do," Father said. He put a large piece of mutton in his mouth, chewed meticulously. Swallowed. Drank some water. Alys almost smiled. She ate instead.

The lines at the corners of Mother's eyes multiplied and she put down her fork. "Eldred." This was father's given name, and it was Mother's signal to him that her patience was at its end.

Father lifted his gray eyes to meet Mother's brown. "I was helping Lloyd mend his roof."

Mother seemed to shorten in her chair. She blinked, glanced quickly at Alys, and then away again when Alys looked back. "In the village?"

"Outside. The old place." Father glanced up at her, then down at his plate again. "Branch fell on Lloyd's roof in the last storm. Ripped a clean hole. Not so bad, but it needed seeing to."

"Did you have permission to go all the way out there?"

Mother asked. Mother surely already knew the answer to that question. There was no granting permission to go out to the old homesteads. It was strictly forbidden. No exceptions. Mother stared at Father, full in the face, awaiting his answer in any case. Alys saw that Mother had yet to eat anything. But Mother never did eat much. She was all bone and sinew.

Father looked at Mother, kept chewing.

"Eldred," Mother said, so quietly it might only have been her lips moving. Alys smelled fear, sharp and nose-curling.

"I know, Heledd. I know." Father's eyes shifted to Alys, then back to Mother. Mother nodded, picked up her fork, and ate.

As Alys walked along she passed the schoolyard, where the youngest children of Defaid had returned to play after finishing their dinners. She saw seven-year-old Ren leaning against the fence that surrounded the schoolyard. He was Madog and Enid's oldest child, and just about to begin watching at night. Alys paused next to him and followed his eyes.

The children of Defaid were all standing in a perfect circle while one sturdy boy walked around them, singing:

> *The Beast is an animal*
> *You'd better lock the Gate*
> *Or when it's dark, It comes for you*
> *Then it will be too late*
>
> *The Beast is an animal*
> *Hear It scratch upon your door*

It sucks your soul then licks the bowl
And sniffs around for more

The Beast is an animal
It has a pointy chin
It eats you while you sleep at night
Leaves nothing but your skin

On the last word—*skin*—the boy touched a small blond girl's shoulder and then he took off in a tear around the circle, chased by the girl. The children all screamed with joyful terror as he ran for the little girl's empty spot in the circle. Alys used to know all the Defaid children by name, but the older she got, the less she paid attention. She recognized the boy, though. He was one of the High Elder's grandsons, a sly bruiser named Wyn. He was the type of boy who always did his worst when the adults weren't looking. He easily reached the little girl's spot before she could catch him, and now the girl was It. Alys shook her head. That poor girl would be It for the rest of the afternoon if she didn't find someone smaller and slower to pick on.

Children and their games. Alys couldn't imagine she had ever been similarly enchanted. Maybe the games had gotten meaner. Then she remembered how she'd taken such pleasure in frightening Gaenor.

Alys looked down at Ren, who was leaning his chin on the fence. "Where's your mother?"

"The babies," Ren said, his eyes fixed on the children. Enid and Madog had just had twins, boy and girl. Alys supposed that meant that Enid was busy. She looked at Ren closely. He was thin, not so pink and bright-eyed as usual. She rested her palm on his brown cap of hair and felt his weariness in her own bones. She felt something else, too—a yearning that stretched and stretched and made Alys feel the tiniest bit dizzy. Ren looked up at her, surprised. She pulled her hand away.

"There you are," a woman's voice said behind them. It was Enid. "I've just got the twins down for their nap. Come, you." Enid was twenty-five now, and starting to show her age. "We're getting Ren ready for watching," she said. "He's learning to sleep when the sun's up."

With all the wanderings of the older children, the Elders had begun to look to the next generation of Gwenith children to guard the pastures and the Gate. Fifty of them had made the journey from Gwenith eight years ago. There were only twenty-five left—fully half of them had been lost to accident, illness, or wandering. Ren was the first of the new crop.

"Oh," Alys said. "I thought he looked tired."

"Yes, tired. Well, aren't we all?" Enid had been given special permission not to watch while she was pregnant, but once her babies were a year, she'd have to mount the Gate again and the twins would be left with one of the village families each night. At least, Alys supposed, Enid and Madog could keep an eye on Ren if they were all on the watch together.

"Will they let you keep Ren with you," Alys said, "when you watch?"

"Madog's asked the Elders about that." Enid smiled tightly. "We'll see. Come, Ren."

"I could help," Alys said, without thinking. She thought about Delwyn, how he'd saved her that first winter. "I could keep an eye on him, too."

Enid gave her a real smile now—no teeth, but soft, rounded cheeks. She even reached for Alys's hand for one brief moment, and Alys felt the rasp of Enid's calluses. Then Enid turned away and pulled Ren along behind her. The boy slowly peeled his eyes away from the children, and Alys watched mother and son walk away. She noticed how Ren's trousers bagged around his hips, pulled tight by an old belt of his father's. His cuffs were folded up several times. Room to grow, she supposed. She could hardly believe that she'd been so small once. That at Ren's very age, she'd first climbed the Gate herself.

THIRTEEN

Alys's boots crunched in the frost that laced the dirt beneath her feet. The basket was heavy on her hip, and though she'd wrung Father's linen shirts until they no longer dripped, still she felt the moisture seeping through her wool overcoat. It was just past dinnertime, but the sun looked weak and tired, as if it had held its weary head up long enough and it could hardly stand the effort.

Normally Mother would have had the washing hung when the sun was still on its rise. But she was feeling poorly today and she asked Alys to wash Father's shirts and then hang them up to dry. It had taken Alys twice as long as Mother to perform the same task, and to do it half as well. Alys figured the wash would be more frozen than dry when she retrieved it by supper, and would end up dripping in front of the fire, a grand, steamy mess.

In planning out Defaid, the Elders had declared it slovenly and unseemly for laundry to be strewn about the village. Clothing touched skin, and skin was a private matter. So the women were instructed to do their washing in their own kitchens and yards and then hang their laundry to dry on the communal lines in the southern corner of the village. Only women were allowed there, lest a man catch sight of a woman's limp underskirt hanging from a line. The women were expected to be able to control themselves around the men's saggy braies.

The washing lines were strung between tall posts and each family had its own stretch of line, some longer than others depending on how large the family was. Mother's line was short. The nearest line to hers belonged to pinch-faced Mistress Daniels, and next to her was Mistress Hardy. When Alys arrived with her bundle, both women were there. Their youngest children hung miserably at the two women's legs, sniffling and crying to go home. Lined up around all the other washlines, the same scene unfolded in dreary progression. Gray-faced women were hunched over baskets, and were clung to by wet-nosed children.

Neither Mistress Daniels nor Mistress Hardy nodded or spoke to Alys, nor did she expect them to. Anyway, the women were too busy gossiping about the travelers who'd just arrived that morning to pay Alys much mind.

Alys's trip to the washlines hadn't allowed her time for a curious stroll past the travelers' caravan, so she hadn't yet laid eyes on them. She wondered if it might be Pawl and Beti. They were due for a visit.

"Is that boy their son, do you think?" Mistress Hardy

said, pinning up a pair of her husband's massive trousers.

A son? Well then it couldn't have been Pawl and Beti. And she'd so hoped it was them.

"It's all the same to them, I imagine," said Mistress Daniels. She stopped her own pinning and lowered her voice. "You know them travelers marry their brothers and sisters, don't you?"

Mistress Hardy clutched a damp apron and widened her eyes. "You don't say?"

"I do say," said Mistress Daniels. "Sons, nephews, daughters, nieces. It's all the same to them. Foul creatures. And I've heard tell that the men lie down with men, and the women with women."

"What for?"

Mistress Daniels cut two hard eyes at Mistress Hardy, who appeared no less confused as a result.

"But here's the thing," said Mistress Hardy. "Why would the Good Shepherd keep safe such savages?" She shielded her daughter's left ear with one of her hands, and pressed the child's right ear into her skirt until the girl struggled. "How is it they can travel anywhere they please, but aren't taken by *them*. The soul eaters?"

"Travelers are The Beast's wicked stepchildren, that's how." Mistress Daniels nodded her head short and sharp, and Alys found herself slowing her hands despite herself, taking longer with the washing than she ever needed to. The nonsense that these women talked. That all of them talked. As if they knew anything about soul eaters. Or travelers. Or anything. It was no wonder Mother called Mistresses Hardy and Daniels the Blind and the Dumb.

"You don't say," Mistress Hardy said. Her eyes were so wide, so thirsty for more, Alys thought they might loosen in their sockets and fall clean out of her head.

"I do say," said Mistress Daniels. "Mistress Miles told me they sacrifice their firstborn children to The Beast. Chop their heads right off, and say a toast to The Beast with their babies' own blood." She hissed her words now, and didn't notice her son had stopped crying and was staring at her, mouth open, nose running thick and yellow. "Ay, and after that they dance naked under the moon."

"The Good Shepherd help us all," said Mistress Hardy. "And what do you suppose they do with the heads?

Mistress Daniels wrinkled her brow. "What heads?"

"The baby heads, Agnes. The ones they cut off?"

That's when the screaming started. Boy and girl let up such a shriek and a howl that Alys nearly dropped her basket.

"Whatever are you shouting about, child?" Mistress Daniels pushed the boy off her skirts and wiped his face roughly with a linen. "Why can't you be more like your older sister? Quiet as a mouse that one is." Then she looked up at Alys, her face sealed at the lips. "What are you looking at, girl?"

Alys looked back at her line and hung the last shirt in her bundle. "Nothing, Mistress."

As Alys walked away, Mistress Daniels raised her voice over her weeping brat. "That one's just like them travelers. Mind your children around her, Della. Mark my words."

FOURTEEN

As Alys walked home through the village, the sun sliced sideways across the horizon, casting long, cold shadows. Instead of cutting straight through the village, Alys perched the empty basket on her hip and took the long way around the perimeter of the Gate so as to get a look at the travelers.

It was Pawl and Beti. She'd recognize their four strong, ugly horses anywhere. And of course she always knew Pawl by his red hair—now shot through with more white than when she'd first met him eight years before. Alys had grown fond of Beti over the years, as well. She'd never known a woman to laugh more often, or at less. Beti was nearly as strong and broad-shouldered as Pawl himself was, and it would be a charitable way of saying it to call her disheveled. In truth, Beti wasn't simply sloppy, she was unconcerned.

With them, there was indeed a boy. Or not a boy, exactly. He stood half a head taller than Pawl. Those women at the washlines were ignorant fools, and no surprise there. Even if Alys hadn't known that Pawl and Beti had no son, anyone could see that the boy wasn't the couple's natural child. His skin was the brown of buckwheat honey and Pawl's and Beti's complexions were as pale as Alys's. The boy's true parents must have been from the mountains. One of the things villagers from Defaid didn't trust about travelers is that they came in so many colors. The people of Defaid only came in shades of milk, but travelers from the Lakes were those colors and more. Folks were drawn there from all the far corners of Byd.

Alys tried not to stare at the boy, then discovered that she was doing so anyway. The boy's eyes were the darkest brown. With a start, Alys realized the eyes that she was studying so intently were looking straight back into her own.

Alys peeled her gaze up and away as if she hadn't been looking at all, and then she turned her attention to what they were selling from the other villages. There were saddles and shoes from Tarren. Also bags of ground hard winter wheat. There were woven grass baskets and salt fish from Pysgod, the village that clung to the river. The wares weren't so interesting that Alys needed to be perusing them for long, and there was no sense pretending otherwise. She glanced up at the young traveler again and saw the slightest flicker of a smile playing around the edges of his mouth.

"Our lass!" Pawl poked his head out of one of the caravans,

rushed over and grasped Alys around her middle, and picked her up off her feet.

"Oh, we've been looking for you, child." Now it was Beti's turn, and she lifted Alys just as easily. Alys felt the itchy snarl of her gray hair where it leapt free of its bun.

"Now look what we've brought with us, Alys," Pawl said. "Not pots and pans, no, this time we brought a nice big boy. And what do you think of him?"

Alys felt herself blush crimson, and when she glanced up her gaze stopped at the boy's mouth, where she saw that same lip curl of amusement that she'd noticed before.

"He's a handsome lad, isn't he, Alys?"

"Oh now Pawl," Beti said, punching him hard enough in the arm that she tilted him just slightly off his feet. "Leave her alone. She'll run away if you keep teasing her like that."

"I'm Cian," the tall boy said. "And you're the fair Alys that Pawl and Beti can never stop talking about."

"Ay," Alys said, "I suppose I am." She couldn't bear even to glance in Cian's direction. The heat in her face had traveled to her stomach, and Alys felt the urge to run. "Well, I should go now. Mother will be waiting for me." She glanced at Pawl and Beti. "And I'm in the pasture tonight so I'll need to bundle."

"Ah, well then I've just the thing for you," Pawl said. "Something I've been saving for when you were a bit older. And bigger." He dashed into one of the caravans and then was back again with a wool coat. Mam's coat. The one she'd left in Pawl's wagon eight years ago.

Alys touched the coat, looked at Pawl, nearly threw her arms around him but didn't. "Mam's coat. You kept it for me?" She pressed her face to it, but no scent of Mam remained. Silly to think there might be.

"Ay lass, I did. I remember like it was yesterday. You such a wee thing, and it was all you had of her. Didn't realize I had it until I was a day or more away from Defaid. And then I thought to myself, Pawl, the lass will grow into it someday, and then you'll give it to her. And now I have." He laughed and chuckled, wiped his eyes.

Beti patted his arm, wiped her own. "Ay dear lass, you run along then," Beti said. "The shame of it, sending you children out on a night as chill and damp as this one's likely to be. The coat will help, won't it? And we'll look for you tomorrow day, all right?"

"Ay," Alys said, and then she did hug Pawl, swift and hard, and hurried off relishing the cold on her warm cheeks.

As she rounded the corner toward home, Alys saw Enid emerging from Mother and Father's front door. Enid paused for a moment and looked around her as if unsure what to do next. When she caught sight of Alys she walked toward her, head down. It had been a month since Enid had returned to the watch, leaving her twins to the care of a village woman all night. Ren was on the watch now, too, and his company might have been a solace to his mother, but the Elders had turned down Madog's request that the boy be allowed to watch alongside one of his parents. Madog took the news quietly, but Alys sensed something different about him lately, a set to his jaw that she'd not noticed before and a scent like wet metal whenever she drew near him.

"Alys," Enid said when she was close enough to whisper, "I have a kindness to ask of you." Enid squeezed Alys's hand briefly, and she felt the tickle of Enid's rough fingers on her palm. "It's Ren. He's feeling poorly." She looked at Alys meaningfully. When children of Gwenith took sick in their first years on the watch, they often didn't recover. "He's to be out in the pasture tonight and Madog and I are on the Gate. You said once you'd help look after him, and I'm asking if you'll do that tonight. Keep an eye on him?"

"Ay," Alys said. "I'll look after him."

Enid nodded. "Good. I'll tell Madog. He'll be grateful, as am I."

As they walked to the pastures at sundown, Ren pursed his lips and blew misty clouds of hot breath into the cold dusk. He tilted his head back and watched the puffs of warm, damp air turn white and then disappear above him. He blew long slow puffs, then short fast bursts.

What a thing to play at, Alys thought to herself as she watched Ren puffing along. He should know by now that seeing your breath meant a long, cold night ahead. A child of Gwenith shouldn't find joy in the cold.

Puff. Puff. Ren skipped along beside her, occasionally running the back of his hand across his nose and coming away with a long ribbon of snot. Alys dug out a linen from deep in her pocket and handed it to him. "Wipe," she said.

"Thanks," Ren said.

"Keep it. And where are your mittens? I know your mam

didn't send you without them." Ren didn't reply, he just kept skipping along next to her. "You'll get tired doing that."

Skip. "Doing what?"

"Bouncing like that. There's no need for bouncing. Walking is better." Again the boy didn't answer. He'd tire soon enough, Alys thought, and then she wondered what she'd do. She wouldn't be able to carry him. Not all night. "We'll walk your pasture first, then mine, and we'll need to be quick about it so we're never long away from one pasture or the other. We're lucky ours are next to each other."

"Dad did that. Switched me with Lyneth."

"That was smart of him," Alys said. She gently pushed Ren toward his field. Their two dogs were already far ahead, no doubt circling the herds as Ren and Alys should be doing. But Ren was slow, despite the skipping. The night had fallen fast and black, and thick clouds obscured the moon that should have been shining on them full and bright. The grass and frosty earth crunched like broken glass beneath their feet. The moisture in Alys's nose turned to crystal and her eyes burned. She smelled snow. "Cold?"

Ren looked up at her from beneath the brim of his too-large hat. He nodded. She pulled off her own mittens and gave them to him. "Put these on." Then she pushed her hands into her pockets. The boy didn't smile or answer, but he put on the mittens.

Alys noticed that he'd stopped skipping. She pulled out a hand and felt his forehead. There was heat in there, like a coal in a pot. "Feeling poorly?"

He shrugged. She took one of his mittened hands in hers and held it as they walked. His fingers softened in hers and they kept on like that in silence. Every once in a while the wind picked up and bit her cheeks and brought tears to her eyes, and once it lifted the hat off Ren's head so that she had to chase it and bring it back to him. She felt the heat rising off him when she returned the hat to his head. This wouldn't do. She'd promised Enid to care for him.

The children of Gwenith were given tents where they could warm themselves in the dead of winter. They weren't allowed to sleep in these winter shelters, but they could take brief refuge in the worst weather. If Alys could get Ren settled into one of the shelters, then she could watch both pastures while he slept.

Alys switched her bag so it hung down her front and she kneeled in front of Ren and hitched him onto her back. She tucked her arms securely under his knees and felt his arms tighten around her neck. He was heavier than she expected. The tent couldn't be far, she told herself.

And yet it was. By the time they reached it Alys's arms were burning and trembling and she sank to her knees with relief. She untied the flap and pulled the boy inside.

The floor of the tent was layered with animal pelts that smelled of damp. The walls and ceiling were made of tallowed hide that did little more than break the wind and keep out the worst of the rain and snow. Beneath the pelts, though, Ren would be warm enough, and dry.

She took off Ren's hat and boots and stuffed the mittens back into her own pockets. Then she cocooned him in her wool blanket and settled him in the skins. She couldn't see his face in the dark, but she felt his trembling. Then one of his thin hands tightened around her wrist, not letting go.

"You'll be fine," Alys said. "I'll come for you in the morning."

He held on harder, his grip stronger than she would have thought possible for such a slip of a boy. His fingertips dug into the cords of her forearm.

She could have wrenched her arm free, but instead she sighed. "Ren, if I stay here and they find out, I'll be punished."

Ren loosened his hold on her and curled in on himself. She touched her wrist where his fingers had pressed into her, and hesitated. She would go now, she told herself. And she'd come back for him at dawn, just like she'd promised. She would say goodnight and leave. That is what she would do.

She felt around with her hand and found the silky cap of his hair just peeking between the pelts. She wondered briefly whether it was brave or foolish for Madog and Enid to have had children. If Ren had belonged to Alys, she couldn't imagine sending him out here all alone. But then again, he wasn't alone now, was he? And Alys had a choice about that.

Then she was decided. She turned toward the tent flap and tied it shut from the inside. She pulled off her own boots and crawled between the pelts. She'd never slept beside anyone before, unless she counted the time that she'd sat up all night with Delwyn. But then she hadn't been asleep herself. She drew Ren to her and wrapped her arms around him, so close that she could feel his trembling in her own body. She pulled the pelts up so that only their noses and foreheads emerged. "Go to sleep," she said.

"I don't want to sleep," he said. "If I fall asleep, you'll leave."

"I won't. I promise."

Ren's body gentled, and he slid his hands under hers. She closed her eyes and wondered if she might actually sleep.

"Alys," he said.

"Yes, what?"

"Have you ever thought of running away?"

Alys sucked in a breath and felt it steam around her when she exhaled. "Yes," she said.

"Why don't you?"

"Afraid to go off alone, I suppose. But if I could go anywhere, and without a worry about the distance, then I suppose I'd want to go to the Lakes."

"I want to live by the sea. Dad said you can see it from the mountains. He said you can see for miles up there. You can see all of Byd, and the sea beyond, and there's always snow. He said we can all go there and he'll build us a house and then we'll never be tired again because the twins and I can sleep all night and play all day. But every time Mam says we should leave, Dad says it's not time yet. We should wait until the twins are older, he says. But I don't want to wait. I want to go now."

All the while Ren spoke—more words at once than she'd ever heard spill out of him—Alys held herself still. She didn't breathe, or blink. "Your dad and mam talk about running away?"

She felt the boy stiffen in her arms. "I'm not supposed to talk about that."

"I'd never tell, Ren. Not ever."

He relaxed again. "You could come with us. Dad said he'd show me the sea."

Alys had to laugh at that. The sea. She'd heard tell such a thing existed, that Byd was surrounded on all sides by a vast border of blue, deeper and wider than any lake. She felt a sudden urge to see it herself. Just to think of all that blue water.

Maybe she'd go there, she thought to herself. Someday. Maybe Pawl and Beti would go with her. She smiled at the thought of them. And then at the thought of that brown-eyed boy and his black brush of hair. So black it was like starless night. And then, something about his black-as-night hair, and the wanting she felt inside of her, the yearning and the hoping, something about all of those things made her think of the hole. And of time running out. Of Alys's hourglass tipped over. Alys almost never dreamed anymore, but when she did, it was of that hole, that bottomless rip that needed mending, that she felt growing all the time, fraying and rending. She closed her eyes and tried not to think of all that nothing.

"Go to sleep now, Ren. No more talking."

FIFTEEN

She woke to muffled quiet. Ren had pulled away from her in the night and he lay flat on his back, arms and legs outstretched, snoring. His hair was damp against his forehead and he no longer shivered.

Alys untied the flap to the tent and snow spilled in on her feet. A foot at least had fallen in the night and the world was white outside. Dawn was just beginning to blush the horizon. They'd almost slept too long. She shook Ren awake and tossed him his boots. She'd have to hope that no ill had befallen the sheep. If it had, she'd be better off freezing to death in the woods than going back to Defaid.

As she and Ren made their way through the snow, they were joined by the dogs, and the sight of them unstitched the worry in Alys's chest. The dogs were too placid for there to have been any trouble in the night. She and Ren might make it through this unscathed.

She gestured at the dogs with her chin, squeezed Ren's hand. "Notice the dogs," she said, "how calm they are. That means the sheep are fine. That's good."

Ren nodded, hummed, kicked snow, showed no sign of interest. Alys spied the gray of rabbit fur, a flash against the snow not twenty feet ahead of them. She tapped Ren's shoulder, pointed. The rabbit sank into the snow and was gone. "He's going to be some owl's dinner before the day is out," Alys said. "And that rabbit will never hear it coming. Or see it." Alys spread her arms and blew a silent puff of air between her lips, then quick as a flash she wrapped herself around Ren and lifted him in the air until he cackled. As she set him down, she saw his cheeks flushed with cold and delight. He reached for her hand again and they walked on.

"I had a dream last night," Ren said. He kicked more snow. "I was watching the sheep and I was so tired and I just couldn't stay awake. I was sitting under that tree right over there." He pointed to a large evergreen with branches as wide as a house just at the edge of the sheep pasture. "It was summer and everything was green and soft and warm. And then a lady came and told me that I should follow her and then I could sleep."

Alys stopped. "What sort of lady?"

"A strange sort, I reckon. And she floated, so quiet. I've dreamed about her before."

"When was that?"

"Last time I was in the pastures." Ren squinted, thinking.

"I was right in that field over there, under that tree, like I told you. I thought the lady was real, because she seemed so real, but then I woke up."

Alys looked down at Ren. Enid and Madog must have decided not to tell him about the soul eaters. But how could the child protect himself if he didn't know? Then Alys chastised herself for judging them. What did Alys know about being a parent? And what good would a warning do the child anyway? If the soul eaters wanted him, they'd surely have him.

"Did the lady tell you her name?"

Ren smiled. "Not this time, but last time she did."

Alys stopped and turned Ren to her. "What was her name, Ren, do you remember?"

"Of course I remember. It was Angelica, and she told me not to forget. She said I should come and find her."

Alys gripped Ren's hand so tightly that he yelped, and she apologized. "Don't you ever tell anyone from Defaid about that dream. And if you ever see one of those floating women . . ." Alys held him by the shoulders. "If you ever see one, Ren, promise me you'll run."

Enid's worried outline was the first that Alys made out as they approached the Gate, and at the sight of her, Ren trotted ahead. Enid seemed as if she were about to run toward him, but then Alys saw Madog place a hand on her shoulder and she stayed put until Ren reached her. Then Enid felt his forehead and bent down to wrap her arms around him, looking at Alys over his shoulder. Madog reached down and picked up the boy to carry him home.

"I'll find you later," Enid said to Alys.

"Ay," Alys said. She must tell Enid about Ren's dream.

When Alys reached home she was met by Father, who was headed outside the Gate for wood. The kitchen was cold and empty. "Mother's feeling poorly again today," he said. Then he was gone.

Alys thought she might not be able to sleep, and yet she did, fitfully. She found herself dreaming not of the hole, but of floating women. In snow, in mud. Made of leaves, made of feathers. And right in the middle was the sensation of being shaken from sleep. But it was too soon, too soon for waking. Alys felt as if a great weight were on her, pressing down her limbs, even as another force was trying to drag her up. She struggled to open her eyes, to speak.

"Wake up, child. I need you."

Alys felt a hand clamping her shoulder and she looked up at Mother, or at a version of Mother unlike any she'd seen before. She still wore her nightclothes, and her usually calm, implacable face was clenched. Her hair, which Alys had only ever seen coiled and pinned at the base of her head, hung down around her shoulders, long and unkempt.

"It's early still, child. But I'm ill and I need you. Get yourself dressed and come out to the kitchen." As Mother left, she held onto the doorframe for a long moment before continuing on.

Alys assumed Mother would need her to take over the day's chores, so she dressed for work, and in layers of wool stockings to keep out the snow. She nearly forgot her whistle, but at the last moment she pulled it on.

Mother sat at the kitchen table with nothing in front of her. At Alys's place she had set a cup of strong tea and a plate with a thick slice of brown bread and some cheese. "It's not much, child, but you'll need it. Now eat it quick." She nodded at Alys, short and sharp like always, but Alys could tell there was something terribly wrong with Mother, and she felt a nugget of fear in her chest. She'd never in her life had to worry about Mother. Mother never got sick. But now Mother clutched her belly as if she were trying to hold her insides together. "I need you to go to the old place."

Alys stopped chewing for a moment, but she knew better than to ask a question that was about to be answered.

"There's something I need you to bring me from the root cellar. Something it's not safe to keep here," Mother said. "And I need you to do something else for me." Mother put her hands on the table and forced herself to standing. She went back to the bedroom she shared with Father and returned with a small bundle wrapped in layers of rough cloth. She retrieved a basket from a hook in the kitchen and placed the bundle inside. Alys watched Mother's movements while she ate, not really tasting the salty cheese and days-old bread. Then Mother sat down, the basket in front of her on the table. "In back of the house there's a large oak tree, you remember the one. I want you to bury this parcel beneath that tree."

There were many things Alys could have said or asked, but she stuck to practicalities, because she knew that's what Mother wanted her to do. "The ground will be hard."

"Ay," Mother said, "but you'll manage. Go into the house

through the kitchen door and get yourself a shovel. Father keeps tools there still. Dig a hole deep enough that the wolves can't get to it. Then I want you to go in the root cellar. You'll find a shelf with some jars. The one I need has a label on the bottom with scratches on it. Six scratches. Inside you'll find some roots. Knobby old things. I want you to put one of those roots in a piece of linen. Tie it up good and tight and tuck it away on your person. Don't put it in a basket, not even in a pocket. Put it somewhere private, do you understand?"

Alys did. Mother didn't want Elder Miles poking his nose into it, whatever it was.

Mother shuddered, and Alys nearly reached out to her, but didn't. Mother had never liked to be touched. She had a yellow cast to her skin that Alys didn't like. If Alys had seen anyone else in the village looking like this, she'd think the person was dying. That the poor soul had the fever, or worse. "Mother," Alys said.

"Ay, child." Mother looked up at Alys and there was pain in her eyes.

"Are you sure you'll be all right here, alone? Should I get someone to come stay with you?"

Mother closed her eyes briefly, breathed in and out. "No, child, there's none can help me now. None save for you."

SIXTEEN

Alys walked out into a village coated in white from last night's snow. The sky was gray but bright, and light reflected from every surface. Alys pressed mittened hands to her eyes. This was morning, she thought to herself. True morning, not the twilight of dawn that she was used to. Around her, villagers went about their morning business. Women taking their wash to the lines. Older girls carrying buckets to the wells. Not a single child of Gwenith was among them—they were all still asleep in their beds.

There was a jar of dark honey in Alys's basket. The parcel that Alys was to bury was still with Mother. It wouldn't do to knock on the Elder's door and explain that there was something Mother wanted her to bury at the old place. Instead, Alys was to explain that Mother was ill—which was true. And that this was why Alys had been awakened early to go in search of something to make her feel better—which was also true. And that was the end of the truth. Alys was also to explain to Mistress Miles that Mother was sending her in search of slippery elm.

When the door opened, it wasn't Mistress Miles, as Alys had been expecting. It was her youngest daughter, Cerys, the girl Alys had once dreamed of frightening with her tales of The Beast. Cerys was the same age as Alys, and not quite so tall, but her body curved in and out the way a woman's did. Alys didn't spend much time pondering her own body in the seconds it took her to dress and undress, but she knew its outlines well enough, and that it was as straight up and down as it ever was. The blue wool dress that Cerys wore was finer than any of Alys's, but not so much finer as to explain why it moved so differently on her. And even for a child of Defaid, Cerys was rosy. The word *ripe* came to Alys's mind. Cerys's lips were red like the High Elder's apples, and her cheeks were pink. There was a dusting of freckles on her nose and her hair was buttercup yellow. Golden curls sprung loose from her braid, and here and there along her hairline.

When Cerys smiled, she showed teeth. "Oh Alys," she said. "I didn't expect to see anyone here. I was just on my way to see Mai." Mai was Cerys's special friend, daughter of another of the town's Elders. Alys didn't say anything in response, because there wasn't anything to say. Then Cerys laughed, wrinkled her brow, and looked at Alys as if she weren't sure what to make of her visit. As if it weren't obvious why Alys would be standing on Elder Miles's doorstep.

Finally, Mistress Miles filled the doorway behind her daughter, and Alys explained to her about the slippery elm. She took the basket from Alys, then looked at her daughter. "Don't be late for supper."

"Course not, Mam," and Cerys laughed and waved a hand and rushed off, her skirts swirling in the snow. Alys looked after her for one long moment, then back at Mistres Miles's charmless face. She wondered how soon Cerys might begin to resemble her.

"Wait," Mistress Miles said and closed the door. Then after some minutes the door opened again. Mistress Miles shoved an iron bracelet at Alys. It was engraved with the number one. "Elder Miles says you should be quick about it. You're to be back through the Gate by the noon bell, no later. Or he'll send riders after you."

Alys bit her tongue. "Thank you, Mistress Miles. That's very kind."

Mother was waiting for Alys when she returned to the house, and once she saw the basket safely hooked on Alys's arm, she turned and retreated to her bedroom without another word. Alys might have told her that there wasn't near enough time for her to get to the old place, bury the parcel, retrieve the medicine, and make the long walk back by noon. It would take her twice that time. But Alys could see that Mother was past caring. A sour scent rose off her, and something else, too, something that Alys didn't want to think about. There was nothing for it—Alys had the time she had. She would just have to hope that she wasn't caught where she shouldn't be. She'd take the long way around the fields, through the fforest if need be. She'd purposely sprain her ankle by way of explanation for her delay, if it came to that.

As Alys reached the Gate, she saw the bottom half of her least favorite guard sticking out of one of Pawl's caravans. The guard's name was Ffordd, and he was the worst of an unpleasant bunch, taking far too much satisfaction from his power over the comings and goings of travelers, and Gwenith children especially.

His front half was buried inside the wagon, where he was no doubt examining its contents and possibly taking a stealthy cut for himself. Beti perched on the front seat of one of the wagons, and she looked surprised to catch sight of Alys so early in the day. She waved and smiled. Cian sat in the other wagon and Alys sensed anger rising off him. He seemed to loathe Ffordd as much as she did.

Meanwhile Pawl stood behind Ffordd with hands on hips, waiting for Ffordd to finish. Pawl glanced over at Alys, caught her eye and winked, grinned, mimed kicking Ffordd in the arse. Alys would have liked to laugh, but she could only smile a little and wave before moving on. Her worry for Mother rose in her belly like floodwater.

Once through the Gate, Alys made straight for the stand of elms that delineated here from there—the borders past which no child of Gwenith or person of Defaid should be traveling. She pulled off her mittens and the cold nipped her knuckles as she peeled off several curls of slippery elm bark. All the while she worked, she listened and looked for villagers. All was quiet in the snowy fields. Mother had warned her to keep an eye out for the village's deer hunters. They'd travel farther afield than the other villagers, and quiet as they kept, they might see Alys before she spotted them.

One road led from Defaid to the old farmhouses and beyond, and Alys stayed off it. She kept the road to her right shoulder and shielded herself among the trees. This slowed her down, but also kept her hidden. After a mile of hopping narrow streams and ducking branches, she was hot and sweating in her wool, despite the cold. Finally the trees opened up into meadow and rolling fields that used to be cultivated but had since gone to weed. Now Alys was as exposed as the rabbit she'd pointed out to Ren as it hopped through the snow.

The first of the old farmhouses she reached was a sad, sunken creature that crouched on the landscape, gray and dead, shutters akimbo. The next of the farmhouses was the same, and the one after that. Then finally came the house that Alys remembered from her first months in Defaid. In case Alys lost her way, Mother had told her to look out for the house with the white front door. Not chipped white, or cracked white, or the pale gray of white gone to dust. This door would be white, pure white. And the house's roof wouldn't sag.

And there it was. Alys wouldn't say that it looked well, but it looked well enough. And livable, even after all these years of emptiness. All the shutters hung straight and even, closed tight against whatever might try to batter them. Alys wondered how many secret trips Father had made here. Many, from the looks of it. She took one last, long look around her, reassured that the world was quiet except for the flight of a few birds. Then she walked around the house and saw the tree, just as big as she remembered it. It was as wide around as a barn door, with a tangle of limbs that looked as if they were all reaching out in different directions and would have split apart if only they could.

Alys turned away from it and twisted the knob of the kitchen door, and walked inside. It was damp and chill, as Alys expected, and empty of furniture. The closed shutters kept out the light, so Alys left the door open. The room was swept clean and the hearth was empty of even a single log or pile of ash. Father was careful. But not so careful. Along one wall was a stash of tools, unrusted and well-used—saws of various sizes and shapes, hammers, an axe. Alys lifted the shovel and carried it and the basket out to the massive tree.

Alys held the shovel vertical and felt around through the layer of snow for a soft spot in the soil. The tree's roots were as thick and tangled as its branches, but soon Alys detected some give beneath her, and she shoveled away a mound of snow to find a spot of soil roughly the right size and shape. She began digging, using her foot to press down on the shovel, through the chill, hard earth.

About a foot beneath the surface, just at the point where Alys might have buried Mother's bundle, there was already a bundle, wrapped in linen that had gone as brown as the earth that covered it. One more strike of the shovel and Alys might have torn right through it, but she stayed her hand just in time. Alys knelt down in the snow and stared, and for the first time she allowed herself to ask the obvious question, here where there was no one to answer her. *What was Mother having her bury beneath this tree?*

The snow melted cold beneath Alys's knees and shins and spilled into the tops of her boots. Alys told herself that she should cover this up and find someplace else to bury Mother's bundle. That would be the wisest course. But instead, Alys lifted the stiff little bundle from the hole she'd dug. She set it in her lap, then carefully unwrapped the aging linen. Inside, she found a tiny, baby-shaped skeleton, small enough to fit in her palm and as light and fragile as a bird.

Alys wrapped it up again, gently, and put it back in its resting place. Then she lifted the bundle Mother had given her this morning out of the basket and placed it next to the other. She didn't need to open the fresh bundle to know what was inside. Brother or sister, they could rest there together. Alys rose to her feet, brushed the snow off her legs, and buried them both. When the dirt was in place, Alys covered the mound with snow and pressed it down smooth. She looked around her at the gently undulating whiteness. The tracks of birds and her own footprints were the only signs of movement or life. Beneath the snow, though, all hidden by the smooth whiteness, Alys imagined a dark tangle of roots, grasping and curling and reaching, each cradling a bundle wrapped in linen.

This was why Mother never smiled.

Alys wondered how many miscarriages Mother had endured. How many times Mother had stolen through the Gate and made a furtive trip out here to bury another bundle under this tree. It was no wonder she kept the bundles secret, no wonder she buried them where no rule-abiding villager would ever find them. No woman would want Mother to birth her baby into this world if she'd known how many of Mother's own babies she'd lost.

But that wasn't the reason for Mother's silence. No, Mother never told a soul about those bundles because they'd surely call her a witch if they found out. The Elders would say she'd caused this, that a woman who knew how to bring babies into this world knew just as well how to do the reverse. If the Elders knew what Mother had done here, they'd say she was a bride of The Beast. They'd accuse her of dark magic. They'd burn her. Or crush her under stones, or drown her first to see if she'd float. And if she floated, then they'd burn her.

Alys thought about the root Mother needed, and Mother's yellow skin and pained eyes this morning. The odor of rot and blood. She remembered what Mother had done for Mary all those years ago. The tea she'd brewed to help Mary pass the afterbirth so she wouldn't succumb to fever. Alys needed to do the same for Mother now. She turned back toward the house and returned the shovel. She opened one set of shutters to let in more light, then lifted up the door to the root cellar, right in the center of the kitchen floor. Scents of earth and damp rose up to meet her. She climbed down the ladder to a room just wider than her armspan, just tall enough for a grown man to stand in. The floor was packed dirt and the walls were lined with shelves, mostly bare. There was one shelf full of canning jars, and Alys set to finding the one that Mother needed.

It wasn't easy in the dark. The small space seemed to snuff

all light, air, and sound. Alys quickly felt suffocated, her heart beating too fast in her chest, making it difficult to concentrate. She was too conscious of the passage of time and what it might mean if Elder Miles sent riders after her. It was causing her hands to shake, her bladder to weaken with dread. She had to lift each jar into the slender shaft of light from the kitchen above. There must have been twenty different kinds of roots, all equally knobby and desiccated. Most were labeled with names. A few had only scratches on the bottom. Finally she found the one with six parallel scratch marks, and she withdrew one of the roots and wrapped it in a bit of linen. She unhooked her coat and then the front of her dress, and she tucked the linen inside her shift, next to her skin. Then she hooked herself up again. Finally, she climbed up into the kitchen, breathing deep gulps of fresh air. She wiped her forehead where cold sweat slicked her skin. For a short moment she sat on the edge of the root cellar, her legs dangling down. Her heartbeat still thrummed in her ears but two distinct sounds pierced through and caused Alys to clutch the kitchen floor.

Footsteps and laughter. Both right above her head, inside the house.

SEVENTEEN

Alys thought quickly. It was a long, exposed walk back through the meadow. She needed to be quiet, quiet as a mouse to get out of the house unheard. And then pray that whoever was upstairs didn't think to open a shutter and look out while she made her escape.

She looked at the open cellar door. Mother's roots were down there. She'd have to close it if she wanted to protect Mother's secret. Alys tried to remember if the hinges had squeaked when she'd first opened it. She had no memory. Quiet hadn't been her goal then, speed was. Now she needed both.

There was high-pitched laughter and low-pitched murmuring. Feet moving across the floor in a shuffle step and then coming to a halt. More murmuring, a giggle, a soft thud. Then silence. *No,* Alys thought. *Don't stop moving.* She needed their noise. But more so she needed to leave. She touched the center of her chest, felt the tiny bulge where she'd tucked away the root. Thought again of Mother's sallow skin, and the sweet stink of death rising off her. She pushed up from the floor with her hands and brought her feet to a crouch. Then she stood, never making a sound.

She reached for the cellar door latch and lifted. The hinges squealed. Alys dropped the door, left Mother's basket, and ran back the way she'd come.

Behind her she heard the pounding of boots on wood, but there was no time to look for who might be emerging from Mother and Father's house. It certainly wasn't Father, and that was all she needed to know. Her skirts dragged in the snow, and she yanked them up. The frozen air burned shallow in her chest.

Then she heard horse hooves, and she knew she was being run down, knew there was no hope for escape. Still she ran and kept running until the hooves were so loud in her ears that she thought she might be trampled, and a hand yanked her by her braid and sent her sprawling face-first into the snow.

The hooves stopped pounding and she was dragged up and found herself staring into the reddened face of the High Elder's youngest son, Rhys. He was tall and solid, and although only seventeen he had every ounce of his father's unforgiving nature. He'd never spoken to Alys, never so much as looked her way, but even so Alys knew his eyes were a transparent blue. Something about those eyes had always chilled her. There seemed to be nothing behind them, they were like looking into rock. He held Alys in two meaty hands, one twisting her arm behind her back and the other gripping her throat. It was the closest she'd ever been to a boy her own age since she and Delwyn had held each other on the Gate. And then she was just a child. A sharp, musky tang rose off Rhys and Alys tried to pull away, but he only twisted her arm harder, squeezed her throat tighter. It felt as if he'd surely separate the two halves of her arm.

Still he hadn't spoken. He examined her face as if looking for something. Then he shoved her away from him. "What did you see?"

Once free of him, Alys briefly considered running again, but Rhys's horse stood at the ready and Alys knew it would be pointless. Her only hope was to talk herself out of this somehow.

"I got lost," Alys said. "Took a wrong turn and found myself here."

He exhaled through his nostrils. Then he hit her, a hard, backhanded smack against the side of her head that sent her reeling and nearly falling sideways into the snow. She turned and spun, dizzy on her feet. The horizon tilted and Mother and Father's house listed at an angle. Then the world righted itself again and Alys saw a figure in blue emerge from the house. A woman's shape, topped by golden tresses and a rosebud mouth. Cerys. It could be none other.

Alys turned back to Rhys, her eyes widening. She thought back to the giggling and murmuring, the shuffling of feet, the soft thud. Cerys and Rhys, in a house where they thought they'd be alone. Cerys, youngest daughter of Elder Miles. And Rhys, youngest son of the High Elder. Unmarried. They shouldn't have been alone together at all, much less alone together out here, where all were forbidden to go. Alys sniffed the air and wondered how she could have missed the scent before. The scent of fear. Rhys was terrified, even more than she was.

"I saw nothing," Alys said. "And if you just let me go I'll say nothing."

Now the scent that rose off him turned acrid. Before Alys could brace herself, Rhys hit her again, and this time she went all the way down. A loud whistling filled her ears. Then silence.

"She's not dead," Cerys said.

These were the first words Alys heard when she came to, lying sidelong in the snow where she'd landed.

"I didn't think she was," Rhys said.

"Well you needn't be short with me," Cerys said.

Alys touched her face where Rhys had hit her and felt skin but the skin didn't feel her back.

"Get up," Rhys said.

Alys crawled to her knees and stood up, her stomach rising into her mouth and then pouring out at Rhys's feet. He jumped backward, and she retched until nothing more would come up. She wiped her mouth on her sleeve. "I swear, I saw nothing. I shouldn't be here, and I know that. I just need to get home." Alys looked up at the sky. The sun was arching toward the west. "I was supposed to be home by the noon bell."

Rhys shook his head. "It's too late for that. You're coming with me. I'll tell Father I caught you wandering."

Alys's scalp tingled and she felt light-headed. "Please. You don't have to do that. I promise I won't say a word."

Rhys's eyes were as blank and cold as the snow. "Say a word about what?"

Alys looked between him and Cerys. The girl twitched like a stalked bird. "You can't trust her," Cerys said.

"Go home," Rhys said to Cerys.

Cerys looked back at him, her pink lips opening round and startled. "Walk all that way? Alone?"

Alys had the strongest urge to slap Cerys's pink cheeks. "Are you frightened of what's out there, Cerys?"

Cerys's eyes narrowed and her upper lip thinned. "Don't you speak to me. You're evil, and everyone knows it."

Alys smelled burning, like a cinder, or as if her own skirts were on fire.

"You watched while the soul eaters killed your parents," Cerys said. "You invited them in. Unlocked the door for them, showed them the way."

"That's not true," Alys said. Although if Cerys knew what was actually true, she'd think Alys just as evil. And Alys couldn't have argued with her.

Cerys crossed her arms over her chest, and suddenly Alys saw her resemblance to her mother. How she'd grow into that square face and that starched apron. Alys saw Cerys for exactly what she was. Thin and transparent as glass. She saw her vanity. Her smug confidence that she was cared for. Her belief that she mattered. Everything that Cerys was—everything that Cerys might become—was laid out before Alys like food on a table.

Alys inhaled it, and it warmed her—first from the inside, the blood that flowed through her veins. Then the warmth spread to her skin, like a blush.

Cerys's rosebud mouth faded from pink to white. Her cheeks, the same. She clawed her chest, and a sound like choking escaped her lips, which were now bluing at the edges.

"Cerys?" Rhys said. His horse reared and screamed.

Cold washed over Alys like a dunk in an unheated bath and she shuddered. She staggered backward, away from Cerys.

Color rushed back to Cerys's cheeks and lips. Her mouth twisted, her breathing too ragged for speech. She lifted one arm straight ahead of her and pointed at Alys, her finger hanging in the air while she struggled for the words. Then the words came to Cerys, and Alys found that she knew what they would be even before Cerys uttered them. "Soul eater," Cerys said. "Soul eater."

This time Alys didn't feel the blow before the world went black.

EIGHTEEN

When Alys woke up she was tied, hands in front of her, and a long strip of cloth was wrapped tight around her mouth. She lay on her side in the snow and her layers of wool were wet through. The light was horizontal, a weak, midafternoon sun that would set in perhaps an hour, maybe less. Mother and Father's house rose in the distance ahead of her. And behind it, the tree where all their babies were buried.

"Get up," Rhys said.

Her feet weren't tied, so Alys was able to get to her knees and then stand. Rhys stood back from her a good ten feet and Alys saw she was tethered to him by a long rope. He was frightened of her still. Frightened of what she might do if he got too close.

"We're taking you back to Defaid now, and you'll stay exactly this far from me, do you hear?" Rhys was trying too hard to look intimidating. The effort gave him away. Alys nodded anyway. In truth, she was at his mercy.

On the way back to Defaid, as Alys trudged in the snow behind them, Cerys occasionally looked back at her. She was up on the horse and Rhys walked alongside her, holding fast to Alys's rope. At first they had kept up a steady murmur, words that Alys couldn't hear but could only imagine were full of calculation. Then they fell into silence.

Soon Alys lost all sense of what time it was. The sky had grown steely gray and heavy. Snow began to fall in fat flakes, thickening so that the way ahead closed in and Alys felt she was being marched into a void, into nothingness. That would be a blessing compared to what awaited her once they reached Defaid, once Rhys and Cerys told the Elders what Alys had done.

The air was still and the snow sifted down fast, straight, and quiet, coating the trees on either side of them in white. As they emerged from the thick band of fforest that divided the abandoned farms from the fields that spread out from the Gate of Defaid, Alys heard the muffled clop of horses' hooves in the distance.

Alys heard men's voices and then she saw there were two riders, one of them another son of the High Elder. The other was the blacksmith. Alys had never spoken two words to either of them.

"What's happened?" the blacksmith called out first. "Are you all right?" The men looked confused, then horrified, as their eyes traveled first to Rhys out in front, then to Cerys in the saddle, and finally to Alys, attached to Rhys by a rope.

Rhys's older brother was a big boy of about nineteen with sandy blond hair. Alys recalled his name was Alec. "Rhys, where in Byd have you been? Elder Miles and his wife are just about out of their minds. Every man in the village is out looking for Cerys."

"Well I found her," Rhys said. "Saved her from that one." He jerked his chin at Alys.

"Whatever's she done?" the blacksmith said, squinting at Alys from beneath his broad-brimmed hat.

"I'll tell you later," Rhys said. "But I'd advise you to keep an eye behind you. She's a crafty one."

Alec looked at Cerys, and then back at his brother, wrinkling his brow.

"Don't be an idiot," Rhys said. "I meant Alys. Now let's get home before dark."

They all headed toward the Gate in silence, and not long after, they approached the first children of Gwenith headed out to the pastures for the night. Alys saw them in the distance, felt them as they grew closer, but she kept her eyes on the snow in front of her feet. She assumed they did the same. She didn't blame them for it. There was nothing to be done when the son of the High Elder had you by a rope.

Then she heard a small voice. "Alys?"

She looked to the child it belonged to, and it was Ren. He'd not only spoken to her, but stopped in his tracks, staring. She shook her head at him, short and sharp. *No, Ren,* she wanted to say. *You mustn't.*

And then she was past him and she hoped he'd walked on

and forgotten about her. Poor Ren, she thought to herself. Leave it to that little one not to know how to save his own neck.

When they reached the last long stretch of road to Defaid, the sky was as dark as smoke, and there were no more children of Gwenith heading toward the fields. The doors were closed. Alys was delirious with cold and fear, and yet she might have laughed if she hadn't been bound. In all their lives, these men and Cerys had never known what it was like to have the doors close behind them, to find themselves on the wrong side of that reassuring Gate. The High Elder hadn't kept the doors open for his own sons. She wondered how Shoulder Miles felt about that, if his heart quaked even a little bit when the High Elder gave the order to shut the doors, even though his youngest daughter was still out there, unprotected.

Rhys and the other two men raised their voices in unison, shouting for the doors to be opened. From his perch in one of the watchtowers, Madog called down to the night guard, telling him to open the doors, that the men had found Cerys. He said nothing about Alys. She supposed there weren't words for that.

NINETEEN

Once the Gate doors were opened, there was a chaos of pointing and exclaiming that grew as word spread. Villagers lifted lanterns and gathered close to catch sight of Cerys, then withdrew respectfully when the High Elder arrived. Alys supposed that if any of them knew what had happened they might not dare come so near, for fear Alys would try to suck the souls out of them, as well.

Cerys was lifted down from Rhys's horse and passed to Mistress Miles's wide bosom. Cerys looked entirely well to Alys's eyes, but she allowed herself to be carried as if she might faint, and she leaned into her mother, who wrapped stiff arms around her. Elder Miles told her to take Cerys home. Alys could see how Mistress Miles bit her tongue, fighting the impulse to argue for her place among the Elders. She gave her husband a dark look and then turned away with Cerys. The other wives took this as their signal to depart as well, and they peered back at Alys over their shoulders, their eyes narrow and curious.

A strange feeling of distance settled over Alys. Voices were muffled and even the people and things that were closest to her seemed farther away than they should be, as if the world were withdrawing from her. She watched the men gather around Rhys. While he spoke, the other men looked at her, clutched their chests, raised their eyebrows and opened their mouths into round caverns. The High Elder was the only one who didn't move or react. He was the still center, and while Rhys spoke he turned his eyes to Alys and stared.

"Stone her."

"Burn her."

"Drown her."

"Crush her."

These words emerged from the murmurs.

"We will try her in the light of day," the High Elder said. "In the meantime, lock her in a cellar where she can do no more harm."

The men exchanged looks and finally one spoke. It was Elder Yates, the oldest of them. "In whose cellar shall we put her? Surely none where there are children in the house, lest she cast a spell on them. And one of the other children of Gwenith might be tempted to release her."

Elder Couch said, "Why not her parents? She's their punishment, not ours. Have them take her."

The other Elders nodded and grumbled.

"It's no matter," the High Elder said. "As long as she is guarded. Elder Yates, I leave this in your able hands." The High Elder nodded to the men, then left them.

Rhys watched his father walk away then looked toward Alys. "You'll be dead by this time tomorrow."

Alys sensed a wishful uncertainty in him, as if he were hoping to make it so with his words.

"Best not speak to the witch," Elder Yates said. His shoulders were sharply bowed as if time were pressing his head down to meet his bottom half. He looked up at Alys through furry white eyebrows. "Alec, run ahead and tell her father what has happened. Have the cellar open and ready. Elder Couch, go get Vaughn and Sayer. They'll be her guards tonight."

Vaughn and Sayer were two of the day guards, bland and oafish but not cruel. Alys supposed it didn't matter who guarded her. They would be above, and she would be below. And soon enough, she would be judged and found guilty. And that thought shut down something inside of her, put a stopper in her panic. There was too much to feel so her heart simply closed up and felt nothing at all.

Rhys tugged her forward, toward home. It was slow going, following behind Elder Yates. Alys wanted only to be warm, and to have the cloth removed from around her mouth.

A shaft of yellow light stabbed across the darkness ahead of them, through the door of Mother and Father's house. Elder Yates went in first, then backed away to give them room to enter. Rhys bumped into Vaughn and Sayer on the way in, and they in turn backed into Alec. All but Elder Yates looked unsure of themselves and of what to do with their own limbs. The familiar room was rendered strange to Alys, too full of men and the scents of leather and wet wool. Father stood in his shirtsleeves and work trousers, his hair uncombed and his back to a hearth fire too weak to have cooked anything. Mother wasn't there. The door to their bedroom was closed. *Mother,* Alys thought. The root was still in her dress. Father was right here, and Mother was on the other side of that bedroom door, and there was no way for Alys to give either of them what Mother most needed. After all of this—all of this pain, this hope—there was nothing to be done. If Alys tried to give Father the root, she'd only doom him as well. Even if Father could make the excuse that he knew nothing of it, simply possessing the root would be seen as proof that Alys was a witch. And maybe proof that Mother was as well—if they thought to wonder where Alys had gotten the root. If they thought to lift the door to Mother's root cellar and paw through all her jars.

The stopper in Alys's heart loosened again, and she felt terrified and grief-stricken and angry all at once. Father stood there, looking like he'd seen something so awful that there were no words for it, and no actions either. Alys had such a desperate yearning to talk to Mother, to see her, to tell her how hard she'd tried.

The cellar door was open, and the damp scent of soil rose into the room from its dark cavern. Elder Yates told Alec to remove the cloth from Alys's mouth. Alec looked at Elder Yates for a moment, his mouth open, but Elder Yates said only, "Do it."

The moment it was off, Alys felt relief. She felt certain she could bear anything so long as she was able breathe unencumbered.

Elder Yates stood just beyond the open cellar, dipped his chin at it. "Down you go, girl. Rhys, hold on to the tether. Vaughn and Sayer, you pull up the ladder when she's reached bottom."

Alys climbed down the ladder grasping each wooden slat with her bound hands as she descended. She stood at the bottom and looked up into the brightness of the kitchen. The five heads of Rhys, Alec, Elder Yates, Vaughn, and Sayer stared down at her. Then the ladder went up and Elder Yates himself took the tether from Rhys and fastened it to the handle of the door, several feet above her head and unreachable without the ladder.

The door closed over Alys's head and she was submerged in black and a still, chill dampness. She continued to look above her while the men's footfalls circled and stomped, accompanied by low murmurs too muddled for Alys to make out words. She heard the scraping of chairs and imagined them huddled over hot tea, staring at the floor beneath their feet and wondering what powers a soul eater might have to penetrate air and wood.

Alys struggled with numb fingers and bound wrists to open the front of her dress and retrieve the root. She tucked it onto a shelf, behind a crate of potatoes. Perhaps, if they ever let her talk to Father, she could tell him it was here. Or maybe, if Mother had been able to tell him what she'd sent Alys to do, maybe then he'd think to look for it here.

Alys heard herself whimper. It was hopeless.

She was so cold. She fastened her dress again. It hung heavy on her, damp enough from melted snow to soak up the cold and suck it through to her skin. The tether was long enough that she could let her arms hang down while she stood, but when she sat on the hard dirt floor she found it was too short to lie down.

She felt around in the dark for a basket of apples and then a round of hard cheese. How she could be hungry, she had no idea, but she found herself so starved that she could think of nothing else. She bit through the cheese rind with her teeth, then chewed off a salty chunk and swallowed it nearly whole. She ate three apples down to the seeds, and more cheese until her belly was hard and full.

She sank down to the floor and leaned against the vertical beam of one shelf. She pulled her knees up to her chin and hugged them with her arms. Eating had warmed her so that her shivering stopped, but only for a while. Then a deeper sort of shuddering took over, waves that seemed to start in her heart and travel to her gut. She was well-clothed, she told herself. She had survived far worse nights than this out in the pastures and up on the Gate. At least here there was no wind.

I'm doomed, Alys thought. *That's why I'm shaking.*

The shuddering ceased, and Alys felt calm and emptied. There was nothing for it. Tomorrow would come and then she'd know what her future held. And everyone would know what she was. And maybe there was some strange comfort to be found in that. For just the second time since she was seven years old, Alys closed her eyes in the night and drifted to sleep, still as a stone.

TWENTY

The women came for her the next day. Alys had been awake for some hours, staring into the darkness and interpreting the sounds overhead. Chairs on wood, shuffling feet around the hearth, low voices. Then a knock on the door that was louder than it needed to be, more men's voices, more sets of feet. A bit later, the number of feet halved again, and there was a long window of silence. Then there was the knock that brought the women and their higher-pitched voices and footfalls.

Alys was standing and ready for them when the root cellar door was jerked upward. As much as she wanted to see who looked down at her, she pressed her hands to her eyes to block the light that sliced the solid darkness and sent a stabbing pain into her temple. Peering through her fingers, she first made out four black wedges, then the shapes formed themselves into broad skirts and rough aprons. The ladder dropped down in front of her.

"Up, witch," said one of the women, and there was a sharp jerk on her tether. As Alys climbed she saw Mistress Miles on the other end. Next to her was Mistress Ffagan, who held a basket covered with a linen. Mistress Daniels and Mistress Hardy backed away as Alys rose.

The kitchen was bare and cold. The table was empty and there was no fire in the hearth. Father was absent, although Alys saw his hat and coat hanging on the wall. As Alys scanned the room she saw that Vaughn and Sayer had been relieved of their guard duty by two fresh guards, Ffordd and Enrik. Alys felt certain that she was losing her mind, because she noticed, as if at a distance from herself, that it gave her a tickle of pleasure how Enrik shrank from her, avoiding her eyes. Ffordd stared right back at her, but he kept the heavy kitchen table squarely between them, and his knuckles whitened where he gripped the back of Father's chair.

Father emerged from the bedroom he shared with Mother. He looked diminished, shrunken, and his skin was pale, his face unshaven and bristling with gray.

"How is Mother?" Alys asked, before anyone could think to silence her.

Father looked at her, an expression on his face that was anguish mixed with apology and disbelief. "She's not well, and I haven't the skill to help her. She burns with fever and moans in her sleep. I've sent twice for help, but none will come."

Oh, Mother. Alys remembered the odor that rose from her the day before, like a rot coming from the inside. Alys stared down at the floor, willing Father to look there, too, to know what she'd left down there. But Father was too stricken. And with a certainty that felt like sinking, Alys knew that Mother's fever was raging too hot for any root to help her. Mother had taught her what happened to women when the afterbirth fever got into their blood. Once that happened, nothing could be done.

Mistress Ffagan widened her eyes and clucked her tongue. "Oh dear. Dear, dear. Poor Heledd."

Mistress Miles didn't take her eyes off Alys, as if Alys might vanish were she unwatched for even a moment. "How could any of the good women of this village come to this house of evil? How could you ask it of them? They have their own families to care for. There's naught here to be done. This is a cursed place, as are all who reside in it."

Mistress Ffagan rested one hand on Mistress Miles's forearm. "My husband asked me to thank you for your work in the meetinghouse last night, Brother Argyll. The structure you built for us is more than adequate, and that will not be forgotten."

Father sagged, grew smaller yet. "And what about my Heledd? Will you forget her? What has she done but care for all of you? She sewed you up and cured your fevers. She brought your babies into the world and lost hardly a one of them."

"Ay, but she never had a one of her own, neither. And that's an unnatural thing." Mistress Daniels cut her eyes at Mistress Hardy, pointed her chin at Alys. "And now we know the reason for that. No seed could catch with that creature here."

Mistress Ffagan sighed and shook her head. "Mistress

Daniels, please close the shutters. Mistress Hardy, if you would, light some lanterns." She looked at Father. "Brother Argyll, you should be with Heledd. We women have work to do here." Enrik and Ffordd exchanged looks, and Enrik rubbed his nose as if he had a furious itch.

"What sort of work," Father said.

"That's naught of concern to you," Mistress Miles said.

"Ay, it is. This is my house, and that's my daughter."

"As shall be noted when the witch is put to trial," Mistress Miles said.

Mistress Ffagen formed her mouth into a round O and covered it with a smooth, plump hand. "Oh dear. Oh dear, dear. Brother Argyll, I'm sure Heledd needs you. Do go to her." She widened her brown eyes at him.

Alys felt Father's gaze on her as he left the room, but she couldn't bear to look at him now. She thought she might shatter if she did. She kept her eyes on Mistress Hardy, who finished lighting a second lamp just as Mistress Daniels shut out the winter sun. It spilled through the cracks between and around the shutters, but the room was cast in gloom. Alys heard the bedroom door open and close and when she turned Father was gone.

Mistress Miles stood with her back to the front door, facing the table. "Sit down." While holding onto the tether with one hand, she pulled one of the heavy chairs from the table. It was Alys's own chair, the one she sat in for dinner and supper each day.

Alys sat, and against her will she felt a hard squeeze of fear inside of her, and her heart began to beat just a bit faster. Her back was to Mistress Miles and the other women, and she faced the cold hearth across the room. No fire was lit, so at least there would be no torture by burning, she told herself. She could face anything but burning. She had helped Mother with burns before. Mother had said there was no worse pain. If it didn't kill you, you wished it would.

Enrik and Ffordd stood to her right, their backs to the door that led to Alys's bedroom. Enrik pressed his lips together so tightly he looked on the verge of crying or throwing up. Ffordd was no longer squeezing the back of Father's chair. Instead, he was holding a thick hoop of rough rope. Alys's heart thumped painfully. Her eyes traveled to the basket that Mistress Ffagan hugged tight to her belly. She wondered what was in there.

"Bind her," Mistress Ffagan said.

Ffordd leaned in so close to Alys that she might have bitten his ear if she'd had a mind to do it. She imagined the taste of his blood, the tearing of his flesh, and most of all, his terror and pain. She shocked even herself amid all these thoughts. Is this how evil worked as it grew inside of you? Once it rose to a certain level did it spill over, and then there was no more controlling it? What would The Beast think of her now? Then she realized, it hardly mattered. There was nothing Alys could do about that hole now. Probably there never was. This creature she'd become—this is who she really was.

Alys stayed still while Ffordd tied her to the chair back, once around her shoulders and again around her waist, and then another time around each ankle, fastening her to the front two legs of the chair. Ffordd was unmarried, Alys remembered. She could smell his breakfast on him. Mutton and cheese. And the stench of a shirt worn too many times. When he'd finished, he looked up at her with his turnip face and his little rodent eyes. She smelled his fear. It was rank on him.

Or no . . . not rank at all. It was sweet like honey. And warm. Alys had been so cold for so long. She drank up his fear and heat filled her chest.

This was what soul eating was, Alys realized. This, right here. This warmth, this rush of blood and feeling, this blooming inside of her. And why shouldn't she do this if she could?

Ffordd hurled himself away from her. He gasped and pointed, clutching his chest, his mouth moving but no words coming out.

Mistress Hardy cried out and fled across the room, followed quickly by Mistress Daniels. "Soul eater," she cried out. "That's what she is. We should burn her and be done with it before she kills us all."

Alys felt her head yanked back by her braid, and she stared up into the upside-down face of Mistress Miles. "We know she's a soul eater, you fools. Now help us here and stop cowering in the corner."

"I think we have this well in hand," said Mistress Ffagan, bending over Alys. "The bridle is all that's needed." She pursed her lips in concentration while she held over Alys's face a small, head-shaped iron cage with a door in the back. In the front of the cage was a flat, spiked bit about three inches long that pointed inward. While Mistress Miles pulled down on Alys's braid so hard she felt her neck might splinter, Mistress Ffagan forced Alys's entire head into the iron cage, pressing the bit into

Alys's mouth. Alys gagged and pushed with all her might, but there was no good direction to push in. Up only forced the bit deeper into her mouth, and her neck couldn't bend any farther back without breaking. Shaking from side to side scraped her tongue. She heard bells ringing and realized the cage itself was hung with them, front and back and one on each side. With a click, the cage door was fastened and locked in back of her head. "There," Mistress Ffagan said. "All done. There's nothing to fear now, sisters and brothers. She is subdued."

Mistress Miles let go of Alys's braid, and Alys lifted up her head, wobbling under the weight of the iron and the jangling bells.

"This," Mistress Ffagan said, "is a witch's bridle. We haven't had cause to use one in quite some time, but it fits her perfectly, like it was made for her. You see how the iron wraps around her neck and the vertical bars are set close to her head so she can't free herself from the bit. It's locked tight in back, and I have the only key. She can't talk, and she can't free herself from the bridle even if we release her from her tethers. Please untie her from the chair, Mistress Miles."

Alys might have struggled against Mistress Miles. But the urge to recoil from her was squelched by the pain of even the smallest movement of her head. Alys found that if she kept quite still the agony of the metal bit in her mouth was just bearable. Even the slightest tip of her head forced the bit deeper and caused her to gag. Panic also caused her to gag. Only calm concentration allowed her to swallow her own spit without the use of her tongue.

"Stand up, witch." Mistress Daniels yanked on the rope tied to the front of the bridle, and Alys lurched up, the bells clanging loudly in her ears, the bit raking against the roof of her mouth.

Mistress Ffagan nodded to Ffordd to open the front door. "Now ye shall be judged," she said.

TWENTY-ONE

A steady rumble of noise had penetrated the room even through the closed shutters, and it vibrated through Alys like a hum. The sound magnified when Ffordd opened the door, and Alys saw that it belonged to a throng of villagers gathered around, waiting and staring. Ffordd and Enrik went out first, affecting vigilance and strength with crossed arms. The voices from the crowd rose like thunder, and a tide of up and down movement rolled across them. Some recoiled at the sight of Alys, others leaned forward. When Mistress Ffagan emerged, they all fell back to clear a path for her. Mistress Miles snatched the rope from Mistress Daniels, and she yanked Alys forward leading her out into the snowy street behind Mistress Ffagan. Wails of terror went up from the crowd at the sight of Alys and her iron witch's bridle. The path widened farther.

Alys couldn't close her eyes now or she'd fall. Instead, she stared ahead at Mistress Miles's broad black back. The bridle bells jangled with every step she took, and she heard the squealing of children all around her, though she refused to look left or right. The villagers on either side of her were a solid mass, no single face emerging more than any other.

Alys felt a prick of something familiar, though she couldn't have said what it was. It nudged her like a memory. She turned suddenly to her right, setting off a peal of jangling bells and a surprised, high-pitched shriek from the crowd. Standing in the snow, crammed in among the legs and feet of curious villagers was little Ren, white-faced and wide-eyed. This time he didn't call to Alys, and when she caught his gaze, he turned and ran.

The meetinghouse rose in front of her now and the crowd closed in behind Mistress Daniels and Mistress Hardy, who both held the rope fastened to the back of the witch's bridle and made a great show of the effort. More villagers milled about in the meetinghouse yard. Enrik and Ffordd rushed forward to fling open the double doors to the meetinghouse, and Mistress Ffagan's steps quickened to enter. Mistress Miles yanked Alys forward to match Mistress Ffagan's pace and Alys nearly fell but caught herself just in time. The bells crashed in her ears.

Walking through the entrance, Alys saw the nine Elders facing her, seated in oaken armchairs that Father had made for them when the meetinghouse was first built. Behind them, a roaring fire burned in the wide hearth. Its warmth died long before it reached Alys.

Several feet in front of the Elders was something that Alys

had never seen before. It was a wooden cage, still smelling of sawdust and fresh pine. It stood perhaps a foot higher than Alys's head and three feet wide. This must have been the structure the High Elder had asked Father to build last night.

Mistress Ffagan walked toward it and opened the door to the cage. "Sisters, give the ropes to Enrik. Ffordd, put her inside."

Ffordd shoved her hard from behind, and Alys might have fought him, but with her hands tied and the iron bells ringing in her ears, she couldn't think of a reason to bother. One more shove and she was in the cage. The door closed behind her and fastened with an iron lock. The ropes attached to the bridle front and back now fell freely and puddled at her feet.

The High Elder nodded to Ffordd. "Now ye may call in the faithful."

Alys could hear the doors swing open behind her and a shuffling of feet and buzz of voices that grew in volume as the benches filled with villagers. Once again Alys felt as if the world were pulling away from her, as if the distance between herself and those around her were a chasm too vast even to call across. She felt herself fall, her knees bending, and it was all she could do to straighten them again. She leaned against the side of the cage, and her bells jangled. There was a hiss and a squeal behind her.

The doors to the meetinghouse were shut behind the villagers and the room dimmed. Lanterns were lit and hung from hooks around the room. The air was chill and damp despite the fire.

The High Elder stood. "Brothers and sisters, we are brought

here today by the discovery of a great Evil in our midst. It is a powerful Evil. An Evil that if left to its own devices would spread amongst us and defile us all." As he spoke, Alys felt his voice vibrate in her chest. His face seemed to dissolve, shuffle its parts, and reassemble, and Alys thought again that she might fall. Her forehead tingled and her cheeks felt hot although she shuddered with cold.

"It is an Evil that we know by many names." The High Elder paused and looked around him. "*Witch*," he said.

There was a gasp, a stifled cry.

"*Soul eater*," he said.

There was a murmur, a collective sucking in of breath.

"But the Good Shepherd has taught us that no matter what we may call it, there is truly only one Evil. It is The Beast. And just as our flock follows the Shepherd as He leads us on the path of righteousness to His loving protection, The Beast's children follow It on a path of perversity and eternal damnation."

Alys stared into the fire that crackled and smoked behind the High Elder. Still she felt no heat. Her nose ran, tickling her lip. She tasted iron.

"One of The Beast's children has grown up among us. We have been kind to it. We have fed it. Nurtured it. Given it shelter and protection. It is crafty, this one. It has laughed at us, scorned us. And we have been trusting, but we have not been wise. We have not seen through its vile cunning to The Beast inside.

"Now, though, we have seen. And we can no longer hide our eyes from the truth. The Good Shepherd is calling to His flock and we must hear His voice and follow Him. Only He can lead us on the path away from Evil.

"We know this Evil now. It is here in this room. And we must cast it out." The High Elder sat down and folded his hands in his lap. He held Alys with his pale blue gaze and Alys felt nothing, sensed nothing. It was as if she were staring into rock. There was no seeing through it.

The room rumbled and shook with voices.

Elder Yates stood, unrolled a sheet of parchment, and cleared his throat. "Sister Cerys Miles, step forth and offer your witness to the Evil."

Cerys sat next to her mother on the women's side of the meetinghouse. She wore a sober gray dress and her hair in a tight braid that yielded not a tendril. She looked up toward Elder Yates, then bowed her head and rose up, swaying just slightly, as if she weren't quite steady on her feet.

Elder Miles leaned forward. "Are you quite well, my child?"

"Ay, Father, I am," Cerys said. She pulled herself up, breathed deep.

The High Elder stared at the girl, his eyes opaque. Unmoved. Then Alys stopped looking into his eyes, and she looked into him instead—into his hard heart. *He knew*, Alys thought to herself. He knew the boy he'd raised, what he and Cerys had been getting up to. Of course he did. She could read the lies he concealed as clearly as if his chest were opened up in front of her. If she were closer to him she felt sure she could smell all those lies. They would smell like vinegar.

"It happened yesterday," Cerys began. "I was out looking

for apples as a surprise for Mother and Father." She glanced quickly toward Alys and then just as quickly away. "Alys told me there was a tree that hadn't been picked clean yet and the apples were still good. And she told me where it was, and so that's where I went."

Elder Yates drew his eyebrows together until they formed a single white shelf. "Apples this time of year, child?"

There was murmuring on the women's side of the meeting-house. Alys wondered which idea struck them odder—apples in the snow, or Cerys doing anything that resembled work.

"The child is trusting," Elder Miles said, looking not at Elder Yates, but at the High Elder who sat next to him. "And the evil one is sly."

"Ay," Cerys said. "She misled me. I couldn't find the apple tree, so I turned back for home. And then suddenly, there she was. I hadn't heard her, nor seen her up to that moment." Cerys looked around her. "It was like she just appeared out of nothing." Mistress Ffagan clapped a hand to her open mouth, and fast intakes of breath hissed around the room.

"And so I said, 'Alys, you frightened me!' And then it happened. It was like she reached right inside me. I couldn't breathe. I couldn't call for help. If Brother Rhys hadn't come upon us she would have ripped the soul right out of me, I know she would have." Cerys dropped to her seat and buried her face in her mother's bosom.

Alys closed her eyes. Cerys had lied about everything that didn't matter, but she'd told the truth about the one thing that did. Alys had tried to eat Cerys's soul, there was no denying it to herself. And she'd enjoyed it. She remembered the warmth inside of her, the flush that spread to her skin. She had never in her life felt so awake, and now there was no going back to that sleepy time before she knew what it was like to sniff out another's soul. She was no longer merely like the soul eaters, as The Beast had said she was. She was one of them. Alys looked toward the windows. The sky was bluing to twilight. The other children of Gwenith would be heading toward the fields, mounting the Gate, to protect the village from creatures like her.

"Brother Rhys Ffagan," Elder Yates said, "offer your witness to the Evil."

Rhys rose from his seat on the front bench. "I was hunting for deer when I came upon them," Rhys said. "And when I saw what that thing was doing to Sister Cerys, I knocked it down. Then I tied it up and brought it back here." He sat down again. Alys noted the looks of disappointment around her. The villagers had been hoping for more detail.

In the silence that followed, Mistress Daniels jumped to her feet. "Soul eater," she cried and pointed at Alys. "Witch! Burn her before she kills us all." She looked toward the Elders. "We must ask ourselves, how much illness has she caused among us? How much misfortune has she brought on us? How many women are barren because of her? Her own mother can't catch a baby. And why, I ask you. I'll tell you why. That one's sucking the babies out of her while she sleeps. There's naught but skin and gristle left of Sister Argyll after all these years giving shelter to that witch. We all know it. That poor woman won't last the night."

"Ay, it's true," Mistress Hardy said. "And the witch tried to take Ffordd's soul, too." She pointed her chin at Ffordd, and he grunted and nodded, looked around him at the assembled and puffed up his chest.

Voices from around the room rumbled and thrummed in Alys's ears. She felt the meetinghouse tilt around her, and she lost the thread of what she'd done and hadn't done. It hardly mattered anymore, there was no point parsing it in her mind. It would all end the same. She sank to the floor of her cage, the cage Father had built for her. *Father.* Father had built her a cage. He'd had no choice, but still. It hurt her more than anything yet.

More voices rose up above the others.

"Wasn't she the one awake when the soul eaters descended on Gwenith?"

"That's what the traveler said, isn't it? That she was out wandering when he found her, while all the rest of Gwenith was dead or sleeping."

"I heard she was skipping through the village like nothing was the matter."

"I heard she was singing."

"It was an incantation!"

A shriek, a cry. First a woman's voice, then a man's. And back and forth it went. Alys closed her eyes.

"She killed her own parents, danced around their dead bodies."

"She ate their souls!"

"Ay, she ate them all!"

"Why'd she leave the children alive?"

"To bring them over to the soul eaters, to turn them unholy like herself."

"And hasn't she done it? Haven't the children of Gwenith been wandering away from us, one after the other?"

"Ay, she'll lead them all away before long, and then we'll have no one to guard the Gate."

"That's when she'll bring the soul eaters back here to take us all!"

So many people speaking at once, and yet Alys could identify each of their voices like individual needles piercing her skin. She heard Mary whose baby she'd held while Mother healed her. She heard Brother Ellis who'd taught her sums. She heard Elin and Fflur, girls her age who'd never in their lives had to climb a frozen Gate.

The High Elder's voice lifted above the din. "Silence, brothers and sisters." More grumbles, questions, but quieter now. "The wolves gather around us, but all those who follow the Good Shepherd are safe in His loving arms. This child of The Beast is merely a test of our faith. It is naught but a wolf that threatens our flock. And when we destroy it, our flock will be safe in the Good Shepherd's arms once again."

More murmuring. Back and forth and back again.

"Burn her."

"You're daft. And set the whole village ablaze?"

"Drown her."

"What if she floats? Then what? Anyway, nearest pond's still frozen."

"Stone her."

"Ay, that'll work. Or crush her."

The High Elder lifted his arms, palms outward, and silence fell. The lamplight cast stripes of light and shadow across his face. "This creature wishes to frighten us. So we shall destroy it in the way all creatures like it fear the most. By fire. At first light, all able-bodied men shall load three wagons with wood. Then the creature shall be taken outside the Gates to the northwest clearing. There we will build a fire so hot it will cleanse us of this filth forever. And by the light of this great blaze we shall sing a hymn of thanks and praise."

Alys was cold, so cold. Crouched there on the floor, chill drafts creeping under her dress and crawling across her skin, she tried to imagine hot licks of flames rising around her, but she found she could not. As the villagers filed out of the meeting-house, Alys felt the cage vibrate around her. She watched the passing feet, skirt hems, and boots turned gray from mud. She had no thought for tomorrow. This chill, and the gaping empty space in her chest, were all that she knew for now.

TWENTY-TWO

The villagers were long gone, the lamps that ringed the meetinghouse burned out. The shutters were closed to the cold, and moonlight glowed blue through the cracks.

Otherwise, the darkness inside the meetinghouse was thick and black. Still, Alys's sharp eyes made out the lumpen shapes of her guards. Vaughn and Sayer had been left behind to watch her through the night. They huddled under blankets near the cold hearth, which had burned to ash hours before. At first the two men had whispered to each other, occasionally glancing back at her nervously. Then they lapsed into silence pierced every so often by snoring. When Alys shifted minutely and her bells rang, they jumped in place and reached for their bows. Alys wondered if a soul eater could be killed with something as simple as a bow and arrow. She had no idea, and doubted whether Vaughn and Sayer knew, either.

There was a pounding on the meetinghouse doors. Alys turned toward the sound, bells clanging, and Vaughn and Sayer murmured and shifted, sat up in their seats and stared. "Ay," Sayer said. Then he rose to his feet and walked toward the doors, while keeping to the perimeter and making a careful arc around Alys's cage. He listened through the doors, bolted shut from the inside with a long wooden beam. "Who's banging?"

"It's Brother Argyll." Father.

Sayer looked back toward Vaughn, eyebrows raised, though Alys didn't imagine that Vaughn could read his expression through the black.

"What's he want then?" Vaughn said, his words hissing through the cold flat air.

"What you want then?" Sayer said through the door.

"I've brought you wood for the fire," Father said.

"Let him in," Vaughn said. "I'm like to freeze."

"Are you sure then?" Sayer called back to Vaughn. "It's the creature's father."

"Way I see it," Vaughn said, "creature killed its father back in Gwenith. You know Brother Argyll well as I do. And you're cold well as I am. Let him build us a fire. He ain't like to do us harm. Anyways, there's two of us."

Sayer shrugged and lifted the beam from the door. It swung open and cold wind rushed through the opening, tearing through Alys, so sharp that it hurt her teeth. Sayer slammed the door shut behind Father and put the beam back in place.

Father carried a pack of wood slung across his shoulder and

made his way up the aisle, past the cage, not looking at Alys. As he walked by, she held onto the wooden rungs of the cage, so hard that she felt splinters piercing her skin.

Father shrugged down his load in front of the hearth and set to building a fire. He placed a heavy jug on the floor at his feet, pulled off his gloves, and knelt down to press his hands to the jug as if to warm them. Sayer and Vaughn sat down and pulled blankets up to their chins.

"That tea?" Vaughn said.

"Ay," Father said. He stacked kindling, arranged it with care.

"Hot?"

"Ay," Father said. "Help yourselves." He stacked wood, pulled out some flint, struck a spark that flashed. He leaned forward and blew.

Vaughn and Sayer's heads bent in the same direction and Alys heard pouring and murmuring, and "Oh, that's lovely" from one of them. The men sighed and shifted back in their chairs. Time passed while they sipped tea and the fire grew big and orange, so hot that Alys felt an occasional lick of warmth, just enough to make her shiver and remember how cold she was. Father sat still and crouched before the fire, watching the flames.

"How fares Sister Argyll?" It was Sayer's voice, thick and drowsy.

Silence from Father.

Sayer seemed to have lost interest in the answer, because he didn't ask again. Alys heard a metal cup clatter to the floor. Then another. Father stood and righted the cups. Picked up his jug and his bundle, looked toward Alys. "Oh child," he said.

That's when Alys knew he was there to save her. A groan rose out of her that she didn't recognize. This was crying, she realized. It was high time, she supposed. Eight long years since the last time.

Father jabbed the tip of a knife into the heavy lock that hung from the door to the cage and wiggled it around. Then he unlocked it with a sharp tug. He did the same to the lock on the bridle, and then pulled it from her face and took the same knife to the ropes that held her wrists. Her hands freed, Alys wiped her nose and mouth on her sleeve, coughed and spat. "Mother," she said, her voice a burnt whisper in the back of her throat.

"Heledd is dead," he said. "Now come. Quickly. I'm no expert at mixing a sleeping draught and we must get you out before they wake."

Mother. Alys had not even been able to say good-bye. Or to thank her for all she'd taught Alys . . . or to tell her how she'd grown to love her. To tell her she knew about Mother's secret suffering and that she loved her all the more for it. To tell Mother that Alys thought she was the bravest, truest person in all of Defaid.

Alys pictured Mother's face, so still and yet so restless. She'd learned to read Mother's moods in the subtlest raise of eyebrow or drop of chin. She wondered what Mother's face would have looked like now, if she were still alive and knew what Alys had done. Alys felt shame, burning shame, and then the shame burned itself out and a heavy stone dropped into place inside of her—cold and dead—where her heart and stomach should be. It was all she could do to carry herself forward. But she needed to keep moving, if only for Father's sake.

Father lifted his pack to his back and she followed him through the doors of the meetinghouse and out into the silence of Defaid at night. Moonlight glowed across the snow that crusted the roofs. The lamps from each of the Gate's three towers shone north, south, and west. They walked west, toward the town doors. Alys wrapped her arms around herself, felt the cold sifting through the rough cotton of her shift, the wool of her dress. Her heart felt tight and frozen. She couldn't conjure the warmth of the fire that Father had built, or the relief she'd felt when he released her.

When they had gone as far as home, Father stopped walking. He stared ahead while he talked to her, not looking at her, not really seeming to look at anything. "Go to the doors. Enid will meet you there. She has clothes and food for you. Then you must go. Far as you can, away from here."

Alys stared at him for a long moment. "Come with me."

Father leaned forward and pressed dry, trembling lips to her forehead. She breathed deep and smelled wet wool and wood shavings. Then he pulled away from her. "Go, child. Quiet and quick now. Heledd asked me to bury her beneath the tree behind the old place. I'll take her there at first light."

"They won't let you," Alys said.

Father pushed the door open to their dark kitchen with its empty hearth. "They'll not stop me." He closed the door behind him.

TWENTY-THREE

As Alys approached the doors to the Gate, she saw Enid holding a sack and a dark bundle. The wind whipped the skirts around Alys's legs, and she bent her head into it, walked faster, her eyes burning. Enid's face was white, her lips pale blue lines, sewn tight shut. Over Enid's shoulder, Alys saw Madog and some of the older Gwenith boys and girls lifting the massive beam that held the doors closed all night. She glanced toward the guardhouse and realized that whoever was on duty there must have been given a sleeping draught as well.

When Alys drew close enough to touch, Enid reached for her wrist, pulled her in so near that Alys could feel her breath puff warm and damp around her face as she spoke. "Go to Pysgod. Tell them your family are travelers. Tell them soul eaters got them, and you were the only one that lived. It's close enough to true, isn't it?"

Alys didn't speak the obvious, that Pysgod had no good reason to take her in. She was barely a child anymore, they would feel no obligation. At best they might give her a meal and send her on her way.

Enid squeezed Alys's wrist, bringing her back to the moment. "It's the only thing. Now go." But instead of releasing Alys, Enid pulled her even closer, wrapped her arms around Alys tight. She whispered into Alys's ear. "Don't you ever come back here, Alys. We'll come find you. And then we'll be together again." Alys was afraid to tighten her own arms around Enid, afraid that if she did she wouldn't be able to let go. She'd feel like a child again in Enid's arms, the child she was before. Wishing for her mam. Wishing for Mother.

Enid set the sack down at her feet and unfolded the bundle, which contained a wool dress of Alys's and Mam's heavy coat, a scarf and her gloves. Enid helped Alys into them, her breath making white clouds in the night air as she spoke. "Keep to the fforest and follow the river. I don't think they'll send anyone after you, but if they do, the road won't be safe. The river will take you straight to Pysgod. Keep moving. Don't you dare rest while it's dark."

Enid didn't need to say out loud what she and Alys both knew. If Alys so much as sat down in the snow to rest her eyes, she'd surely freeze to death. Then she'd be food for the wolves. The air was so cold that Alys's eyes teared and the tears froze on her cheeks. When she breathed in through her nose, her snot turned to ice. That was not a good sign.

There was a low whistle behind them. It was Madog. He looked to the sky, still pitch black, but his message was clear. There was no time for talk, she must go.

Alys nodded to Madog and the other children as she walked through the Gates. She looked behind her long enough to wave to Enid, who stood watching her. Then the doors closed, and Defaid was a wall of black, shut tight in front of her. She looked up to the nearest watchtower, the lamp glowing orange, and made out the outline of a hand. She raised her own in response. Then she turned around and looked to the world in front of her, a world of snow, dead fields, and the black spikes of trees everywhere the sky met the earth—south, north, west, it was all the same. She looked south, toward Pysgod, which was days away she figured. She'd never been there before, but she knew the reason no one ever traveled there—no one except a traveler. It was because you'd be forced to make camp in the wilderness between here and there. The wilderness where wolves roamed and soul eaters hunted.

Alys curled her toes in her boots, stomped her feet to shake feeling back into them. She expected to hear the hard thunk of packed snow, beaten into ice by feet and hooves and wagon wheels. But instead her heels sank into slush. She looked down to see a black circle of melt around her feet, as if she had burned a spot into the earth. And then the spot spread out to her right, forming a long, black path in the white snow leading to the north fforest. She looked south again toward Pysgod, the way she was supposed to travel, and the wind picked up hard and howling, blowing snow and ice into violent, opaque swirls. It bit her cheeks like teeth, blinded her. Alys staggered backward, her feet sinking into slush again, and she turned to put the wind at her back, even for just a moment, to catch her breath. It bellowed behind her, and nudged her north, forcefully, unmistakably.

But north there was nothing. North was wilderness and the corpse of a town that was once called Gwenith.

The wind blew and screamed in Alys's ears, like a human howl. The cold dug its fingers under her coat, raked its nails across her skin, stabbed straight into her heart. She shivered and shook. There was nothing for it. She had to move, to get away from here. Then she could figure out a path back toward Pysgod once this storm was over. She took to the black, melted path north. At least, she told herself, no man or woman of Defaid would ever follow her there.

And the sisters would feed on the fear . . .

The sisters moved through the fforest, snowflakes parting before them like sheep. They looked at each other, blinking crystal lashes over ice-gray eyes.

A small boy with white-blond hair floated between them.

Something drew the three. It was a scent. Their eagerness grew stronger along with the scent, and soon they no longer floated. They sailed. They flew.

"The fear, Sister, do you smell it?"

"I do, Angelica."

"This is not our fear," the boy said. "We did not make it."

"No," Benedicta said, "the other made it. The green wood girl."

Sister nodded to sister. The green wood girl. They scented her. She had left her mark.

"Alys," the boy said. "That is her name. Alys."

"She is like us now," said Benedicta.

"More like us, but not us yet." Angelica sniffed the wind. "She leaves them now. But she leaves them huddled. They lock their doors and windows. They pray."

The three stopped. They had arrived. They stood in the snow, in the dark. Lanterns flickered weakly in towers above them. The three looked at the great wooden Gate, the pile of sticks these villagers had erected to keep them safe, to contain their fear. But the fear was too much to be held now. It oozed and rolled over the Gate, it coated the land like mist. It filled the soul eaters' nostrils, and the scent was sweet.

"It's time then?" the boy said to the sisters.

"Yes," the sisters said. "It's time."

*It sucks
your soul
then
licks the
bowl*

TWENTY-FOUR

Alys followed the dark ribbon of melt straight into the wilderness. She had been in the fforest to the south many times, but she'd never been in this fforest before. This was the black bristle of land that divided the safety of Defaid from the dead patch that once was Gwenith, her home.

This was the fforest that mothers and fathers warned their children about, the one that all the stories were told about, the place where nightmares hatched. It was just a fforest, Alys told herself, no different from any other. Yet somehow it seemed darker than any fforest she'd ever been in before. Branches clung together overhead and roots locked together underfoot. The tree trunks seemed to writhe and bend around her, beckoning her in and closing up behind her. It felt like being swallowed.

The wind muffled to a hum and a whine. She still felt the

cold clean through to her bones, but now it was more of a settled ache than the sharp pain it had been before. Snow and ice crusted the fforest and the moon reflected off the white surfaces so that Alys could just make out the path in front of her, the path that stayed damp and black no matter how icy and white the rest of the fforest remained. She looked behind her and the black ribbon that led back to Defaid was gone, iced over and white again.

Alys shuddered and quaked, a shiver that started in her gut and spread outward. Her teeth banged together, and she lost her footing more than once because she couldn't feel her feet.

This was hopeless, she knew. It was too cold, and the way was too far. If she could make it all the way to Gwenith, she might find shelter there. She might be able to build herself a fire in one of the houses that hadn't yet sunk into the ground. But she'd been walking for hours already, and she couldn't imagine walking hours more. She'd die before she even made it halfway. And that was assuming she knew where she was going, which she did not. Already she felt the awful temptation to sink to her feet, to curl up here among the roots and drift away. Maybe the roots would wrap around her, pull her down and under where the earth was still warm.

She heard the long, looping howl of a wolf. It was off to her left, and not far away at all. Another howl, in answer, to her right. She looked into the wilderness, but as sharp as her vision was she could only imagine their outlines. Two different howls, two different wolves. And where there were two wolves there were surely six or more.

Running would do her no good. The wolves would want that, then they could nip at her heels, take her down from behind. The hair lifted on Alys's arms and a shiver rattled in her chest.

She heard the crunch and swish of paws in snow, fur brushing against bark. The sounds came from both sides, circling her. She stood still and waited.

The crunching and swishing took shape around her, and hunched forms emerged from the trees, white and gray, black and mottled. There were six wolves. No, eight. They whined and yipped, uncertain and excited.

One was bigger than the rest. Braver, nearer. Eyes locked on Alys.

She had never been this close to a wolf before. It was nothing like a dog, there was no dog in it. There was nothing at all in it that Alys recognized. Alys had never felt terror like this. She lost herself to it.

Wolf lips lifted over teeth, wolf nose twitched and sniffed, wolf tongue licked the air. Wolf fur bristled over back and haunches. Wolf felt no cold.

Now Alys felt no cold. She had no memory of cold. Only blood. The hot scent of urine in snow. The pack. She sniffed the air. Panted. Growled low. She felt a hunger in her belly, a gnawing. She hadn't eaten in so long. She felt the fur on her back lifting and reaching, excited and wary. She salivated. Wolf breath filled her chest and wolf blood flowed through her veins, and she pawed the snow with her wolf feet. She took it in. The wolf was her, and she was the wolf. Its wolfness filled her like smoke. She smelled it in her nose, and tasted it bitter in her mouth. And she found that she loved the bitterness, she burned with it.

And then she was no longer wolf anymore, she was Alys again, but sharper and stronger and more awake than she'd ever been before. She was Alys, but not tired. Not questioning. She was Alys, but not sad. She felt herself rising off the ground with joy. The night was black around her, but she could see through it. The cold raked her skin, but did not penetrate. Her toes grazed the ground, but did not need to rest.

The big wolf was down, deflated, emptied. It lay in the snow like a pelt stripped of flesh. The other wolves yipped and cried, then withdrew into the darkness of the fforest and were gone.

The sound of their yips brought Alys back to herself. The cold bit the inside of her nostrils. Her feet sank into snow, and she shook as if she'd been stripped of all her layers of wool. There was a dead wolf in the snow just in front of her, and she knew that she had killed it. Sickness rolled from her feet to her bowels to her stomach and then into her mouth, and Alys fell to her knees retching. What came out smelled like death. It steamed and sank into the path in front of her.

Alys looked at the big wolf and reached out to it, laying her hand on its muzzle. She stroked its belly and spine with her other hand. Alys had seen death before, too many times. But she had never before been the cause of it. She had drained this wolf of what once made it alive. Not its blood, or its flesh. Something else. Something more important. This dead thing in the snow wasn't a wolf anymore, it wasn't anything at all. The creature that had bared its teeth at her just minutes ago, that had looked bigger and broader than a man, now seemed insubstantial in her hands, as if she might pick it up and toss it away.

Even worse than killing the wolf was an awareness that made Alys recoil from herself in shame: She had enjoyed it. She could still conjure the blood and fur heat that made her forget what cold was.

Alys's guilt and horror at what she'd done were so immense that at first she thought she would curl up against the wolf's thick fur and die here herself, but she no longer wanted to touch it. She wanted only to get away from it, to get away from the truth about herself.

She was a soul eater.

And yet she couldn't be.

And yet she was.

She didn't want to be. The brief flush of pleasure she'd felt was fully erased by her remorse. She wanted to believe that her sadness over the wolf meant she wasn't yet too far gone. That there might be some other way through, between the good child she could no longer pretend to be and the evil thing she did not want to become.

She got to her feet, and her ears closed to the sounds of the night, wind rattling tree branches and skating through leaves. There was nothing else to hear or feel or touch or see. There was just her own breath in her ears, her feet numb and too far away from her knees. She stumbled on.

The pack that Enid had given her had been light at first, but now it weighed against her back, pulled on her shoulders. She felt an urge to take it off and leave it here. After all, only the living needed food.

Her skin hurt. The muslin and wool of her clothing rubbed against her shoulders and torso, and the shudders she'd felt in her body now went as deep as her bones.

A little farther. Just a little farther.

It was a voice inside of her, but not her. It was strange and familiar. She knew its rumble in the spot in her chest where it had vibrated before. And each time her knees buckled and her footsteps slowed, the voice came back.

A little farther. Just a little farther.

She imagined The Beast perched in the trees above her. Thought she heard the flap of Its leathery wings overhead. But when she looked up there was only night, only snow.

The black ribbon carried her forward and forward, over branches and around stumps and between trees and around rocks. Up and over and around and the numbness in her feet traveled up her legs until she fell more than she walked. Her head swirled and pounded with each jerk down and up again. She was sick, very sick. Alys had witnessed too much fever not to recognize it in herself.

She was climbing, had been climbing for some time. She remembered there was a mountain between Defaid and Gwenith, a black mound against the sky to the north. The land rose to her right and the path led her in a gradual slope that occasionally spiked and pitched up, and she used her hands to pull herself forward. Through the wool of her gloves her fingernails dug into bark and scraped over rocks. The numbness spread up her arms.

The path pitched up even more steeply. She sat on a rock, put her head in her hands, felt the cold of the stone through her wool, straight through to her butt and thighs. *I can't*, she thought. *No more.*

Then she caught the scents of earth and rain, felt claws on her shoulder, and one thin claw raking her cheek. But there were no claws there, just the voice in her head and her chest.

A bit farther, girl. Over there. Almost there.

Alys thought about rising to her feet again, willed her legs to hold her, to carry her on, unsure if they'd obey. They did, and she climbed. Then she crawled, pulling herself along over rocks, dragging herself through mud and dirt, leaves and sticks working their way into her clothes, her hair. She stopped looking forward. There was only the spot of melt beneath her, and then the next and the next.

When the climbing ceased, Alys felt a moment of disorientation. The way ahead of her was a clear and gentle slope to a small wooden shack tucked into the side of the mountain. The black ribbon of melt led straight to its door.

Alys thought she might be dreaming. Perhaps the fever had finally taken its hold and she was really back there in the fforest somewhere, curled up in the snow, sleeping to her death. She got to her feet, looked to the shack in front of her, and then to the sky. It was just bluing to dawn, the stars beginning to fade. The snow shone white around and over the shack, its roof a shelf of white. Alys pushed open the door and saw that the shack had been built at the opening of a small cave. There was a rough hearth of stacked stone, and in the hearth was a neat pile of wood and kindling. On its ledge was a flint.

She dropped to her knees in front of the hearth, pulled off her muddy gloves and took up the flint with stiff fingers. She couldn't make her hands work, they were too thick and dull. Then a spark caught the kindling, a flame blazed and spread. When the wood began to crackle to life, Alys sat back on her heels and waited to feel warm.

The fire grew and glowed orange and Alys looked around her. There was a wide pile of straw covered with fur pelts. The shack tilted a bit to one side and seemed barely standing, as if no one had lived here for years. She leaned forward and smelled the straw. Old. Musty. The pelts felt at once damp and stiff with age. There was another pile of straw near the door, and Alys sifted through it. Some animal had lived here once, but that was a long time ago.

She shivered, drew close to the fire again. She should eat, but the thought of it made her stomach turn. The heat from the fire only warmed her skin. She was still cold under the surface, so cold that she couldn't imagine being warm again. She pulled off her boots and set them near the fire, but not so close that they might burn. She forced herself to peel off her damp clothing, and once she was down to her shift she crawled under the pelts and put her pounding head down. She turned on her side, pulled her knees up to her chest, and pressed her cold fingers to her hot cheeks. She stared out toward the fire.

There was a flat rock to the right of the hearth, not even knee high and just wide enough to set a pot on. There was something resting on top, and as the fire licked and Alys shook and shuddered, she wondered what it was. Her eyes closed, once, twice, but she decided she needed to know what that thing was, even if it meant crawling out of the pelts to find out.

She reached forward and forward the short way across the room to where the rock sat and the thing rested on top. It was more than one thing, it turned out. It was two things. She felt along with her fingers, grabbed them, and pulled them back toward her.

The first: a small, sharp knife, with a wooden handle that had been carved by hand.

The second: a heavy iron bracelet engraved with the number nine.

Alys heard the flapping of broad wings and a thump like some heavy bird landing on the rooftop. She set the knife and the bracelet on the floor. Then she pulled deeper under the pelts, drew them up to her eyes, curled her icy fingers under her chin. She shivered and quaked and each time she blinked, her eyes wanted to stay closed, but she forced them open again, because there was something she was seeing in this shack. Right there in front of her—close enough to touch if only they were touchable.

There was a woman—a mother. And a goat and two girls. The goat sighed and rested its head in the hay. The woman sat and stared into the fire. The girls lay their heads in the mother's lap and stared only at each other. And then reaching across the space between them, the girls held hands.

The girls were mirror images of each other and yet Alys would know them each anywhere. That one there was Benedicta.

And the other was Angelica. And they were linked by hands and by heart. This was before it all went wrong. When there was still a choice to be made.

Alys closed her eyes and slept.

Father told Mother and Alys to get in the wagon. Father clicked his tongue and jerked the reins and the old dray horse pulled forward.

It was nearly dusk and Alys knew without being told that they were late, very late, and they were in danger of the Gate closing with them still outside. She sat in the back of the wagon, watching the ground roll away from them. Then she turned and it was only Father on the seat. "Where's Mother?" she said.

Father looked back at Alys, his face blank. "She must still be back there."

Alys turned back to the darkness, which seemed to be thicker and blacker than what lay ahead. She turned to Father's broad, black-coated back. "Stop the wagon, we must go back for her." Alys felt as if she were calling to him through mud, as if it took her voice too long to reach him.

He pulled the wagon to a stop and Alys leapt from the back, running and calling for Mother. She ran through a field and she could barely see her feet, and there was a fforest to her left, so deep and dark that she could only make out the first layer of trees. But there in the depths of that fforest was a flash of white and Alys saw Mother, there in her nightshift. And she ran into the fforest for Mother, but there were so many trees in the way, and for some reason Mother couldn't hear her and instead of coming closer she grew farther and farther away.

And then there were others in the trees. Women with long rivers of hair down their backs, all interwoven with leaves. They floated through the trees, so much faster than Alys, never tripping on roots. Then all the women turned to Alys and Alys saw her own face on all of their faces. Her and her and her. Mother saw them now, too, and she turned to Alys, a question in her dark eyes, and Alys tried to call to Mother but her voice died in her throat.

Then the others that were Alys were all around Mother and Alys could no longer see Mother, because Mother was swallowed up in a sea of Alyses with leaves in their hair.

TWENTY-FIVE

Alys woke to a dead fire and a cold room and weak, watery light leaking between the cracks in the shuttered windows. Her hair was damp through and her shift stuck to her skin. Her forehead blazed and her head rocked with pain when she sat up. She must move, or she would die here, and she thought perhaps she did not want to die. Perhaps she could carry herself a bit farther.

Alys shivered and quickly pulled on her clothing, which was now quite dry, if not warm. It would have been better if she'd had a dry shift as well. As it was, when she was fully dressed, she was uncomfortably aware of the damp muslin clinging to her back, chest, and arms. She crouched on her haunches and opened the bag that Enid had packed for her. She reached for the iron bracelet and the knife, dropped them inside, and pulled out a cloth-wrapped chunk of bread, some dried meat, and an apple. She should eat, she thought. That is what she should do.

She was too sick to be frightened. The fever seemed to have dulled her ability to worry beyond what was right in front of her. And in front of her was bread. She pulled it to her mouth, bit some off, and chewed. It tasted like dust and her throat closed to it. She folded it up again and put it in the bag. She would need water if nothing else, she thought. She could melt some snow in her mouth. She slung her pack onto her back, pulled on her mittens and scarf, and emerged from the shack into weak afternoon light. She hesitated for a moment. The wind penetrated her clothes and she wondered if she should stay another night.

There was no trace of the black ribbon of melt that had led her from Defaid to this shack. In the other direction, though— toward the dead town of Gwenith—there was a new ribbon of melt. Alys hesitated a moment longer. *Stay, or walk*, she wondered. Then a gust of wind rose up behind her and shoved her toward the wet black path. Alys heard the flap of enormous wings and she looked up at the roof of the shack. There was nothing there, only a thick layer of snow. She looked up at the sky, half afraid and half hoping to see The Beast flying over-head. There were only clouds.

Alys pulled off a mitten and reached her hand into the snow. She put a small handful into her mouth. It burned cold down her throat. She took another handful. It's what Mother would have told her to do.

Then she once again allowed the wind to direct her. She

walked along the path of melt and into the fforest. It was so cold that where the damp path met the snow, a crystalline edge of ice formed. Ice coated the tree branches, the leaves. She might have thought it beautiful if she weren't so wracked by chills. The weak winter afternoon light grew even more filtered here. She couldn't possibly have much sunlight left in the day and had no idea how long it might take her to reach the town and some shelter.

So she did as she had done the day before, and thought of nothing but the path in front of her—the wet rocks, the frozen streams she stepped over, and catching herself when she slipped.

The fforest was silent, not even a bird call cracked its surface. There was only the in and out of Alys's breath and the friction of her steps. It was as if everything here were frozen solid. Or perhaps had fled. She wondered if all the animals had left when the people did.

It was odd to think that each step brought her closer to a home that she now barely remembered. But she didn't linger on those thoughts. There was no point. There was only walking and fighting the cold.

It began to snow. Thick, fat flakes sifted down through the trees, and the late afternoon was so quiet that Alys felt certain she could hear the flakes land with soft pats. The snow caught in her eyelashes and she breathed it into her mouth. Something about the white upon white upon white and the soft patting flakes made her want to sleep, to lie down and rest her head.

She began to struggle with herself, part of her willing to go forward, and some other part pulling her down. She reached out to the trees for support as she walked between them, using each as a lever to propel her on. Then slowly, gradually, she realized that she was no longer using the trees to pull herself up. The path had begun to descend.

She couldn't see more than a few feet in front of her. If she broke through the fforest edge, she wondered if she'd even know it. She wondered how she'd find a house in this. Then she stopped wondering, because the pain in her head was so great and the shiver in her bones was so powerful that she thought she might simply leave her body.

The sky was turning the gray of snow-filled night. The path grew steeper and Alys felt that she was falling downward and down. Then the air changed.

Alys couldn't see the fforest open up to fields, but she could feel it. Although the snow obscured all, she sensed that trees were no longer closing around her, that the world was now a wider place. She looked down. The black ribbon was gone. She looked behind her, and she could find no trace of it there either. She'd lost the way.

She stumbled forward, could have been walking off a cliff for all she could see or imagine. She spoke to herself, begging herself... *I can't... I can't any longer... I can't... don't make me...*

She sank to her knees. A mistake. It was so hard to pull herself up again. The next time she went down she'd surely never get up.

She walked on, thought she felt old road beneath her feet, under the snow. It was rutted but still too steady and flat to be field. If she could just keep to it, she might find some shelter.

But that plan was forgotten, because soon all was white in front of her, and all was white and cold inside of her. Her lungs were made of snow and ice. She was becoming snow and ice. Then it seemed to her that a tree was emerging from the white in front of her, dark against the snow.

The tree moved, and trees don't move. But it was a tree and it was coming toward her and toward her and then she sank into the snow and then the tree took her away.

TWENTY-SIX

Alys lay on a mattress on the floor, examining them through her eyelashes. Their voices had awakened her, but she remained still, delaying as long as possible the inevitable moment when they realized she was no longer sleeping.

Her nose twitched at the smell of gamey stew. The three travelers sat at a wooden table eating and talking about snow and weather and Alys.

"And there she is," Beti said. "I see your eyelashes flickering, no use pretending otherwise."

Cian glanced in her direction and then cast his eyes down at his bowl again. Alys became painfully aware that she was lying in bed in front of three fully clothed people in a shift that wasn't her own. She was covered with blankets, but still. She certainly hadn't put the shift on herself. She rose to sitting, pulling the topmost blanket with her, doing her best to cover herself and drawing the collar of the shift closer to her neck. Her hair was loose and unbraided, something else that had been done for her.

"Lass! You're looking better!" Pawl rose halfway out of his chair and surely would have pulled her into an embrace if Beti hadn't held his arm. He shook her off. "All right, all right, Beti, I'll leave her be. Rest, child. You'll give yourself a headache shooting out of bed like that."

It was true, her head did pound when she first sat up, but then the pain subsided and now she felt almost right.

Beti bent down in front of her and pressed a hand to Alys's forehead. "You'll live," she said. Then laughed.

Cian hadn't looked directly at her yet, and then he did. Alys felt a rush of heat to her skin—face and body—as if she held a fire within her. That boy had some power over her, and she did not know what to make of it. She felt such a combination of fear and fascination . . . and something else. Something that made her tingle.

Alys shivered. Noticing her quake, Beti said, "Here, let's get you properly dressed and fed." Alys's eyes widened in alarm and she gripped the blanket tighter. "Come now, don't worry about the men. They're just leaving." Beti looked toward them, raised her voice. "Aren't you? Go check your traps. Fetch some wood. Make yourselves useful."

"Ay woman, we'll do that. And you take care of our Alys." Pawl pushed himself up from the table, retrieved his hat and coat from a hook on the wall, and Cian did the same. Then they

228

opened the door to the outside and a fierce wind blew in. They shut the door quick behind them. It was night, Alys knew now. She hadn't been sure before, because the room's windows were covered with blankets, no doubt to keep out the draft.

Beti brought Alys her clothes. She'd let them sit by the fire so they were warm to the touch. Then she turned her back and began to busy herself at the hearth, giving Alys a view of her stout back and the opportunity to remove her borrowed shift and put on her own clothes without feeling watched. Alys wanted to braid her hair back but didn't know where her leather laces were. The fire blazed and the room was blissfully warm but still she shivered. Although she'd thought she was better, the effort of standing and dressing nearly sent her back to the floor.

"Here child, sit here." Beti pulled one of the heavy chairs away from the table. "I'll make you some tea. And there's stew."

"Just the tea, please," Alys said. "I don't think I can eat quite yet."

"Well, we'll have to work around that, because you need to eat. Maybe we'll just try some toast and cheese for now. You need some hot food in your belly."

Alys nodded, tried to look grateful. Her stomach turned at the thought of eating. She couldn't.

Beti sliced cheese onto bread, put it in a frying pan with a knob of butter, and set it over the fire.

"How long was I asleep?"

Beti poked the bread in the pan, shifted it to keep it from burning. "About a day."

"And we're in Gwenith, aren't we?"

"Ay. Aren't too many good houses left standing, but this is a sturdy one. We often stay here when the good folks of Defaid send us packing. It's a nice place to rest a bit in the bad weather."

The smell of hot bread and cheese should have made Alys's mouth water, but instead it made her feel ill. "When he comes back I must thank Pawl for saving me. That's the second time in my life he's done that."

"It's still only once, my love. It was Cian who found you in the snow. He saw you staggering in all that white, picked you right up and brought you here. You're lucky he's such a big strong boy, else we wouldn't be talking right now." Alys's cheeks flamed hot. Cian of the brown eyes had picked her up in his arms and carried her here. She wanted to fold in on herself from the embarrassment of it. And then that other thing again. That . . . tingle.

Beti set a mug of hot, milky tea and the plate of toasted bread and cheese in front of Alys. Then she crossed her arms over her rough apron and smiled.

The front door flew open with a bang, and icy wind blew into the room again. Pawl and Cian both had big bundles of wood and kindling strapped to their backs.

Beti rushed over to close the door behind them.

Pawl and Cian dropped their bundles near the hearth. Cian pulled off his gloves and set to building up the fire. Alys found herself transfixed by his hands as he worked. They weren't freckled farmer hands. Or callused carpenter hands. They were smooth and quick and nimble and a beautiful brown. . . . *Tingle.*

Beti sat down at the table, and once Pawl had shed his coat and boots he did the same. They both looked at Alys expectantly, as if waiting for something remarkable and entertaining to occur.

Alys felt herself blushing and didn't know where to set her eyes. It was too unsettling to look at Cian, and too burdensome to look at Beti and Pawl with their hopeful expressions. So she looked down at her plate. A slick of oil separated from the browned and melted cheese. Her stomach turned. Still, she forced herself to reach for it. She broke the hunk of bread in half with her hands, hoping that a smaller portion might not disgust her so. The bread was thick and gave off yeasty clouds of steam as she tore it. She hadn't eaten in how long? But it was as if the longer her stomach had gone without food, the less she wanted it.

Still, she felt sure that eating some of this bread and cheese would make Pawl and Beti happy, and she found herself wanting to do so. That's what a good girl would do. She picked up the smaller of the two pieces and brought it to her mouth, took a bit between her lips and teeth. Chewed.

But instead of tasting bread and cheese she tasted dust and ash.

Cian sat down at the table and smiled at her. Alys's stomach cramped forcefully. She thought she might cry. She pushed the plate away. "I'm sorry, Beti. You've been so kind. But I can't. I can't seem to taste anything."

"Oh tosh now child, no reason to get upset about it." Pawl patted her hand. "Drink your tea. That'll cure what ails you. And when you're ready, you'll eat." He rose to his feet and pulled a large jug from a shelf. Then he poured a clear liquid into two mugs and gave one to Beti, kept one for himself, and set the jug in the middle of the table. He didn't offer any to Cian or Alys. At once Cian looked less happy.

Beti took a long sip from her mug. She regarded Alys thoughtfully. "You haven't got a fever anymore. It broke in the night. And anyway, fever takes away your appetite but it doesn't take away your taste. How long haven't you been tasting anything?"

Alys thought back. There were the apples and cheese she had eaten when she was tied up in the cellar. That had tasted just fine. Then there was the bread in the small shack in the fforest where she'd spent the night. That had tasted like dust. And in between those two meager meals were the trial and the cage . . . and the wolf. Her mind traveled to that poor animal, and it was like an arrow shot, straight and true. This was her punishment for the unnatural thing she had done to that wolf. She had turned it into nothing, and now that nothing filled her mouth.

"It's been a few days," Alys said.

Beti shook her head. Took another long sip. Pawl poured himself more and topped off Beti's cup. "Well," Beti said, "you've had a shock, no doubt. What those sour-faced Defaiders did to you I can only imagine. We heard what happened when we went back the next day. I thought Pawl was going to do something awful to those Elders. It was all Cian and I could do to hold him back. So we got in our wagons and came here."

"I said to my Beti, 'I know where she's gone. Back to Gwenith. Back home.' And I was right, weren't I?"

"Ay," Beti laughed. "You were!"

"Good child," Pawl said, patting Alys's arm. "Another night

of resting up here, and we'll all be well fortified. Then on to Pysgod in the morning. We need more fish, eh, my love?" He reached over and tucked one of Beti's errant strands of hair behind her ear. "I do love to trade when it's good and cold like this. And this winter's dragging on something fierce. Should be spring by now. But that's good for us. The cold makes people desperate. You know, Alys, some Lakers like to trade in the spring and summer when the weather's warm and the roads are easy. But I say, better to enjoy the nice weather back in the Lakes and take sinful advantage of all the hungry villagers in the winter. Don't I always say that, Beti?"

"Ay, ya do," Beti chuckled.

Alys felt herself smiling while Beti and Pawl talked. She imagined going to the Lakes with them and how it might be. An impossibly happy life unspooled before her like thread.

And then the thread turned knotty and Alys remembered why she was here instead of Defaid. Because she was a soul eater. Because she was evil. And how long would it be before Beti and Pawl found out? How long before Cian saw her for the monster she was? And what if . . . what if she did something awful to one of them? What if Cerys and Ffordd and the wolf were only the beginning? What if she were turning, slowly but surely, into a creature like Angelica and Benedicta? What if that was why she couldn't eat? Because food wasn't what she hungered for anymore?

Pawl had continued talking. "I'll teach you everything I know about trading, Alys. You'll be a fine foxy dealer by the time I'm done with you." He gave her a broad wink.

"I can't go with you to Pysgod," Alys said.

Cian glanced up at her, wrinkled his brow, but said nothing.

"Whatever do you mean, child?" Beti said. "Course you will. Where else have you to go?"

Alys reddened. "It's not that I wouldn't like to go with you. I used to long to live in the Lakes with you. But . . ." Alys looked around her. "Perhaps I should stay here. Maybe this is where I belong?"

"Ooooh," said Beti. "No, child. No. This ghost town's no place for you."

"No ghosts here," Pawl said, gulping more of his drink. "Soul eaters saw to that. No soul, no ghost. When a soul eater gets ya, poof. Yer gone."

Cian gave Pawl a dark look.

"I'm not afraid of it here," Alys said. "It's my home, isn't it?"

"You're not staying here, child, and that's final." Pawl's voice was firm in a way she'd not heard it before. She wanted to yield to it, rest into it. But she couldn't let herself.

"Listen to Pawl, child. And in this cold?" Beti said. "You'd never be able to keep yourself warm and fed. No offense to you child, but even I couldn't. Not to mention, well, child. There's things out there." She glanced toward the door as if one of those things might be standing just on the other side. Little did Beti know, Alys thought to herself, that one of those things was sitting right across from her.

Alys couldn't let herself give in to the temptation to go with them. She wouldn't.

Then she felt Cian looking at her. "You should come with

us." That was all he said. Nothing more. Alys's heart squeezed and released. Squeezed and released again. A quake. *Tingle.*

"It's settled then," Pawl said. Nodded to all of them.

Relief washed over Alys like warm water. She had no decision to make. There was no struggle that would convince them to let her stay here. They wouldn't let her stay, and in truth she didn't want to. She would just have to hope for the best, as she'd always done. Hope that whatever monstrousness lurked within her, she could keep it at bay. And if she couldn't . . . well then she'd run away. But at least she would have tried. Would have known what a happy life felt like, if only for a while.

"Of course it's settled." Beti smiled and reached across the table to pat Alys's hand. "Never any doubt." Then she pulled her hand back and drank deep.

Pawl and Beti talked more of trading, of all the villages that Alys would see with them, all the places they'd take her. She felt her eyes grow heavy, and as Pawl and Beti's words seemed to slur together, Alys wondered if she were even fully awake—if she might be asleep already and only imagining this. But their voices grew louder and more insistent, and just when Alys's eyelids were starting to droop shut, Beti burst into a guffaw and Alys jerked awake in her chair.

Pawl took a long gulp from his cup, then he gestured with it to Beti. "Now, love, didn't I tell you we'd find our girl here? Didn't it happen just like I said? I knew they wouldn't burn up my girl. It would take more than that load of tight arses to do my girl in. I always say, it's a wonder those Defaiders can walk in a straight line with their arses sewn up so tight. Ya'd think they'd fall right over. It's a wonder they don't sneeze shit right through their noses, considering it's got no place else to go. Don't I always say that, Beti?"

"Ay," Beti laughed. "Ya do. Ya most certainly do."

Something odd was happening to Pawl. This wasn't the gentle man she knew. And Beti's voice was louder and faster and harder than it had been before. It hurt her ears. Alys glanced at Cian and his face had grown closed, his mouth a flat line.

"The lot of them act like they don't shit brown and through their arseholes the same as the rest of us. But we know different, don't we girl?" Pawl nudged Alys with his elbow. She withdrew her own.

Beti chuckled and coughed, drank some more. Pawl slapped the table to put the cap to his joke. Cian closed his eyes.

There was a change in the room, like a turn in weather, and Alys could feel it on her skin. Cian, who'd seemed so open-faced and pleasant when she first awakened, had turned to stone before her eyes. And Beti and Pawl had become freakish versions of themselves, laughing too long, asking questions and not waiting for the answers. She'd thought they'd be pressing her for details about what she'd done to be punished, but they seemed to have forgotten all about it, and about her. They drank up, poured more, talked louder and less intelligibly.

Alys now wished she hadn't given in to them so easily. Wished she'd insisted upon staying here by herself. Who were these people she'd thrown in with? Was this what she really wanted? She hardly knew anymore. She wondered if she'd made a mistake, or if she simply didn't know her own mind. She missed Mother and Father. Powerfully. Missed the quiet of their home in Defaid. Missed knowing what would happen every day of her life. It wasn't a happy life, but she could trust it. With Pawl and Beti the landscape felt shifty. Unreliable.

Cian reached for the cork and put it in the jug. "That's enough. I'll build up the fire for the night. Time for bed."

Pawl followed Cian's hands with his eyes, lowered his eyebrows and seemed about to argue, but shrugged instead. "Come along, Beti."

Beti glanced behind her at the hearth, squinted and seemed to have trouble focusing. "Well, but the dishes need scrubbing."

"I'll do it," Cian said.

Beti rose from the table, pushing upward with a great effort. "You're a good lad. Bless the day we found you." She hooked one foot on the leg of her chair and nearly went over, but Alys jumped to her feet and caught her in time. Beti breathed out heavily with an oof and a grunt, and Alys smelled something familiar on her breath. She tried to recall the scent and it came to her that it was much like what Father used to thin the whitewash for doors and fences. Her nose curled and she fought the urge to pull away. Beti threw an arm around Alys's shoulder, and Alys led her to the wider of the three mattresses on the floor. Beti dropped onto her butt and began to struggle with her shoes, so Alys set to unlacing them for her. Then, to Alys's horror, Beti undressed down to her shift, exposing great folds of flesh in the process. Alys averted her eyes while Beti crawled under the blankets and commenced to snoring as soon as she was horizontal. Pawl managed to take off his own boots. When he reached for his pants buckle, Alys fled across the room. Within seconds, his snores matched Beti's.

Alys looked back over at them. Cian was leaning across Pawl and had two arms under Beti. "What are you doing?"

"Turning Beti on her side. That way she won't choke to death if she throws up in the night." Cian grunted a bit under Beti's weight, then stood up.

"Is she sick?"

Cian looked at her, wrinkled his dark eyebrows. "Drunk. Never seen drunks before?"

"You mean, what they were drinking from that jug made them that way?"

"Yup." He sat down at the table and ate the bread and cheese that Alys had left on her plate, wiping the plate with his finger and licking off the crumbs. He seemed calm and open-faced again now that Beti and Pawl were off to bed.

"Why do they drink it if it makes them sick?"

"Because they like how it feels on the way there." Cian looked straight into her eyes when he spoke to her.

Alys found it was impossible for her to do the same and still speak words that made sense. She glanced just a bit away, into the fire. "How does it feel on the way there?"

"Wouldn't know," Cian said.

"They're awfully loud when they drink," Alys said.

Cian laughed. "That's one way of putting it." He stood up and made a neat stack of the dirty plates and mugs.

"I can wash those for you," Alys said.

"No need. I'll leave them until morning." He built up the fire and stretched.

Alys hovered uncertainly near her mattress. Cian's bed was perpendicular to hers. So close. She wanted to take off her shoes, stockings, and dress, but the very thought of doing so with him near her made her face burn. She was deeply conscious of his body and hers in the same room.

She snuck a glance at him and he was looking back at her, his face once again impossible to read. "I'm going out to fill a jug with snow so we'll have water for tea in the morning."

"Oh," Alys said. "Yes."

He moved past her and was gone in a rush of open door and wind. Alys quickly unlaced her boots and pulled off her stockings and dress, then slid under the covers in only her shift. She closed her eyes and pulled the covers up to her nose. She could be sleeping by the time he returned, she thought. Or at least she could pretend to be.

TWENTY-SEVEN

Cian came in and brought the cold air with him, and although Alys had every intention of staying motionless as death she couldn't help flinching and pulling the covers around her.

"Sorry about that," Cian said. "But think about me out there walking around in it."

Alys lowered the blanket to her chin, glanced up at him and then away. "I'm . . . thank you."

He laughed. "Eh, it wasn't so gallant. I had to lift a leg anyway."

Alys's scalp heated up, blood rising to the roots of her hair. She felt as stuttering and stupid as she ever had around Cerys or any of the children of Defaid who seemed always to be laughing at something. Alys couldn't remember the last time she'd laughed. Certainly not since she'd left Gwenith at the age of seven. What had there been to laugh about since?

Cian sat down on his mattress. "All right, Alys. I am about to remove my trousers. You may watch, or you may close your eyes. Either way I'm going to do it. I just figured I'd give you fair warning."

Alys closed her eyes. But the degree to which she felt a tickling urge to open them, to see what that boy looked like under his clothes, brought that tingling feeling again. She squeezed her eyes tighter. She heard the swish of blankets, and then a sigh.

Alys opened her eyes. The room was dark except for the orange glow of the fire. Cian lay with his feet toward the hearth, his head just an arm's length away from hers. She'd only slept this close to someone once before, and that one time it was Ren, and he was just a child. But Cian, he was no child.

Now Alys felt no desire to sleep at all. She was feeling better, and her old rhythms took over. The night was for watching. But there was nothing to watch here. Nothing except the fire, and the thick thatch of Cian's black hair where it rested on his pillow. She stared at the fire, let the quiet settle and wrap around her. She waited for Cian to fall asleep so that she could relax the muscles in her belly that seemed to hold tight whenever he was in the room.

The telltale slowing of his breath never arrived. She was certain he was awake. She looked over at him and saw the firelight reflected in his dark eyes, which were open and staring.

As if sensing her watching him, he turned over on his belly

and put his chin on his crossed arms, looked at her. "So what happened, Sister Alys. Why'd those Defaiders do you like that?"

"Don't call me that." Alys looked at the fire, refused to look at him now.

"Isn't that what young ladies of Defaid are called?" His voice was full of laughter, even though he wasn't laughing.

"I'm not a lady of Defaid." She was something awful, but she wouldn't tell Cian that. "You're keeping me awake."

"Liar. You're used to being awake at night."

Just then a loud snore rose up from Pawl, ending in a cry and a wail and a hum. Alys thought for sure that Beti would wake up, but she didn't. "How can Beti sleep through that?"

"Oh, that's the miracle of liquor, fair Alys. Once they're good and drunk, they feel no pain and they hear no cries in the night."

Alys wanted to look at him just then, but still she didn't. She kept staring at the fire and listening to his voice. "How did you come to be with Beti and Pawl?"

"They took me in when I came to the Lakes last summer."

"Where'd you come from?"

"The mountains. I lived there with my parents."

"Where are your parents now?" Alys was afraid she knew the answer already, and wondered if she shouldn't have asked the question.

Cian was quiet for a long moment. "Dead. Same as yours."

Now she did look him straight in the face. "Soul eaters?"

"My parents and I were out hunting deer. We camped in a clearing in the woods. We were sealed up tight in our tents, them in one, and me in another, all of us asleep. I dreamed two beautiful, wild-haired women were singing to me. They moved through the trees like they didn't need feet. When I woke up the next morning, I was shivering in my bed. My tent flap was open. I went straight to my parents' tent. Their flap was open, too. They were both lying there. Dead. Wide-eyed and open-mouthed."

"What did you do?"

"I ran. I ran and I ran and I ran. I don't remember how long. Maybe a day, two days. Then I arrived in the Lakes and met Pawl and Beti."

Alys turned over and mirrored him, rested her chin on her crossed arms. There was sadness in this boy, hidden away under his calm and mirthful face. Alys felt it in the room, settling around them, in them. He wouldn't want her to ask him about his sadness, though. He closed it up behind his laughing brown eyes for a reason. Instead she wondered about all the places he'd seen, places she'd allowed herself to hope that she might see as well. "What are the mountains like?"

"The air smells different up there." Cian closed his eyes and opened them again. "Like pine trees and cold water. In the Lakes, mostly it smells like people. I'm fond of some of those folks. But I get tired of smelling them."

"Why not leave?"

"And go where? I've been nearly everyplace on Byd now. Been to Pysgod, Tarren, even been back to the mountains. But still I stick close to Beti and Pawl. They're not always easy, but they care for me. I've grown accustomed to their ways. And no matter how sick I get of their drinking, I know why they do it. It's the same reason I've never lit out on my own."

Alys held her breath, knowing already what he would say, but asking him anyway. "What's the reason?"

"The singing and the whispering," he said. Then he rolled over on his back and stared up at the ceiling so that once again all Alys could see of him was his black hair. "They sing at night, Alys. The soul eaters. Just like the night they killed my parents. They sing and they whisper your name and it feels like fingers crawling inside of your head. It's all you can do not to scream."

Alys had the strongest desire to reach out her hand and touch his hair. "And that's why Beti and Pawl drink? So they won't hear it?"

"It's why they all drink," he said.

"Does it help, do you think?"

"Some say drunks sleep deeper. But I like to keep my wits about me."

"I don't think I like it when they drink," Alys said.

"No. I don't expect you would. I don't suppose there's much drinking in Defaid. But Lakers don't have Gates to keep us safe, Alys. We have nothing to wrap around us and shut out the singing. It's just us and the night." Then Cian turned on his side, faced the wall, and said no more.

TWENTY-EIGHT

They all rose before first light, and Beti and Pawl spoke little until they'd each downed several cups of blisteringly hot tea. Alys helped with breakfast, which was dried fish and mashed potatoes that Beti formed into cakes and fried in a lard-slicked iron pan over the fire. The food seemed a little less awful to Alys, and she managed to eat half of it before pushing her plate away.

They set off at sunrise, Beti and Pawl in one caravan led by two of their stout horses, and Cian and Alys in the other. Pawl said it would take them two days to reach Pysgod, and they'd need to stop before darkness fell each night to make camp.

The day was clear and cold and Alys wrapped a scarf around her neck and face, stopping just south of her eyes. Occasionally she pulled the scarf down to breathe the sharp air, then covered herself again. She kept scanning the trees, the horizon, the murky depths of the fforest on either side of the road. She knew it made no sense to look for the soul eaters now. They wouldn't be out in the daylight. Still she watched. But the only movement belonged to the occasional scamper of dun-colored deer. And the only sound came from black crows perched thick in the trees, cawing their hunger.

Before starting off this morning, Alys had worried that Cian might want to talk to her. Talking about nothing with boys had never been a particular talent of hers. But she found they fell into an easy silence. It seemed that he was content to sit next to her, hold the reins, and breathe the air. Hours passed this way.

They stopped once to rest and feed the horses, and to relieve themselves. Alys went so far into the woods to do so that Pawl called after her and said she might as well walk to Pysgod. Once back in the caravan and moving again, Alys broke the quiet between her and Cian. "What's Pysgod like?"

"Oh, it's a village like any other."

"Well I've not been to any other villages."

"Fair enough," he said. "It's bigger than Defaid. Busier because of the boats and the dock. Psygoders travel farther afield than Defaiders, but not because they're so brave. They've got their boats to take them up- and downriver, but they make sure they get home before dark, just the same as any tail-between-his-legs Defaider does. The Psygoders built their Gate right up to the river, so it's open on one side to the water. I guess they figure soul eaters don't paddle boats."

He laughed, quieted, then looked at her for a long beat. "It doesn't hurt, you know," he said.

Alys flushed warm, familiar now with the look on his face when he teased her. "What doesn't?"

"Smiling. Laughing. I don't think I've once seen your teeth. Have you got any? It's nothing to be ashamed of if you don't. Some of the nicest Lakers I know haven't got any teeth."

"I have them," she said. "Teeth."

"Won't believe it until I see it."

Mother had made Alys smile sometimes. Mother could be very funny in her way. Alys shut that thought tight, put it away. "Anyway," she said, "I never thought there was much to smile or laugh about." She'd grown to be like Mother that way, she supposed.

Cian kept his eyes straight ahead on the road. "Well, fair Alys, you are just exactly missing the point."

Cian built a blazing fire when they made camp, and Beti piled blankets onto a few logs and low rocks so they'd each have a place to sit.

"Lucky it ain't snowing," Pawl said. Then a few minutes later he said it again. Alys was learning there wasn't anything Pawl would say once that he wouldn't say twice. Or three times.

They ate bread and beans with mutton for dinner. Beti and Pawl also drank. And drank.

"Alys dear," Pawl said, "you have yet to tell us what you did to scare them Defaiders."

Three sets of eyes looked at her now, and once again Alys

had no comfortable place to rest her own eyes. She focused on the fire that blazed at their center.

There were too many awful answers to give, so Alys chose the one that would frighten them least, but was nonetheless true. "I saw something. Something I shouldn't have."

"Oh, ain't it always the way," Beti said. "Girl sees something she shouldn't and they call her a witch." She tutted and shook her head, drank.

"And who'd you see doing what they shouldn't have been doing?" Pawl squinted at her while refilling his and Beti's cups.

"The High Elder's son and a girl."

"Ooooooh," Pawl said. "And I think we all know what they were getting up to."

"Well, being a witness to something like that'll get you burned," Beti said. "Good and crisp."

All the while they talked, Beti and Pawl drank cup after cup. Cian tried to put away the bottle, but each time he brought the cork close, Pawl waved him off. At first Pawl was playful, but then his manner changed. Like the night before, even the air felt changed to Alys. Beti and Pawl's faces looked different, and their eyes grew glazed and unseeing.

"Enough," Cian said. "It's time for bed." He pushed the cork into the jug and picked it up.

With speed that Alys wouldn't have thought him capable of, Pawl jumped to his feet, yanked the jug from Cian's hands, and shoved him backward so hard that Cian tumbled over the rock he'd been sitting on.

Pawl's face was red and angry and unrecognizable. He seemed

to have grown stockier and broader-shouldered. Cian stood, but drew no closer to Pawl. Pawl swayed, struggled to focus. "You're so high and mighty, aren't you, boy? Think you're better than me because you don't need a drink to drown out the singing. Well just you wait. Wait till you've been listening to it for a few more years. Wait till you find a few more orphaned children weeping next to their dead mothers and fathers. You won't be so high and mighty then. You'll pick up a bottle then, boy. And I'll be there to pour for you."

The fire had burned low and the sky had darkened to black and the flames flickered on the two men. An angry light snuffed out of Pawl and he shrank into himself and sank down next to Beti, opened the jug and drank straight from the bottle. Beti's eyes drooped shut. She hadn't moved or raised an eyebrow while the men argued. Pawl nudged her with his elbow and she grunted, opened her eyes and then closed them again.

Cian's shoulders dropped, and he looked back at Alys. "The two of them can sleep together tonight. Let them piss on themselves." Cian went to Beti and lifted her up by the shoulders. Pawl made to protest, but it was halfhearted and he soon lost himself in his jug again. Alys helped Cian guide Beti to the caravan, and they both nudged her up from behind until she was crawling on all fours. "Beti," Cian said, "get under the blankets so you don't freeze."

She waved her arm at him, hello or thank you or go away, it was hard to tell what she meant. Alys climbed in after her, curled her nose when Beti breathed out. She managed to roll Beti up in a warm hide, then used her knee as a wedge to turn Beti sideways so she didn't choke.

When Alys climbed out again, Cian smiled at her. "You're getting good at nursing drunks."

Alys went to Pawl, who sat staring into the dying embers of the fire. She shuddered, but he didn't seem to notice the cold. "Pawl." She touched him lightly on the shoulder, then quickly pulled her hand back. He looked up at her with runny eyes. "It's time for bed. Beti's waiting for you."

"Ay," Pawl said. "Good girl."

Alys didn't know if he'd meant her or Beti, but either way he held his jug under his arm and rose to his feet. She moved to help him but he lurched away from her and staggered toward the caravan where Beti lay.

Cian was busy dousing the fire, so Alys went straight to the empty caravan and climbed in, unlaced her boots, took off her coat, and crawled under the blankets and pelts. She kept her dress and stockings on.

Moments passed and she heard the crunch of Cian's feet. He sat on the end of the caravan to remove his boots and his coat, then he climbed under as well.

Alys had turned on her side so she faced one wall of the caravan. She pushed herself as far away from where Cian lay as she could without pressing her face into Pawl and Beti's pots and saddles and bags of potatoes. Still, she felt such a strong awareness of him next to her that her heart beat into her chin.

She felt a tap on her shoulder. "Yes," she said.

"Might I have a word?"

She buried a smile in her hand and when she was certain it

was gone she turned over to face Cian, who was only a shape next to her, blacker than the blackness around him.

"You see, fair Alys, we are about to sleep side by side in this caravan, and I am a strong believer in talking to a girl before I bed down next to her. Anyway. You don't sleep much, and I don't sleep much, so we may as well talk."

Alys was grateful that he couldn't see her face. "All right. Tell me about the Lakes."

"Well, the Lakes are flatter than here. Flat as anything can be, really. But you can look up and see the mountains where I come from off in the distance. There are five lakes in all, and streams between them. And there are grassy marshes, too. Shallow enough for walking if you don't mind being ankle deep in slime. Deep enough in some places to canoe, and deep enough in many to drown if you don't know where you're stepping and find your feet sinking into the muck. The Lakes are wet, fair Alys. Very, very wet. Sometimes you think you'll never be dry."

"So you don't like it there?"

"Oh you misunderstand me. I love it there. I'm a water boy through and through. Beti says she thinks I squirmed out of my mother a fish and only after that I grew into a boy." He laughed to himself, and Alys imagined what his face looked like when he laughed.

"Do you and Beti and Pawl live in the town?"

"There isn't really a town the way you'd think of it. When the water is high we plant our tents and caravans on the highest ground we can find. And when it's low we pull in closer so we're nearer to the water and the fish and the game."

"No houses?"

"We're travelers, Alys. We move around. And you can't move a house. Anyway a tent can be nice. Sort of like this."

Alys thought to herself, *Yes, this is nice. I quite like this.* "Have you been to the sea?" She thought of Ren's wish for a home in the mountains overlooking the blue that sourrounded Byd. Then she thought of saying good-bye to Enid, of how she might not see any of the children of Gwenith ever again. For one moment, a little flame of hope flared up inside of her, hope that maybe Enid and Madog and the children would leave Defaid, would come find her. But then Alys knew—they never would. Not that she could blame them. She probably never would have either, not until she'd been forced.

"Ay, I've seen it. Not to get close to, but I've seen it. It's something beautiful. I'll go there someday. There's more of Byd to see, and I want to see all of it."

More of Byd. And more beyond that. It was hard to imagine. But Alys found herself desiring to do the same. Then she imagined seeing all of Byd with Cian. This thought came to her with the sudden, shocking heat of sinking into a just-poured bath. Maybe she didn't have to be alone. It was an unsettling thing, to powerfully wish for something that hadn't even occurred to her moments before. This was something she hadn't known was possible for her.

They fell silent again, and Alys found her breath matching Cian's, in and out, and she let her eyelids drop closed. In and out, in and out . . . his breath and her breath, and warm puffs of air between them.

Alys's eyes shot open. She'd been asleep, but didn't know for how long. She knew from his breathing that Cian was asleep next to her.

She could feel how awake she was, knew this would mean long hours of lying here and no more sleep. She became painfully aware of her full bladder. She'd been too embarrassed at bedtime to excuse herself behind a tree, and now the discomfort was beyond ignoring. She'd never make it to morning. She felt around in the dark for her coat and boots and struggled into them, then slid out of the caravan.

The moon was full, reflecting off the snow so the ground was bright enough to make her squint. She thought about squatting right there, but then thought about Cian in the caravan just a few feet away. She looked into the woods. *Well,* she thought, *just a bit of the way in for some cover.*

Ten paces in, her legs sinking into snow, she decided she'd gone far enough. She put a sizable tree between her and the caravans, and she pulled up her skirts.

When she stood again, she saw movement in the trees ahead of her.

Deer, she told herself. That's all there were in these woods. Deer and crows.

Alyssssss

Her name, sung to her through the trees.

Alyssssss

Come heeeeeere

Then the movement materialized into something long ago and familiar.

A boy. A boy she knew.

He ran fast between the trees, calling her name, singing her name. He had white-blond hair that shone in the moonlight. Quick as a rabbit he skittered between the trees.

He poked his head from behind a tree, held up one thin index finger and crooked it toward him.

Come

Alys would know him anywhere. Delwyn, the boy she'd grown up with, who'd saved her from falling off the wall. The boy his twin brothers had called Rabbit. The boy who ran away after his brothers had been killed by the soul eaters.

But Delwyn should have been dead, or he should have been fifteen. There was no in between. And this boy was still a child. But he was also Delwyn. And he was smiling at her now, and crooking his little index finger at her and bidding her come.

Alys stood rooted in the snow.

Then the white-haired boy who was Delwyn, but couldn't be, but was, came toward her. And she saw why he was so fast, because this boy barely touched the ground when he walked.

He floated.

And now he was closer.

Alys shook her head, clapped her hands to her ears, scrambled backward, ran and tripped her way to the caravan.

She climbed in and buried herself under the blankets, boots and all.

And she listened on, although she didn't want to. She didn't think she ever wanted to hear anything again. She wanted the world to go silent for her, forever, so she'd never ever have to hear that singing. It pierced the darkness, tickled her ears, scratched at her temples, crawled under her skin.

Alyssssssss

She didn't breathe.

Come heeeeeeeere

She didn't move.

I missss you Alyssssssssss

Alys reached into the darkness in front of her, blindly, and she felt skin. Warm skin. Warmer than she thought anything could be. Her fingers on Cian's throat, her palm at the base of his throat where it met his chest. She felt his heartbeat. Then his hand on her hand.

"Is one of them singing to you, Alys?"

"Yes," she said. Barely a whisper. She wanted to tell Cian that it was Delwyn, her friend. That an orphan child of Gwenith was now a creature that ate souls. She wanted to say that she knew too well how such a thing could happen. How a heart could turn bitter and hateful. But the words turned to ash in her mouth.

Cian placed his other hand on the side of Alys's head, over her ear. "Don't listen," he said. "Pretend it's the wind."

So she did. She pretended it was the wind, and she kept her hand where it was, on the base of Cian's throat. And she thought again that never in her life had she felt such warmth.

And then he kissed her, sudden and warm and soft, yet not. She tasted sweetness but also sadness, and she wasn't sure if it was hers or his. And then he kissed her again.

TWENTY-NINE

No one spoke much the next morning. Pawl looked sheepish, Beti confused. Alys felt embarrassed and unsettled, and she wasn't at all sure what to make of Cian. For his part, he busied himself with making tea. She tried not to think about the taste and feel of his lips on hers. She failed.

Once on the road, Alys sensed an odd stillness in the woods around them. There were no birds. Nothing scurrying. Only the friction of their wagon wheels. The snuffles and clops of their horses. The sounds of melt. The weather was warming fast, this long winter releasing its hold over the land crackle by drip. The tree trunks were wet and black, and snow dropped from branches in soft plops.

Perhaps two hours along the road to Pysgod, as the sun was arching toward late morning, the silence was broken by a new sound—muffled but rhythmic and urgent. Horse hooves. A single horse, ridden fast, coming from behind them. And the only source of a rider on the road behind them could be Defaid.

Ahead of Cian and Alys, Pawl turned to look behind him and nodded to Cian. Both pulled up on their reins, slowing the wagons to a stop. Pawl hopped down and trotted back to them. "Alys m'love, get inside the caravan and hide yourself."

Alys did as she was told, but kept an ear pressed close to the front of the wagon where Cian and Pawl waited for the rider. Minutes passed, or seconds that felt like minutes, Alys's heart beating hard and sharp in her chest.

"Hey oh," Pawl called out.

"Ay," came the rider's voice. Panting, his horse slowing to a halt. "Ay, brother, can't stop. Can't. Have to keep going."

"Well now," said Pawl. "We won't keep you. But where you coming from in such a tear? And where you going to?"

"From Defaid. What's left of it. Going to Pysgod."

What's left of it . . .

"What's happened?" Cian's voice.

"The Gate's been burned down." His voice was familiar to Alys. It was one of the High Elder's sons—Rhys's older brother, the one who'd ridden out with the blacksmith. Alec.

"It can't be true." Beti. She must have climbed down from the wagon, too curious to stay where she was.

"Ay, 'tis. Middle of the night. Fire tore through it like it was a pile of leaves. And then the soul eaters came."

"Soul eaters," Pawl said. "Did you see 'em?"

"Heard 'em, more like," Alec said. "Singing all weird like,

whispery and coaxing. I seen men and women just walk off into the fforest, gone before we could stop them or hold them back. And them Gwenither kids that should have been guarding the Gate, they just up and left us. Couldn't be bothered to stay and help, not even after all we done for them."

Pawl made listening noises while Alec spoke. Then he said, "Wandered off, you say? All of them?"

"Ay. And while the rest of us were busy trying to put out the flames, keep it from spreading to the village. See now, I must go. I have to make it to Pysgod, ask them to send wagons for the folks who can't ride, so we can take shelter behind their Gate."

"Well wait just a minute. You'll faint if you don't drink something." Beti, urging tea on him no doubt.

"The fire," Cian said. "How'd it start?"

"A witch named Alys did it. She's one of them Gwenith kids. Only turns out she was a soul eater, just that none of us knew it until she went after one of the girls in the village. So we locked her up and she was supposed to have been burned to death but she got away before we could do it."

"And then she came back and burned down the Gate, did she? Well that's a story, isn't it." Cian. Voice flat, tone inscrutable.

"Did the witch have any kin?" Beti.

"Just the man and woman that raised her, none other than them. The woman is dead. The witch poisoned her. And the man's the one who set the witch free. We caught him carting his wife's body outside the town. High Elder thinks he had some unholy purpose in mind."

Alys sank her teeth into the flesh of her thumb, forced herself to remain quiet.

Alec paused for a moment as if waiting for the next question. When Beti, Pawl, and Cian remained silent he filled in the answer himself. "We stoned him," he said. "That was before the fire."

Oh no. Oh no oh no oh no oh no oh no.

"So the witch burned down the town because you killed her father." Cian.

"Witches are vengeful creatures," Alec said.

"No doubt," Pawl said. "Well, we mustn't keep you longer. Thank you kindly for the news."

When Alys heard the last fading of Alec's horse's hooves, she emerged from the caravan and sat in the wagon next to Cian. They all looked at her. She felt their eyes rather than saw them. She kept her own eyes focused on her knees.

"It's terrible what they done to your father," Beti said.

"Ay and they call us savages," Pawl said.

Cian reached for her hand, held it. She squeezed his so hard it should have caused him pain, but still he held on.

"He's dead because of me," Alys said.

"Nonsense," Pawl said.

"He wouldn't be dead if it weren't for me. They killed him for what I did. And for freeing me."

Beti patted Alys's knee and made soft clucking noises. "There, child. Nothing of the sort."

"I should've made him come with me. Or I should've helped him bury Mother. I shouldn't have left him."

"Child," Pawl said, "I didn't know your father well, but I

know you weren't going to make him do anything he didn't want to do. And he wanted to bury his wife and to keep you safe. And you are safe. And we aim to keep you that way."

"But what about the other Gwenith children? What's to become of them now? I should go back and find them. If they're wandering in the fforest . . ." Alys trailed off, thinking about Delwyn floating, calling to her. The world swam around Alys, and she forced it to stop and be still. Where would Enid and Madog go? "Pysgod," Alys said aloud. "That's where they're headed. That's where Enid told me to go when I left Defaid. We can still go to Pysgod and wait for them there."

"Well it pains me to say it," Pawl said, scratching his chin, shaking his head, "but there's no safety for you in Pysgod now. Matters not that we know you didn't burn down the Gate, Alys. That rider thinks you done it. He knows you by sight, I'm guessing?"

"Ay," Alys said. "He does."

"There's something else," Cian said. "If the Defaiders think the Gwenith children abandoned them, it won't be safe for them in Pysgod either. They'll accuse the whole lot of you of being witches."

"Well there's nothing for it then," Beti said. "On to Tarren then?"

"No, I think not," Pawl said. "It's only a matter of time before word reaches them, and we can't know how soon. One fast rider is all it would take. Or if no riders are brave enough to make the journey, then some traveler could carry the news, not knowing any different. No, we must take Alys back to the

Lakes with us. It's the only place she'll be safe. Them Defaiders won't be making their way there. Be hard pressed to know which scares a Defaider more, a soul eater or a Laker." He chuckled. Beti scowled back at him.

Alys had let them talk, let all this happen around her, and she had to make it stop. "No, no, I can't go with you. I have to find Enid and Madog and the others. I must. Please take me to Pysgod."

Pawl shook his head, clucked.

Beti said, "Oh dear no, child. It's not safe. They'd burn you before you could lay an eye on Enid and Madog."

"I'm begging you," Alys said. "Leave me at their Gate and I'll look for them myself. Anyway, you can't stop me. I'll get out here and walk."

"Alys," Cian said, his voice even, his tone no different than if he were pointing out a bird in a tree. "You won't do the others any favors by looking for them yourself. The Pysgoders will know who you are and if you ask after your friends you'll only cast more suspicion on them. They'll end up stoning the lot of you."

Like Father. Oh no. Oh no oh no oh no oh no.

Everywhere she went, death followed. It clung to her, refusing to let her go, to let her take a clean, full breath of air. Alys's shoulders sank, her heart turned to dust in her chest. She could taste it in her mouth, dry and bitter.

"Ah, child, you're breaking my heart just looking at you," Beti said. "Pawl, you and I will go to Pysgod. We'll ask after the other Gwenith children. See what more we can find out. Cian and Alys can take the caravan a ways past the village and wait for us there till nightfall. Till we've seen what's what."

"I should go instead of you, Beti," Cian said.

Pawl shook his head. "Yer daft, boy. Brown as you are, think you'll be able to just wend your way around that village? They're already scared out of their wits no doubt. Now don't get me wrong, boy, I can see how you're looking at me. It's not them I'm thinking of, it's you. Something could happen to you. They could decide you've got the mark of The Beast on you because you're not white as snow. No, Beti's right. She and I will go, and you and Alys wait for us. Just keep on riding when we get to Pysgod. Beti and I will turn toward town and you keep on. Go a good two miles more, I'd say. To the old burned-out tree. You know the one, son. Struck by lightning last year. That's where we'll meet you."

"Ay," Cian said. He picked up the reins.

Pawl started to turn away, then came back and grasped Cian by the arm. "If we're not back by nightfall, you go on to the Lakes without us, you hear me? Don't come looking for us. Just go." He nodded once, twice. Then withdrew his hand and walked to his wagon.

Alys wanted to call after him. Wanted to say something that would be right. But by the time she thought of what to say, he was already climbing in next to Beti, picking up his reins, clucking the horses forward. She looked at Cian. "He's a good man," she said.

"Ay," Cian said. "He is."

Alys and Cian sat several feet apart at first. Then as the sun faded and the afternoon chilled, they grew nearer to each other.

Cian built a fire, and they both stared into its flames. Alys could feel Cian's warmth through her clothes, even though they weren't touching. Then he reached for her hand and held it. She moved still closer to him and put her head on his shoulder. She wondered at this, it was so strange a thing to be doing. Yet it also seemed like something she should always have been doing. She felt that no matter where she was, even with her eyes closed shut, she'd know if he was nearby. She would know him in her skin and her bones, and this baffled her. There was no sense in it. There was no making sense of it. She wondered how she could have such a sudden need for this boy.

Alys wanted to be happy in this moment, but she found herself instead regretting their meeting. This need for him, this place in her heart that he was filling, brought with it a kind of pain, a feeling of loss even before she had lost anything. It was a sort of terror, a dread. She breathed deeply, tried to focus on the salt smell of his skin, the clean animal scent of his hair.

The sun was setting when she heard the sound of wheels on snow. She looked up at Cian and felt such hope that she thought she might cry out. Instead she got to her feet and hid herself in the caravan.

She heard a knock on the side of the wagon. "It's them. You can come out," Cian said.

The wagon pulled up and Pawl hopped down first, then went around and helped Beti down. Their faces were empty of smiles. Like faces that had never smiled. Beti put her arms around Alys, pulled her into a rough, too-hard hug. Beti's ragged strands of hair scratched Alys's face and Alys felt uncomfortably conscious of the outlines of Beti's body, all that flesh, under all those layers of wool. But she didn't pull away, not as much as she wanted to.

"Oh, child," Beti said. "Your friends aren't there."

No, of course they weren't there. They wouldn't be. Not yet. But they might make it to Pysgod by tomorrow, by following the river the way Enid had told Alys to do. And yet Beti and Pawl looked hopeless. Alys looked back and forth between them, waiting for them to articulate some plan by which they'd find the Gwenith children so they could all be together again.

"We made it through the Gate," Pawl said. "Just barely." He sat down, held his hands in front of the fire. His cheeks seemed to have fallen an inch since morning, like some measure of life had been extracted from him over the course of the day.

"I thought them Pysgoders was a better sort than them Defaiders, but no such thing," Beti said, sitting down next to him. "They're not lifting a finger to help. Not a finger. Not even the children. The poor children." She looked up at Cian. "Can you imagine?"

"Ay," Cian said. "I can. They're afraid."

"I don't care if they're scared shitless," Pawl said. "To leave them children out there with no protection. Ay, it'll be Pysgod's Gate that burns next and who will take them in then? Tarren? Like as not. And to think them villagers are always looking down on us Lakers. The things they say about us." He looked at Alys and she couldn't help reddening. "Ay, we know what they say. But we'd never be so cold, so heartless, so evil as them. And evil it is. For all their talk of The Beast, they're the beastly ones." And then he stopped, as if all out of words for his disgust.

Cian handed him tea. "Are they looking for Alys?"

"They're on guard for her. And no girl her age who doesn't live there is going to enter those Gates. No girl her age should get anywhere near. And in the meantime they're doing what all villagers do. They're kicking out the travelers and closing themselves up tight. They threw us out and the rider from Defaid, too. Can you imagine that? Poor sod. Lass, I'm sorry to say, but if . . ." He paused, caught himself. "*When* Madog and Enid and the others reach Pysgod there will be nothing for them there. They'll have to move on. Meantime, we mustn't keep you here. They'll kill you if they should lay eyes on you, lass. I'm sure of it."

They were quiet then, all four of them, and for once Alys felt no eyes on her. She wanted to argue for staying, for looking, but the will to fight had gone out of her.

Cian rested his hand on her shoulder. "Alys, it would make sense for Enid and Madog and the other Gwenith children to go to the Lakes. When they can't stay in Pysgod, Madog and Enid will think of Pawl. They'll know to find him, that they'll be welcome there."

Pawl brightened a bit. "Ay, lass. Ay. The boy's right. And it's warming. There's more light all the time. They'll turn up. Meanwhile they've got each other."

They did, didn't they? Alys tried to reassure herself with that. They had each other. They weren't alone. Then she looked into the fforest. She thought of Angelica and Benedicta. Of little Delwyn singing to her, scratching at the edges of her mind, of her soul. Digging in with his thin fingers.

None of them was alone.

Cian's hand had traveled to her hair, she felt the weight of it. Wanted to be comforted by it.

Pawl kept nodding even though nothing more had been said. "We'll go home to the Lakes. We won't have to find your dear ones. They'll find us. And then all will be right as rain."

Pawl, Alys observed, was a terrible liar.

. . . and they would never, never be hungry.

The flames rose but the soul eaters felt no heat. They watched as it sucked and gasped and swallowed. They felt nothing.

The people fled and the soul eaters embraced them. The soul eaters tasted fear, they drank it up, but it did not satisfy. It burned.

It was then Angelica realized. The burning was in them. *We are the fire,* she said to her sister and the boy. And they would burn and they would burn and they would burn. Burn until there was nothing left to burn.

Burn it all to ash.

PART

5

The
Beast
is
an
animal

THIRTY

Alys had been in the Lakes exactly five days the first time she woke up in a tree.

Her eyes opened to the night. Air moved on her skin. She felt bark under her toes and through the linen of her nightshift. She was sitting. Perched. Like a bird.

There wasn't a moment between sleep and waking that she thought she might be dreaming. Nor was there a moment she thought she might fall. She sensed the ground was far below her, but her feet were sure under her, her crouch steady. She thought if she just opened her arms and tilted forward she might float gently downward.

She didn't though. She clung to the branch. With each passing second she felt more herself, more aware that this was terribly wrong. Girls didn't wake up in trees. Creatures did.

She feared that's what she was becoming—a creature.

It was then that Alys split in two. There was an outside part of her that went on, spoke to people. Ate food—or tried to—and went to sleep under covers, inside a tent. But the inside part of her—the part that was truly her—wasn't present among these people. The inside part of her was in the trees, in the fforest, sniffing the air.

Alys had been hopeful when she first arrived in the Lakes. Despite everything terrible that had happened, she thought her life might be taking a turn. She'd lost Mother and Father, and she ached for them. But Defaid hadn't been her home. She'd never belonged there, had never wanted to belong. From the moment she'd decided to go to the Lakes with Pawl and Beti and Cian, she'd felt such a strong desire to be at rest there. To join them and feel joined to them. That desire was more powerful than any she'd allowed herself to feel before. As a child of Gwenith, a watcher, she'd learned not to look forward. There was no future for her in Defaid—at least not one any better than the present. Those days were behind her now, but from the moment she first awakened in a tree, Alys couldn't deny the sick certainty in her heart that there was no peace for her here, either. She carried darkness within her. She could never get away from it, because she could never get away from herself.

The Lakers had been welcoming at first, and Alys enjoyed how free in their ways they were. Alys expected they'd be different from the villagers, but she couldn't have imagined how different they were—even from each other. Folks from the villages all looked the same. They had the same starched collars, same starched skin, same starched faces. The Lakers were alike only in that they were all a muddle. They dressed in a muddle of shapes and colors, they lived in a muddle of tents and lean-tos, they worked a muddle of occupations that might change from day to day, and at a muddle of hours that might shift on a whim. If they didn't feel like fishing, then they didn't. And they might be up with the sun to weave, or salt, or sew, but if they weren't in the mood to do those things, then they didn't. There was no starch in the Lakes. No collars. There were women with short hair, and men with hair down to their waists. Women and men with beads hanging from their ears, and signs, words, and pictures inked into their skin. There were people who weren't man or woman. They were both, either, neither. Alys was more curious than alarmed by all the variety. She'd even grown accustomed to letting her own hair hang loose, and to dressing as she wished instead of as she ought.

Before, she would have felt uncomfortably exposed without her dress fastened tight up to her throat. But the fresh warmth of spring's arrival, the damp of the Lakes, the hard work of netting fish and cooking over open fires, made her dress hang heavy and confining on her limbs. Alys found herself looking with envy at the Laker women who wore loose shirts like men did, even trousers. On her third day in the Lakes, Beti handed Alys a folded stack of clothing and said, "Here, child, I'm hot just looking at you." Alys flushed crimson and thanked her, and waited until she was alone to examine everything. There were two linen shirts, one a washed indigo blue and one white, also two pairs of thick linen trousers, loose around the thighs and more fitted at the calves. Coiled in the middle of the stack was a brown leather belt for holding up the trousers. That evening while the sky was still light, Alys stole away to her sleeping tent and tried everything on. The shirt was open at her neck, and the evening air kissed her collarbones. The trousers were magical. She bent, she sat, she stood, she stretched. Nothing pulled or draped over her. Nothing stopped her from taking long strides. She felt unencumbered. Nothing but her own muscle and bone limited her movements. The next morning she walked out of her tent dressed like a Laker. Hair loose down her back, throat bare to the sun and breeze, legs moving freely. Cian smiled at her and looped a finger through her belt. "What's this now?" he said. Pawl nearly spit his tea when he saw her. "Our Gwenith lass is a Laker!" he cried out. Beti laughed. Beti always laughed.

Alys had felt happy for a precious, short while—and as free as her legs felt in trousers. She fell into the rhythm of the Lakes so easily it shocked her, like finally resting her head on a pillow after having slept too long on a hard floor. The rightness and softness of the Lakes and the Lakers enveloped her. She admired their easy ways, even if she doubted she could ever feel so loose and open herself. She found herself imagining what a future here might look like. A future with Cian. She thought of sharing all this happiness with Enid and Madog once they arrived. She'd teach Ren to canoe, the way Cian had taught her.

When she woke up in a tree the first time, that all changed. Like wheels in ruts, she sank into old, familiar feelings. Fear. Doubt. Doom. And just as she always had in Defaid, she kept her thoughts to herself.

Then the whispering started.

The Lakers might have dressed differently from the villagers, but they weren't so fearless as they appeared. It had come as a shock to them when Pawl and Beti announced what had happened to Defaid, and that Pysgod had shut its Gates to travelers—with Tarren no doubt soon to follow. The spring thaw meant no one in the Lakes would starve for lack of trading. There was plenty of fish and game, and there would soon be berries, mushrooms, and greens. But the things that Lakers looked to the villagers for—grains and saddles and smoked meats, lard, butter, potatoes and apples—would dwindle. Alys's sharp ears picked up the hushed voices around evening fires. More than once she'd heard her name spoken just a bit too loudly, before the person talking realized that Alys was within earshot. More than once she'd heard it remarked that all their troubles had coincided with the village girl's arrival.

Alys pretended not to hear them, and Pawl, Beti, and Cian pretended the same way. Pawl told stories, Beti guffawed. Sometimes Pawl and Beti drank too much, sometimes they didn't. Cian kept smiling. None of them acknowledged the whispering. Instead they tried to distract themselves as well as her. When silence fell around their campfire, Beti would pipe up with plans for the Gwenith children's arrival. Occasionally this cheered Alys, but just as often it caused her to worry more about what might have befallen them on the way. When Alys counted aloud the days that had passed since the fire, Pawl assured her the children's slowness was as it should be. "They'll be following the river to find their way here. It's awful bendy. And they've got the babies in tow. Any day now, they'll turn up. Patience, lass." She wanted to believe him.

The first time she woke up in a tree, she'd hoped it wouldn't happen again. Maybe a dream had led her up there, she thought. But she didn't believe it. And the very next night—and every night after that—she woke up the same way. She went to sleep each night afraid of what was surely to come. She piled clothes, pots, sacks of potatoes, and blankets in front of her tent flap, thinking the obstacles might slow her down, cause her to wake up and stop herself. She lay in bed, calming herself, touching the bit of linen embroidered with the names of the children of Gwenith—as if they might keep her settled, keep her down. But each night it was the same. She awakened perched on a branch, legs crouched bird-like underneath her, as balanced and aware of the space around her as if she were an owl.

This made her think of the soul eaters, of course. Those sisters, with their owl eyes, their love of the dark. Their comfort in it. She wondered if this was how soul eaters slept—perched high off the ground, watchful even while resting. Alys had thought her days of night watching were over. Alys had been a fool.

The evening of her tenth day in the Lakes, Alys felt that she would surely crawl out of her skin if she didn't get away from all these people. She remembered what Cian had said about the Lakes—so many people and their smells. Her nose was constantly full of their scents, her ears full of their voices. Cian knew how to be quiet, and fishing with him or helping him mend his nets were the few moments of calm she had. But the foulness within her was such a terrible secret that she felt as if she were just acting like a girl. It was a constant effort to appear right.

So instead of trying to appear so, she left camp and walked into the fforest, allowing herself simply to be what she was. The fforest here was even thicker than what grew up between Gwenith and Defaid. Thicker and wetter. The trees themselves seemed more alive, as if they might move around on their roots when no one was looking. Tangles of vines and moss grew from them like hair.

When she had gone so deep into the fforest that she wasn't at all sure she could find her way out again, Alys found a wide tree and she began to climb it. There was nothing about climbing that caused her to feel unsure of herself. No moment when she felt she might put a foot or a hand wrong. She climbed and she climbed, past the first set of outstretched branches, and then past the next and the next. Once she was high above the ground, enveloped by leaves and bark, she perched. She closed her eyes. She listened. She breathed in.

At first she was most aware of sound—of water dripping from one leaf and patting onto another. Of the tick of beetles and the slithering of centipedes and lizards.

Then it was only scent. Everything else withdrew from her. She smelled the water where it sank into wood, the black-shelled insects, the smooth-skinned lizards. The hot breath of weasels and bats. Of wolves.

She thought of the wolf. The one she'd killed. It wasn't the revulsion and horror of killing the poor creature that came back to her now. It was her enjoyment of it, how wonderful it had made her feel. She felt again the intense pleasure of eating the wolf's soul, the shedding of all worry and want. The absence of all fear and weariness. Hunger cramped her belly but made her sick at the thought of real food. This was not food hunger, Alys knew. This was something else. This was soul hunger.

Then she felt she was falling—but she wasn't falling. Gone was sound and scent. Gone was the fforest. She felt rather than saw that she was with The Beast. The Beast was high up on the mountain, and she was there, too, in her mind if not her body. The air was thin and cold. The Beast was talking to her, inside her head, inside her chest, telling her something, asking her something. Asking her *for* something. The Beast was leading her, and she was following. The Beast was just ahead, just ahead. And then Alys opened her eyes and looked down, and there was no fforest there anymore. There was nothing but the deepest, darkest, most enveloping hole beneath her feet. She looked up for The Beast, but there was no more Beast. There was no more anything. Only black nothing above, and around, and below.

Alys gasped aloud and the world came back to her—and she came back to herself. She was a girl made of skin and bone and hair, perched in a tree. And there was a woman who seemed made more of leaf and mud than skin crawling toward her, along the branch.

Angelica.

Alys knew her by name, but more than that she knew her by sense. Alys's skin was on fire.

No, her skin was freezing.

No, it was on fire.

Unlike her vision of The Beast just now, Angelica's appearance before Alys was no vision. It was terribly real.

Angelica crawled like a wildcat, low to the branch, her large, gray owl eyes open and curious. Her hair hung down around her face, and even through the snarl of dirt and bark that seemed as much a part of her as her teeth or fingernails, Alys could see how beautiful she was. More beautiful than any woman—any person—she'd ever seen before. More beautiful than any memory of her mam's face.

"Angelica," Alys said.

"You know me," Angelica said. Her voice was soft and cool like rain. "And I know you."

Every question Alys might have had for Angelica—every accusation—departed her in this moment. Alys only wished to reach out a hand and touch Angelica's face, to step inside of Angelica. To feel what it would be like to be Angelica. And then Angelica was touching Alys's face with her dry mud hands and it felt as if she were reaching inside of Alys, touching her tender parts. Examining them with careful hands.

"You're like me now," Angelica said. "You should come with me. It's time."

Alys caught a scent of something then. An emptiness in Angelica. A vacancy as deep and frightening as the vast hole in her vision. "Your sister," Alys said to Angelica. "Where is she?"

The emptiness in Angelica opened. It screamed, but there

was no sound. Angelica retracted her hand as if Alys had wounded her. "Benedicta has left me."

Alys remembered the thread that traveled from one sister's hand to the other, through Alys, and couldn't imagine how such a thing could be broken. "Why?" Alys said.

For just a moment Angelica's round eyes narrowed and Alys smelled something sharp and bitter in her nose. Then Angelica's gray eyes opened wide and bright again. "The boy. My sister was jealous of him. He followed us. Wanted to join us, be like us. I pitied him. But my sister's heart was hard. She wanted me to leave him, but I wouldn't."

Delwyn. Alys remembered him calling to her, wanting her to come to him. She'd felt his longing inside of her. Crawling.

Angelica's voice sang to her, it caressed her. "Come with me, Alys. You don't belong with them. You have the hunger, too. Come rest with me and never again be hungry or tired or alone."

Night was falling and Angelica's voice was lulling, and it would be so easy for Alys to let herself go, to sink into Angelica's leafy embrace and become whatever she was meant to become. Alys closed her eyes and tried to imagine being like one of these trees, with vines and moss for hair and clothing.

But then the hole. The hole. The horrible hole. It grew larger and more terrible than ever when Alys's eyes were shut, and although it vanished again when Alys opened her eyes, still she felt it. The hole was real, and it was here, and Angelica was a part of it, and she wanted Alys to become a part of it, too. Alys felt that in her gut, which had turned sour and rose to her mouth. "No," she said to Angelica. "No."

Alys scrambled backward and slid and fell and clawed her way down the tree. Angelica's laughter flew at her and cut like shards of glass. "You'll come to me, Alys. We're the same, you and I. The same."

THIRTY-ONE

Alys lost all hope after that day. She wanted to believe that Angelica was lying. She could smell her deceit, little puffs of stink that rose off her. But Alys felt certain that just as with Cerys, the one thing Angelica hadn't lied about was the worst truth of all: Alys was becoming like Angelica.

When Alys returned to camp from the fforest that evening, all of her senses were alive, and in a way that terrified her. Mother had told her to closely guard her ability to sense illness, because that alone would be cause for suspicion of witchery among the ignorant villagers. Even Mother, as sharp as she was, couldn't have comprehended what Alys was feeling now. The Lakes had been a noisy place to Alys before her encounter with Angelica, but now every moment was cacophony. Too much sensation, too much awareness. She sniffed the air more from instinct than desire, and what she smelled wasn't the scent of food or people—meat, sweat, hair. What she smelled was fear, anger, loneliness. It wasn't just her nose that was alive to it. It was her skin. The hair on her arms rose up when the whispers around campfires turned to dreadful things that lurked and crawled in the dark. At those times the gnawing in her stomach was half hunger, half excitement. She recoiled from herself.

Food lost its flavor again. At breakfast the day after her encounter with Angelica, the fish cakes and bread that Beti handed her tasted like ash in her mouth. Dreading that Beti, Pawl, and Cian might notice and ask her what was wrong, Alys forced herself to take bites of food, while coming up with excuses to rise and fetch water or bread or another portion for one of them. She took her plate with her and slipped her own portion back into the pot. After two days of this, she had to tighten the belt around her waist to keep her trousers from falling down.

Worse even than this was how visions of the hole dominated her waking hours. She grew afraid to blink. When she closed her eyes, the nothingess of the hole possessed her. Everything else faded away until the painful thumping of her heart brought her back and she was able to see the Lakes taking shape around her again. She was there, skin and bone, touching and feeling, but she wasn't there. Nothing was real to her anymore. The Lakers, the Lakes themselves, Pawl and Beti and Cian—it all felt like a fantasy that the lightest touch would shatter into pieces.

Everything Alys looked at, or touched, or ate, or heard—it was all dimming. She felt as if a light had gone out inside of her—a light she hadn't even known was there until it sputtered and turned to smoke.

Since she'd tried to take Cerys's soul, Alys told herself that if she ever felt she was a threat to anyone she loved, she would strike out on her own. Now she had to face what she had tried to ignore for too long. She couldn't get away from the monster. She was the monster. She must leave before she did real harm, and she must do it soon. Certainly before Enid and Madog and the other children arrived.

As it was, her departure would be devastating enough. She clung like a child to the bit of comfort Pawl and Beti offered her, and the warmth she felt whenever Cian was near. The thought of losing them was so painful to her that she had to will tears not to form. So instead of leaving immediately as she should have, each night she awoke in the trees. She climbed down from her perch and returned to her tent. She crawled under covers, heartsick and trembling, until sleep overtook her again. Then each morning she woke up and she stayed one more day. At breakfast she looked at Cian and she thought, *Tomorrow I can leave him.* But then she didn't. Nor did she tell him what was happening to her. She imagined his face if she were to tell him about waking up in the trees, about her vision of the hole, of how she'd been drawn to Angelica, and of the undeniable satisfaction of taking a soul. She imagined every good thing Cian felt for and about her turning to horror.

Alys had survived so much, but she would not survive that. It was her conjuring of Cian's revulsion that finally decided her. She would leave the very next morning, early. Before anyone else rose. That evening at dinner, she laughed extra hard and long at Pawl's jokes, and after helping Beti with the dishes, she didn't wait for Beti to pull her into an over-enthusiastic embrace. Instead, Alys reached out for Beti, held her, and memorized her scent of lavender and lard.

She didn't say goodnight to Cian. She waited until he'd gone to retrieve firewood from the lean-to where they kept it dry, and she told Pawl and Beti that she was very tired. Then she fled to her tent and tied the flap good and tight. She thought this might slow her down long enough to think twice if she were even so much as tempted to go in search of Cian in the hope he might beg her to stay.

Earlier that day, she'd filled a skin with water and put together a small stash of food—not that she could imagine eating it. Now she packed the clothes Beti had given her and Mam's coat. She had the knife Father had made and Mother had given her. She conjured their faces, the roughness of Mother's hands, and the sawdust that collected in the whorls of Father's ears. She had the linen with the children of Gwenith's names. These things would have to be enough to keep her company.

She had no thought of where exactly she would go. But it would be far away, where no one she loved could ever find her or be hurt or disappointed by her. And maybe, to satisfy a curiosity that Ren had planted in her, she would try to see the ocean. The blue that went on forever. Whatever happened to her afterward, at least she would have seen that.

She didn't attempt to block the way to her tent flap that night. It hadn't prevented her from waking up in the trees before, so it seemed pointless now. With everything at the ready, she climbed into her bed fully expecting sleep would never come.

She lay in the dark and heard the sounds of the camp rise and fall around her. The soft voices of the Lakers, the loud voices of the Lakers. Occasionally someone breaking into song. More than once she heard Beti's cackle. She kept an ear pricked for Cian's low voice, but she never heard him.

Her eyelids drooped, and she felt sleep coming, which surprised her. Then her eyes closed and she was gone.

Alys climbed and she climbed. The air thinned and chilled her lungs and her breathing was shallow. But she climbed on, because The Beast was leading her. She saw Its furred back and Its leathery wings ahead of her. There was something It wanted her to see. Needed her to see. So she climbed.

Then it was in front of her and it was familiar and awful. It was the hole. Big and gaping and expanding all the time. Around its edges, trees and bushes lost their grip on the land and tumbled down and down to disappear in its nothingness. The Beast turned to look at her.

She fell into Its eyes, wet and black and knowing, and she knew all that It had lost and all that would be lost to that hole. How every soul that was taken made the wound deeper. The Beast looked down at Its own chest, which opened down the center, and where Its ribs and lungs and heart should have been, Alys saw only darkness and emptiness and pain and loss. She cried out, looked around her, as if help might come.

The Beast shook Its head. Breathed in and out. But it wasn't

The Beast's voice that spoke to her. It was Mother's. "No, child, there's none can help me now. None save for you."

Cian's voice. "Alys? Alys, are you awake?"

Alys's eyes flew open and sun flowed through the cracks in her canvas tent. It was full morning. She'd slept in her own bed, long and deep. It wasn't night, and she wasn't clinging to a tree. She was in her bed, like a normal girl—a normal girl who'd overslept.

She sat up, looked around her. Saw her pack by the tent flap. She'd lost the opportunity to leave today. She'd lost the sense of why she must leave.

She reminded herself: Cerys. Wolf. Delwyn. Benedicta. Angelica.

Oh yes. That. Those. But she couldn't leave now, not with Cian calling to her and the camp awake in the bright sunshine.

"Yes, Cian, I'm awake."

"Are you all right? Breakfast is ready. I have tea here for you."

She untied the flap and peeked around it. He stood there, handsome and smiling at her, and handed her the steaming cup. "Thank you," she said.

"It's a fishing day," he said. "I've just decided. Come with me?"

Hesitation wasn't possible when confronted with Cian's kind, open face—his smile that knew nothing of Beasts and holes in the earth. "I'll just get dressed," she said.

She closed the flap, sipped hot tea, and thought. Her heart raced and yet she also felt strangely calm. She'd only believed she was decided before. Now she really was. She would still leave. Tomorrow. But she had a new destination. She would find The Beast and the hole. And she would ask The Beast to tell her how to close it. Alys might still be a monster. In fact she felt quite sure that she was. But healing Byd—or trying to—was the least she could do for Mother. For herself. For all of them.

THIRTY-TWO

Alys and Cian weren't really fishing. More pretending to fish. Then every once in a while Cian would get a look on his face that meant he'd be leaning toward her in just a moment, rocking the canoe, and touching his lips to hers, soft at first, and then exploring. He'd grasp a hunk of her hair in his hand, wrap it around his fingers. Sometimes he'd take her face in his hands, or rest one hand gently at the base of her throat, tracing the notch between her collarbones with one finger.

She wished now that she could go back to that sweet, short time before she'd begun waking in the trees. Cian had been everything to her then. If she'd been asked before she met him what she was missing in her heart and soul, what she craved, she wouldn't have been able to answer. Then she met Cian. And quickly—so quickly, and yet so completely—he had stepped into the yearning place inside of her. And he fit perfectly. He was what she'd craved all along—she just hadn't known it. Hadn't known such a match for her empty places was possible.

But then shadow fell over her, and dread returned. It carved out all the spaces in her heart that she had so wanted to give to Cian.

Cian looked at her thoughtfully, his head just slightly cocked. "You know, fair Alys"—Alys liked when he called her that—"you're not fooling me."

Cian loved to tease her, and loved to laugh. He told her that one day he'd make her laugh, too. It hadn't happened yet—and now, she thought with a pang, it never would. She cocked her head back at him, but said nothing.

"There's something you're not telling me," he said. "I can feel it."

They were so close to each other. She could smell him—she'd know his scent anywhere, a combination of salt and wet marsh grass. More powerful than his skin smell, though, was his worry. She felt it reaching out to her, trying to penetrate her skin, her heart. But she resisted. Even this physically close to him, there was an uncrossable distance between them. Her lies formed a barrier higher and stronger than any Gate. She tried to believe that he loved her. He had told her so, and Cian wasn't a liar like she was. But he could only love what he knew of her—and he knew nothing. She hadn't shown him the monster inside of her—hadn't told him what the monster could do. How could she truly believe he loved her if he didn't know what she really was, and what she'd done? She couldn't tell him how she woke up every night, perched in the trees like something evil and predatory. She couldn't tell him about Angelica and Benedicta and The Beast. How could she tell him these things without losing his regard for her? The terror of loss was mixed up with every bit of love she felt for him. She'd never had anyone like Cian in her life before—at least not that she could truly remember. Someone who was all hers. Who never seemed happier than when she was nearby. Who treated her as if she were something precious.

"Alys," Cian said, "don't you trust me?" There was no laughter on Cian's face now, only hurt.

Alys felt seized by panic and embarrassment—and exposure. The world around her solidified and she felt Cian tugging her into it, insisting on making her flesh and not shadow. She felt as if she were sitting in front of Cian without her clothes on. Naked. Even more than naked—just tissue and bone, stripped down to her insides with nothing to wrap around herself. In this moment of being spread out in front of him, her dark interior showing, she gave up. She felt a new and sharp craving to give it all to him and to see what he did with it. *Take it,* she wanted to say. *Take me. And if you don't want me anymore—after you see what I am—I won't blame you. And then I'll know. No more hoping and wishing for something that cannot be.*

"I'm not what you think I am," Alys said.

Cian wrinkled his brow. "And what's that?"

"You think I'm just a girl, like any other girl. But I'm not."

"Alys, I do not think you are just a girl like any other girl."

Alys felt herself redden. "Well, maybe not. But you don't

know how . . . unnatural I am." She was unable to look at him. She reached her hand into the soft marsh water next to her and stroked it. It felt alive.

Cian reached a finger out, tipped her chin toward him so that she was forced to look at him. "Tell me," he said. "Tell me your worst."

Alys wondered what the worst might be, what would horrify Cian the most. There was too much. So she decided to tell him where it all began. Her badness. Her wrongness. Her guilt. "I saw the soul eaters, Cian. The night my parents died, I was out and awake and I saw them. They let me live, and I watched them go. I didn't even scream. I did nothing. I just watched them float away."

Cian shook his head. "Alys, I know all about that night. Pawl must have told me a hundred times."

Alys was so shocked she stammered. "But . . . he wasn't supposed to . . . he told me not to tell anyone, not ever."

"Oh Alys, you've seen Pawl around the campfire. There's nothing he's heard or seen that doesn't come spilling out of him after he's taken a dozen or so swigs. And your story is the best of the lot."

Well, Alys thought. So Cian knew about that. But he didn't know about the rest. He sat there in front of her looking so calm and placid about the whole thing, so amused, that she found herself wanting to frighten him. To show him how little reason there was to smile. To make him tremble and withdraw from her the way he should—if he only knew. She thought of Gaenor and how she used to squeal in fright when Alys sang to her.

The Beast It is a creepsome sort
It slips among your dreams
Whispers in your ear at night
And all the while It schemes

You think you're safe in your snug bed
On you It will not feast
Is that your Mam just kissed your cheek?
Oh no, my dear . . . The Beast!

"It's not funny, Cian." Alys felt herself grow angry, and it smelled like meat charred black. "I'll tell you what I am if you must know, but you may want to paddle us back to shore right now, because I promise you won't want to be alone in this canoe with me one second longer once you find out."

Cian crossed his arms over his chest, leaned back as if to nap. "I'm not worried."

"*Fine,*" Alys said. "You joke. But know this: I'm no girl. I'm a soul eater." There. She'd said it.

Cian looked at her for one long beat. Then he laughed. Laughed so hard he slapped the water with his hand.

Shame sizzled from Alys's forehead to her gut. It was one thing to be thought evil, and quite another to be thought ridiculous. "This isn't something to laugh at, Cian. You of all people should know that. I'm like those creatures who killed your parents. And I could hurt you, too. Not because I wanted to, mind you. But because I couldn't help myself."

Cian's face changed then, and Alys felt new shame. The

shame of taking his smile away. His voice came out gentle, and Alys felt his sadness wrap around them. "And how exactly would you steal my soul, fair Alys?"

"Well, I'd . . ." Alys thought for a moment. She thought back to Ffordd and Cerys. The wolf. What had she felt? With Ffordd and Cerys it was hatred, simple as that. With the wolf it was fear. Alys sighed, looked up at Cian. His brown eyes were so open and willing to listen. And again she wondered what she was keeping from him—this deep, dark secret of hers. This vile truth about herself. That she was nasty. That she was foul. That she'd caused Mam's and Dad's deaths, and therefore no one else could—or should—love her. That she then brought suffering and death on Mother and Father. That she invited Angelica to touch her face, to examine her heart.

She was wrong inside and out, and to such a degree that there was no seeing her way toward right. How could she ever find her way to right? A girl like her—damaged and damaging.

Cian was looking at her still. Eyes so soft and ready. So she told him. She told him everything. About touching people and animals, and looking inside of them—being inside of them. About The Beast in the fforest. About Benedicta and Angelica, and her terror of being like them—of belonging with them. And then she told him about Cerys and Ffordd. And the wolf. About the hole in the mountain, and how she felt—knew—that it would swallow them all bit by bit. Then she told him about waking up in the trees every night, about meeting Angelica again, about food tasting like ash again, about that other hunger that curled in her belly.

He flinched.

That was it. The look she'd been expecting. The look of disgust—the moment when she was naked and he found her repellent. The moment he realized that she truly was like those creatures who killed his parents. She put her face in her hands. "I'm horrible," she said.

"Oh no, no Alys. Please don't cry." He was leaning forward, as much as he could without tipping them over in the canoe, pulling her hands away from her face, taking them into his own.

Still she couldn't bear to look at him, so she stared off into the trees instead. The way they stood over the water, roots exposed, branches hunched like shoulders, they looked like monsters themselves. "You think I'm hideous, and I don't blame you. I think I'm hideous, too."

"The only thing I'm thinking is it's no wonder you look so sad all the time. How could you look anything but sad when you've been holding all that inside, and feeling so wrong about yourself?"

"Well," Alys said. Shrugged. "It's true. I am wrong inside."

Cian drew her eyes to his, wouldn't let go. "First of all, if you can step inside of people then I call that a gift, not a curse. And what souls have you taken? You stopped yourself before you did anything truly bad to Cerys or Ffordd. And that wolf would have killed you had you not killed it first."

Alys shook her head. "You don't understand. I'm not here anymore, Cian. I want to be here, but I'm drifting away. I can feel it. I'm losing myself."

"I won't let you drift away. You belong here. With me." He reached out and again tilted her face toward him. "Don't you see, Alys? What's wrong is how you've been treated. It's wrong your parents are dead. And you were just seven when the soul eaters took them. What were you supposed to do? Grown men in all the villages hide behind their big wooden Gates at night, and you think there was something you should have done, or could have done? And the mother and father who raised you in Defaid—they loved you, Alys. That's why they did for you. And you loved them back. It's not your fault they're dead. It's your loss. Don't you see that?"

Alys looked back at him, her mouth dropping open as if to fully take in what he'd just said, to eat it up, chew it, fill her belly with it. She had told him every bit of truth about herself, every ugliness she'd ever seen within herself. Yet there he sat, holding that truth in his hands like a present, and pulling it close to him. Pulling her to him. Maybe he could keep her here. Keep her tethered. Throw a blanket over her bad parts. And then maybe the light inside of her would flicker on again.

She willed herself not to argue anymore. Shushed the voice inside of her that said, *Not so easy, girl, not so fast, the monster won't be quieted.* There was only one thing that would shut up the voice, at least for a moment. She stood up from her seat, wrapped her arms around Cian's neck, and kissed him.

Then all was wet, and cold, and shock, and Cian was laughing and holding onto her, and they were in the water, the canoe capsized, and her heart felt almost warm.

They walked back to camp hand in hand and dripping marsh water.

They were just climbing up the last rise that divided the wet land from the dry when Alys heard a hubbub of voices talking at once. The Lakers seemed to be all gathered together in a big bunch. Then someone turned and saw Alys and Cian approaching, and the wall of bodies parted in front of them, and there they were—the children of Gwenith.

Alys saw Madog and Enid first, each holding a baby, and the moment Enid caught sight of Alys she handed the baby she held to Beti and ran to Alys.

Holding Enid, being held by her, Alys felt such a burden of dread lift from her that she thought she might rise off the ground with it.

"I'm getting you all wet," Alys said.

Enid pulled away from her, smiled and petted Alys's cheek with her rough, familiar hand.

"You made it," Alys said. "You found us."

"Alys, love, we'd never stop searching till we found you." She looked up at Cian. "We owe you thanks. Pawl told us how you saved our Alys."

Cian rolled his eyes. "Didn't take him long."

Alys went to the other children then. First Ren. He was shy with her, not like he'd been before. She remembered the last time she'd seen him—in her witch's bridle, bells clanging. No wonder he pulled away. She reached out to touch his silken cap of hair and he submitted for a moment but looked at the ground. Then she turned to the others, counting heads. While she did so, she touched the linen in her trouser pocket, embroidered with all their names, now wet with marsh water.

The afternoon was bluing to evening, and the Lakers lit their fires. Food was prepared while makeshift tents and shelters were raised for the new arrivals. They all sat, talked, and ate. They even smiled. As the sun set and night fell, there was no Gate to guard, no sheep to tend. Alys felt the vigilance in all of them rise.

"Is it safe here?" Madog said. He looked around him. "You've no fences, no shelters?"

Pawl raised his cup. "Lad, there's nowhere safe. I'd think you'd know that by now. We hear tell of the soul eaters preying on the mountain folk. Like what happened to our Cian's parents. And there have been travelers who don't return to the Lakes from their trips to the villages. And then we're left to wonder what became of them." Pawl shook his head, took a sip. "But seems to us the soul eaters don't like a crowd. They aim for easier pickings. Like wolves, they are."

"What about Defaid, then?" Madog said. "Not such easy pickings."

"No." Pawl shook his head. "I grant you that. But if you think about it, well, them Defaiders made themselves like rabbits in a hole. Only one way out, and once the fire started they were trapped. Here, we're not trapped. And we keep our eyes open."

Alys raised an eyebrow at this, but she said nothing. In all the nights she'd awakened in the trees and made her way back to her tent, she'd yet to meet another wakeful, watchful eye. If Angelica, Benedicta, and Delwyn had wanted to attack the Lakes, they surely could have. Like Madog, Alys wondered why they didn't. She thought of the hole. She couldn't let herself become lulled by the return of the Gwenith children. She would still have to go. She must. It was the only way to keep all of them safe.

Conversation turned to the night the Gate burned down. "I was in one of the towers," Madog said. "And I swear to you, I saw nothing, and I heard nothing. It wasn't until I smelled smoke that I knew anything was amiss. Then I blew my whistle. And all the other children on the Gate blew theirs."

"Did the fire move so fast, then?" Pawl said. "Hard to imagine that Gate could come down like that."

"The fire was fast, yes, and it burned in more than one place. But that's not what brought it down." He shook his head. "We children of Gwenith always thought of our whistles as cries for help. But see, I'd forgotten what Defaiders do when they hear a whistle. They hide."

Cian said, "Do you mean that while all of you were whistling and trying to put out the fire, the Defaiders locked their doors and climbed into their cellars?"

"That's exactly what happened," Madog said. "And there just weren't enough of us to fight the blaze. Finally the oaf of a Defaider on guard duty that night managed to beat loud enough on the High Elder's door to convince him that we needed every pair of hands in the village to put out the fire." Madog took a long pause. "But by then the fire was too far gone. We could keep pouring all the water we wanted but we might as well have been trying to douse it with a thimble. So we just let it burn itself out."

Beti coughed, looked uncomfortable. "The Defaid boy, the rider who told us what happened . . ."

"Alec," Alys said.

"Ay, him," Beti said. "He said something about soul eaters luring folks off into the fforest."

"Ay," Madog said. "The soul eaters came then. They started the fire, I reckon. And once the Gate was down, the singing started. I'd heard tell of it before, of course. But if I hadn't heard it with my own ears, I don't think I could ever have believed how terrible singing and whispering could be. It was like something was crawling inside of you, picking apart your heart and your brains, looking for something."

"Did you see them?" Alys said.

"Ay, we did," Enid said. Two women, and a . . . a boy."

"It was Delwyn, Alys," Madog said. "I know it sounds impossible. He left us so long ago. But it was him, I'd know his white-blond hair anywhere."

"And he wasn't changed," Enid said. "He was still a child, even though he should be as old as you."

"He followed us, even after we left Defaid," Madog said. "Creeping after us in the woods at night, calling to us."

Enid patted his arm. "Madog saved us," she said. "When he saw the Gate was lost, he sent Elidir to gather up the children in the pastures, and then we all just . . . left." Enid smiled at that thought.

Alys did, too. After all those years of feeling there was no way out, no end to that life, for them to just leave. To walk away. "Did the Elders try to stop you?"

"They couldn't," Madog said. "The High Elder threatened me with banishment." He laughed. "Can you believe that? Gate burning down around his ears and he's preaching at me. I said, *Begging your pardon, Brother Ffagan, but banishment from what?*"

Alys clapped a hand over her mouth. "You didn't say that!"

"I surely did," Madog said, then looked briefly proud of himself, before his face fell again. "I should have done it so long ago, led all you children away from there. I could have done it." He looked at Enid. "She begged me to. But I was too afraid. I thought, Defaid wasn't the best home, but it was a home. And we were fed and sheltered. But that was no life, and I'm ashamed of myself. I will never, not ever, forgive myself for keeping us there so long."

Alys took Madog's hand then, and he startled. She'd never touched him before. "You did all you could. We all did."

"What kind of life was I giving Ren, though? The babies won't remember. But Ren, bless him. To think of all those nights I watched my boy drag himself up onto the Gate and out to the pastures. All alone and so tired. I'd tell him stories about seeing the ocean, when I should have been taking him there. Not talking about it. Not just promising."

Enid had been sitting next to Madog all the while he talked, one of the twins in her lap. She'd looked more peaceful than Alys had ever seen her. Younger, too. Almost like the sleepy girl who answered the door back in Gwenith, back when it all started.

Now, though, Enid startled. She looked around her as if suddenly waking from a trance. She gripped Madog's arm, fingers digging in. "Where is Ren?" Then everyone began looking around and murmuring, but there was no Ren. And then murmurs turned to shouts and panic, and Enid looked at Alys with wide, terrified eyes. "Where's our boy?"

THIRTY-THREE

While a few stayed behind with the younger children, everyone else spread out with torches searching the marshes and lakes for Ren. Cian led the search—no one knew the danger spots better than he did, especially in the dark. Madog's first thought was that Ren might have been hopelessly drawn to the water, thanks to all those stories he'd told the boy about the blue ribbon of water all around Byd. Ren couldn't wait to glimpse water spread as far as he could see, and farther.

Maybe it was as simple as that, Alys thought. Maybe Ren had just wanted to see the water. In that case, they could hope that he was content with looking from a distance, and not touching. Not tempted to put his little feet in, to feel the mud ooze between his toes. That was what Enid feared, and why Madog held onto her now—so she wouldn't go running off into the muck and mud herself.

Alys tarried behind the others, her stomach sick with certainty that the greatest danger to Ren lay not in the water, but in the fforest. She stepped back and back from the rest, watching their torches swarm forward into the marshes, and then she doubled back, calling to Ren all the way, begging him to come out, to show himself if he was there.

She thought of little Delwyn following the children all the way from Defaid. Had he waited for this moment to lure Ren into the woods? Did he want a playmate, or worse? Delwyn wasn't a child anymore—he wasn't even human. He didn't want to play, did he? He was hungry. That's why he'd called to her that night. Not for love, but for nourishment of a different, monstrous kind.

Or were Angelica and Benedicta out there? Were they singing to Ren even now? Angelica had called to Ren before, asked him to come to her. Alys walked faster, not needing to think about her direction, because she caught a scent in her nose that she knew to be Ren. He smelled like fresh milk and clean soil under fingernails. "Ren!" She called to him. "Ren! It's me, Alys. Please come out." She heard begging in her own voice and she felt a selfish desperation to find him—not for his own sake, but for hers. And not simply because she loved him like a brother, but because she couldn't bear more sorrow.

Then she saw a flash of white among the trees, and at first she feared it was Delwyn. But no, this was a white shirt attached to a dark cap of hair, and not floating, but crouching. Hiding. Relief bloomed in her belly.

"Ren. It's me. It's Alys. You've scared everyone half to death. Come to me now." She held out her hand. She saw him look at her hand, and his round child eyes narrowed. Alys sniffed the air again. His milk smell had curdled. Soured. Turned to suspicion. He was afraid of her.

Afraid of her. That was why he'd run into the woods—to get away from her.

Alys's relief turned to anger. Resentment. This boy, whom she had held in her arms while he slept, feared her. She'd loved him, thinking they were family, thinking that they could be family. And now he looked at her no differently than the other children of Defaid had. Like a monster. Like the monster that she was.

How dare he?

Anger burned to bitter ash and she stepped toward him, and he shrank from her, clung to the tree behind him, searched for someplace to run or to climb. Alys found herself searching, too, amused that he would think that he could get away from her.

If she'd wanted to get him, she could, couldn't she?

This is what she thought—not with horror, but with a flash of satisfaction that made her feel bigger than herself, that lifted her off the ground. He was the contemptible creature, not Alys. How did he come to judge her? The girl who had sacrificed for him? Who'd risked punishment and worse? If even Ren thought Alys evil, well then why shouldn't she be?

The earth was somewhere below Alys, but it was of no concern to her. She wasn't touching it.

Ren slapped his hands to his eyes, unable to look at her, and he cried out for his parents. The scent in the air, rising off him in waves, was nauseating terror mixed with that of a boy who had lost control of his bladder.

His cry was a blanket of shame thrown over Alys, its weight collapsing her down, shrinking her in upon herself. She clutched leaves and dirt with her hands, willing herself to be here, now, flesh and not shadow. She looked up at Ren. Her voice was a hoarse whisper. "Ren, run. Back that way. To your parents. Run."

Alys buried her face in her hands then, and she wept. She knew only by the sound of small feet through rustling leaves that Ren had made his escape.

Alys wandered back to camp sometime later—hours it might have been. She didn't know. All was still and everyone had retreated to bed except for one person who sat before a campfire, waiting. He stood when he saw her. "Alys," Cian said. And that was all he said before pulling her to him and kissing her. "You're so cold. Sit." He guided her to the log he'd been sitting on just a foot from the fire. Then he sat down beside her and wrapped a blanket around their shoulders. She shuddered, and he pulled her closer. She strained to feel the warmth of him. But the cold seemed to have settled into her heart.

"I frightened Ren in the fforest. I think it's happening, Cian. I'm becoming one of them."

Cian shook his head. "No, Alys. You only think you're bad. You would never hurt Ren. That's not who you are. You must know that about yourself. He was alone and frightened, but not of you."

"You weren't there, Cian. You didn't see the way he looked at me. And he wasn't wrong. I felt like a monster. And like I could do monstrous things. Like I wanted to do monstrous things." Cian pulled her close and kissed her hair. She submitted for a moment, but then placed her hands on his chest and gently pushed him away. "You must listen to me now. Ever since I was a child there have been three creatures who have shadowed me. Angelica, Benedicta, and The Beast. Every day of my life I've wondered when I will see them. Why I see them at all. What they want from me. And what I want from them. Every day they've made me wonder who and what I am. And I will never be at peace until I know."

"How will you know?" Cian said. "Can't you just believe you're good? Can't you just believe me when I tell you?"

Alys looked at Cian's face and knew that if he could make everything right for her, he would. She'd never been so sure of anyone's love as she was of Cian's. He wanted her to be happy, and he wanted her to be happy with him. But she couldn't be. And she felt that loss in her chest. "No. I want to. But I can't."

"I don't understand, Alys. You're finally here. The other children are here now. Maybe it doesn't have to be so hard. Maybe you can let things be easy."

Alys took his hand. "There's something I have to do, Cian. Last night, The Beast came to me in a dream. Years ago It told me about a hole on that mountain—a massive hole that Angelica and Benedicta were creating. That hole has grown, Cian. It will destroy all of us if I don't fill it. The Beast has told me so, and I believe It. I've felt it. So whether I stay here or not, there is no happiness for any of us until I close that hole."

"But why you, Alys?"

Alys shrugged. "Because I'm like Angelica and Benedicta. That's what The Beast told me."

"How will you close it? How will you stop them without dying yourself?"

"I don't know. I hope The Beast will tell me."

"You don't have to go alone," Cian said. "And I don't know why you'd want to. I know the mountain, and you don't. I can help you."

She didn't answer him, but instead rested her head on his shoulder and stared into the flames until her eyes burned. He offered more versions of the same argument at least ten times in the next few hours. He wanted to help her on her journey up the mountain. Help her figure out how to close the hole and save herself. Each time she said the same thing in response: Only she could save herself. She knew this. And she knew just as well that if this darkness inside her grew, she couldn't be trusted not to hurt those she loved—even Cian. That was why Cian must stay behind.

"Cian," Alys said finally, using his own words against him. "You trust me, don't you? That's what you keep telling me, that you trust me. That you love me."

"Ay, of course I do, Alys."

"If you trust me, and you love me, then you must believe me. I must go alone. If you don't let me go now, then I'll only slip away when you're not looking." She thought of Delwyn, how he'd vanished—and what he'd become. She grasped Cian's hand.

"It's because I love you that I must go. That I must fix this shadow inside of me. So that I can come back to you."

Finally Cian relented. She gave him no choice. In the hour before dawn, he helped Alys gather what she'd need for her journey. He held her hand in his own as he walked her to the head of a trail that he said would take her the quickest way up the mountain. When they reached it, Alys turned to him and said it was time for her to leave him. She had her pack with some food, a skin of water, also a blanket, and an oiled canvas that she could shelter under.

Cian leaned against a tree, looking at her. He crossed his arms. "I'm going to wait right here for you, Alys."

She crossed her arms as well. "Oh? Are you, now? For days? Weeks? How long?"

"Forever if necessary." He was smiling, just a little.

"You've no food," she said.

"The longer you're gone, the less I'll need food. I'll grow into this tree right here." He pressed his head back into it. "And I'll become tree, and tree will become me. When you come back you'll see just the outline of my face and body in the bark. And then you can live here at the foot of this tree, and sleep under my branches." He reached out and grasped her by her folded arms, drawing her toward him. "And when you dream, we'll be together." And he kissed her.

Oddly, the moment she had made up her mind to do this—to leave Cian and the others and to follow The Beast and confront whatever lay ahead for her—Alys had begun to feel solid again. No longer shadow and ash. Now she closed her eyes and memorized the feel of Cian's lips, the scratch of his cheeks, his salt and water scent. Then she pulled away, turned, and forced herself not to look back.

She'd hoped to climb all that day and then into the night, as long as it took to get to The Beast, but that was folly. Alys's mind was alert with anticipation but her body was failing her. When darkness fell thick and fast, the moon suggested the outlines of things, but didn't reveal the rocks that sent Alys tumbling to her hands more than once.

So she made camp. She hadn't felt hungry, she seemed to have forgotten all about food, but now the shakiness in her limbs told her that she needed to eat. She chewed a few pieces of dried fruit and a bit of oatcake. Then she retched it all out. She tried not to think about what it meant that she could no longer tolerate real food in her belly. She must sleep, she thought. She rigged the oiled canvas into a makeshift tent, then curled up in a blanket underneath.

She woke with a start, perched in a tree.

Alysssssssssss

Alys looked around her through the darkness. It felt natural to be crouched on this branch, to sense air and space around her, the absence of a bed underneath her.

Alysssssssssss

It was Delwyn. Alys remembered that needling voice, like a scratch inside her head.

Alysssssssss

Come heeeeeeeeeere

Alys climbed across the tree branch and slid to the ground. She looked, sharp-eyed, into the crisp darkness. It was colder up here on the mountain.

She saw him, the moon reflecting off his white-blond hair, peeking from behind a tree as if he were playing with her.

"What do you want?" she said.

He floated and skittered to another tree, peeked from behind it again.

"Stop playing, Delwyn. I know what you are."

"Maybe I know what you are, too." He laughed like a child playing a schoolyard game. But sharper. Nastier.

Then he stepped out, floated forward, no hesitation or playing now, and his face, oh, his face was not the face of a child.

How could Alys ever have thought it was? Was it because a child's face was what she had expected to see? Was it because she so badly wanted to find her Delwyn again—the little boy she'd clung to on the Gate, whose heart beat against her own? But this was no longer Delwyn, it wasn't even anything that truly looked like him. His skin pulled taut and transparent over the bones of his face and his once green eyes were black, so black. Black like two holes in his head. Holes you could fall into.

She felt a tug in her heart while she looked into those holes. Then a pull. She clutched her chest. *No.*

"No, Delwyn. You can't do me like that. I'm not like the other poor souls you've taken."

The tugging stopped. He had no power over her, and she knew why. It was his face that gave him away—or it was her ability to see his face that did. Perhaps this was one of the things that had made her so different all along—that she saw the truth of things. That beauty could sometimes be ugly, and that you didn't always find good and evil where you expected to—or where you'd been told to find them. Now, she saw that this Delwyn wasn't her young friend who ran away, mourning for his brothers. That boy had died long ago. This Delwyn was something else—had become something else—and she could see him for what he was. She could see through his skin to where there should be a warm beating heart, but where there was instead only ash.

Delwyn's face crumpled in on itself, he rushed toward her, and Alys nearly retreated but stood her ground. Then just as suddenly he stopped. He touched his face, as if he could see himself and his monstrosity through her eyes. He looked at his hand, which was as skeletal as his face. And as he looked at his hand, he floated backward and backward until he withdrew into the depths of the mountain, beyond where she could see him.

THIRTY-FOUR

The next morning, Alys felt a deep certainty that she would meet The Beast before the day was out. It felt so present to her, so near, that it was as if It were moving right alongside her. Always she scanned around her, either side and above, but there was no sight of It. No sound.

She hadn't been able to eat breakfast, and she felt weak with exhaustion. Seeing Delwyn's dead face last night had sickened her, robbed her of sleep for the rest of the night. While she walked she took a bite from an apple, and her stomach rose up to meet her throat. She spit it out, and then tossed the apple far into the woods.

Where it landed at the clawed feet of The Beast.

Come. It's time.

It leapt straight up and vanished into the tree cover, and Alys dashed into the woods where It had been, thinking of nothing other than the impossibility of following a creature with wings. Then she saw It land again far ahead of her, and she dashed on.

And so they went, beyond the point at which Alys felt her breath burn in her lungs, past caring about how many times she'd fallen and scraped her skin bloody through her trousers. Late afternoon passed into evening and the light shifted golden, then pink. The land grew steeper and steeper until finally Alys looked up and saw The Beast standing over her, on a rock ledge far above her head, the setting sun shining behind It so that Alys had to squint.

She climbed up to It, hand over foot. Once she was near the top, The Beast hinged forward and down and grasped her arm with one long clawed hand, then lifted Alys up and through the air and onto flat rock. Then It released her and Alys looked up at It, The Beast. Tall and furred, winged and fanged, It looked evil but It seemed good. Alys wanted to ask It which It really was, but she knew It wouldn't answer. She might as well ask the wind if it were good or evil. Like the wind, The Beast was neither. At one time she'd wanted to be able to think of herself as good. Now she wished only to be like The Beast. Neither. As it was, she feared she was far more evil than good.

The Beast was not looking at her, It was staring ahead, and It drew Alys's eyes there as well. It led her onward.

Gray rock gave way to grass and low, scrubby bushes. But these were only the shapes of grass and bushes, because everything beyond the rock was ash. Grass-shaped ash crumbled to dust as she and The Beast walked across it. Bush-shaped ash collapsed when grazed by Alys's fingertips. Her hand was ash-gray when she pulled it away, as if she too were turning to ash. She wiped her hand on her trouser leg, wanting it off her.

Beyond the ash was a deep, black hole. Big enough around to swallow all of Defaid inside of it. The scent that rose from the hole was . . . nothing. There was no scent at all, as if no light, or sound, or sign of life at all—nothing that might attach itself to person or animal—existed anymore in that deep place. Even in her dreams and in her worst waking moments of hopelessness, Alys hadn't known the unnatural sensation of emptiness that she felt now.

"I'm afraid," Alys said. "You said that I would know how to close the hole when the time came. But I don't." She felt panic in her empty stomach. She'd thought the same instinctive knowing she felt when she touched someone—the same that Mother felt when she touched a sick person—might fill her when she came close to the hole. She'd hoped she could heal it the way Mother had taught her to heal a wound, that she'd know how to clean out the poison. But the blackness of the hole gaped before Alys like a growing thing that would only keep tearing and tearing. She was certain that before long, all of Byd would sink into it. She cringed from it.

The soul eaters are making the hole. To close the hole you must make them stop. If you don't, we will all become hole. We will all become nothing.

"Why can't you make them stop? Why does it have to be me?" She hated her fear, but nonetheless it bloomed in her chest.

You must be like them to stop them. I am not like them.

"But I am like them," Alys said. There was the nasty truth. She tasted it in her mouth. No matter how many times she'd tried to push it away, spit it out, it always came back to her. This was why The Beast needed her. Because she was evil. And It needed an evil creature to do this evil work.

You are like them. But you are not them.

Like them, but not them. Like them, but not them. Alys spoke the words to herself, tried to believe them. There was some chance for her still. She had a choice. This was what choosing felt like—it was terrifying. The sun dipped below the horizon. The world darkened around Alys, and she felt the hole's hugeness and her own smallness. "Where will I find them?"

The boy soul eater follows you. You will not need to look for him.

"And the sisters?"

One is with me. She will tell you how to find the other.

Alys followed The Beast through the darkness to the entrance of a cave. It pointed to a torch and a flint.

Light and enter. I will not follow. You must go alone.

Then The Beast crouched, and leapt, and It was gone up into the dark sky on Its leathery wings.

Alys stepped into the cave and the air became at once closer and damper and cooler. The torch illuminated only the rock on either side of her and the stone beneath and just ahead of her feet. There was too little air. There was no air at all. She fought the urge to gasp, to turn around. Minutes passed as she made her way forward. Then the narrow passage widened and rounded into a slightly larger room, and seated there was a woman.

The woman sat on the ground, her back against the rock wall. Her legs were pulled up to her chin, her face down and pressed into her knees, arms drawn into her chest. Her hair, sewn through with leaves and twigs, dulled by mud, enveloped her. Alys couldn't see the woman's face, but she knew this wasn't Angelica. The feeling Angelica gave her was altogether different.

"Benedicta?" Alys said.

The creature looked up at Alys then, her hair parting over her face.

Her hideous face. What Alys had once found so beautiful was now grotesque. Desiccated. All shadows and hollows. Bones visible through transparent skin. Enormous black eyes with no white at all, only pupil. Lips purple like death.

Every rational thought failed Alys, and she wanted only to flee.

"Yes. I am Benedicta," she said. "I have been waiting for you. The Beast promised me you'd come."

Alys felt Benedicta's voice more than she heard it. The creature didn't move, and yet that voice was inside of Alys, insinuating itself in her chest, wrapping itself around her heart. Alys absorbed Benedicta's bottomless despair as if it were her own. Benedicta's need pulled at Alys's own longing. Alys sensed how injured Benedicta was—and yet dangerous. Still so dangerous. Alys couldn't allow herself to yield to Benedicta for one moment, or she might never leave this cave.

"Why are you here?" Alys said.

"To be killed," Benedicta said. "Cannot. Cannot go on like this. Lost the hunger. Only tired. So tired. Want to rest."

Benedicta's words hummed in Alys's chest, but Alys didn't trust them. Didn't trust her. Rest was what Benedicta and Angelica had offered the children of Gwenith. But instead the soul eaters gave the children death. Worse than death: They gave them nothing. They made them nothing.

Alys remembered what Angelica had told her about Benedicta leaving her—that it was because of jealousy over Delwyn. She wondered what Benedicta would say. "Why aren't you with Angelica?"

Benedicta shook her head. "I begged her to stop. To let us rest. But Angelica will never stop. Her hunger is never-ending."

"Angelica told me it was because of Delwyn. That you were jealous of him and wanted to leave him behind."

Benedicta arched her back and let out a scream so loud and anguished it reverberated around the cave and nearly caused Alys to drop the torch and cover her ears. When silence fell again, Benedicta held her own head between her hands and said, "It was Angelica who grew tired of the boy. When his scent turned sour and then rotten. When he stopped smelling like anything at all."

Alys thought of long-dead Delwyn, now more ash than child. They had done that to him.

"I left Angelica," Benedicta said, "because I'm finished. I'm ready to be nothing." She looked up at Alys with black, unlit eyes. "I want you to take my soul."

Alys stepped backward, shaking her head hard. "No. No, I won't. Taking your soul will only widen the hole." Alys thought of the hole growing and growing, swallowing Cian, Pawl, Beti. Enid, Madog, Ren, and the other children. She pictured their faces sinking into black. Then she thought again of Delwyn's face, and of what soul eating had done to him. What it had done to this creature in front of her.

"I fear the hole," Benedicta said. "And yet it draws me. That is why I came here. The Beast said I could go into the hole to become nothing. But that won't do for me. I cannot."

"But you must," Alys said. "If The Beast said that was the only way, then you must throw yourself into the hole."

"It's not the only way. The Beast said you would kill me." Benedicta's voice was a hiss now, the bones in her face twisted and contracted. "It promised. It told me if I stayed here you would do it."

The Beast had said Alys would know what to do. But Alys knew nothing, only desperation. "I must stop Angelica. I can't let her go on taking souls. She'll destroy us all. Do you know where she is?"

Benedicta's face twisted some more, her mouth a grimace that looked like an attempt to smile. "A deal. You are offering me a deal. I help you find my sister and then you will take my soul?"

Alys felt defeated. Was defeated. This creature was weakened, but still crafty, and Alys had no skill for it. She wanted only to close the hole, to protect the people she loved. She'd hoped to make herself clean in the process. But maybe she was too ruined for that. She thought of that day in the canoe with Cian—was it only a few days ago? His belief in her goodness. Then she thought of Mother. And Father. Mam and Dad. Little Gaenor. All the people she'd loved and lost and couldn't save.

It had all come to this. If she couldn't save herself, then she would save Cian. She would save Pawl and Beti, Madog and Enid. And Ren. Little Ren whom she'd so terrified. She might be a lost soul—an empty soul—but they weren't. "Yes," Alys said to Benedicta. "I'll take your soul if you help me find Angelica."

Benedicta moved toward Alys on all fours. Not so close, and yet too close. "I will tell you where to look for her. Then you must take my soul. Now."

The hair picked up on the back of Alys's neck. Alys might not be crafty, but she wasn't stupid. "No. You'll come with me. You'll lead me to her. And then, yes, I will take your soul."

Benedicta licked her lips with a black tongue. "I don't like that deal. What if you trick me? My sister and I have been tricked before."

"I won't do that to you. I know you can see into me, Benedicta. You can see that there are no tricks in me. I only want to stop Angelica. And then I will do what I promised." And she meant it. Alys realized that she, too, wanted this all to come to an end. She, too, was tired.

"All right. It's a bargain. But if you betray me I will find your boy—the tall boy with the brown eyes. The laughing boy I see when I look inside your heart. Yes . . . that one." She laughed—all grim, gray teeth. "I see him in you. You hold him close. Betray me, girl, and I will find him and he'll be less than a memory when I'm done with him."

Alys felt anger flare inside of her, smelled it acrid and bitter in her own nose. She tamped it down, squelched it before it engulfed her. "We'll leave in the morning. At first light."

When Alys turned to leave, Benedicta scrambled the rest of the way toward her and gripped her arm with a bony hand. "You do what you promised. Or I'll kill them all."

THIRTY-FIVE

It was blackest night when Alys emerged from the cave, and she sucked fresh air deep into her lungs.

Alys felt the nearness of the hole although she couldn't see it. She was outside the ash line now, in a scrubby area of low trees and large rock formations. But she knew the hole was just beyond. And she knew it was growing still, getting closer all the time. She could feel it in her heart, her soul.

She hung her oilcloth and crawled underneath it, but sleep wouldn't come. She crawled back out and made a small fire, dug into her pack for water. Alys's fear of what was to come sucked all the moisture from her mouth, and the water was cool in her throat.

Time passed, and Alys stared into the flames. Images floated through her head. Cian's face, most of all. The times he'd grasped her hair in his hands, kissed her. She didn't feel the stomach flip of excitement that usually came when she thought of him this way. She felt only sadness and a sure sense of loss. The promise she'd made to Benedicta closed the door on any happiness she might have had with Cian. If she did what Benedicta asked of her, she would become like them. And then Alys would be the one seeking her end in that hole. Maybe that was what The Beast had planned for her—and for them—all along.

Alys allowed her eyes to be entranced by the flames, not even blinking. The heat sank into her skin, burned her cheeks, and she tried to feel nothing else.

Then, through the flame, in the darkness beyond, she saw two small, white feet.

"Alys."

She looked up at Delwyn. His face was as horrifying to her as it had been yesterday, but she felt a change in him. Something that had been closed to her before, the hard black nugget at his center, had weakened. She could sense the cracks.

"Yes, Delwyn."

He was quiet for a long moment, and Alys thought he might float away from her again. Then he said, "Do you remember the Gate?"

"Of course I do. And I remember how you saved me. Do you remember that?"

Delwyn cocked his head. His black eyes widened with effort. "I remember my brothers. How the Elders blamed them for dying. How they looked at me like I was wrong on the inside. How I hated them."

Hate. Alys knew hatred. She remembered how powerfully she'd felt it with Ffordd and Cerys. How it warmed her belly at first, but then how it turned to ash in her mouth. "Albon and Aron were sweet boys. As were you," Alys said.

"Were," Delwyn said. "Sweet boy no longer, am I? I am old now. Old and . . ." He held his hand in front of his face ". . . ugly. I can remember when I was a child, Alys. But I can't feel it anymore. Being a child is like a story someone once told me. A story I don't believe anymore."

Alys looked at him, tried to conjure the Delwyn she'd known. Tried to erase this face and these hands and skeletal feet from her mind and see only his white-blond hair, his quick, nimble body. She managed for a moment. "Sit with me? Here, by the fire."

Delwyn hesitated for a moment, then crouched down opposite her, the small fire between them.

There was something that Alys needed to ask him, although she dreaded his answer. "The other Gwenith children, the ones who wandered. Did you kill them all?"

Delwyn nodded. "Some I did. Some Angelica and Benedicta took."

Alys reached into her trouser pocket, pulled out the bit of embroidered linen with the names of all the Gwenith children. She ran her finger down the list. Those poor children, she thought. So tired, and wanting only to rest.

"I didn't mean to do wrong," he said. "I only gave them what they wanted. What everyone wants."

"What is that?"

"To have no fear. To sleep."

"Is that what Albon and Aron wanted when Benedicta and Angelica killed them?" Alys knew it was cruel to say this, but she reminded herself that she was speaking to a monster, not a boy. A monster who had killed so many times. She thought of all the poor souls he had sung to in the fforest, and then sucked from this life and disappeared forever.

Delwyn put his head to his knees, reminding Alys of Benedicta. It was as if neither of them could stand to see themselves, or to be seen. As if they had looked into a mirror for the first time and been disgusted by their own reflections.

"They aren't tired anymore. Or frightened," he said.

"No, they aren't anything at all. They're gone."

Delwyn lifted his head from his knees. "I want to be gone, too, Alys. Can you make me gone? I'm dead already. Dead in my soul. Turned to ash and yet somehow still here. It would be a small thing for you to kill me. Hardly a killing at all."

She'd promised to take Benedicta's soul. And she would do it. But she couldn't kill Delwyn. Not him. There had to be some other way. The Beast told Benedicta she could throw herself into the hole, put an end to her suffering that way. It was horrible to imagine that for Delwyn. But then Alys reminded herself this wasn't Delwyn. Not anymore. "You could go to the hole. It would be quick, and painless. And then you'd be gone."

Delwyn squeezed his purple lips together. "I'm frightened of that hole."

"You made that hole, Delwyn. You and Benedicta and

Angelica. It's a part of you. And I think it can give you what you want." Alys felt a clench of disgust in her belly, offering nothingness this way, as if it were a gift. But if Delwyn could help sew up that wound in the earth, maybe something living and real would fill that space again. And maybe Delwyn would be a part of that.

"Will you go with me? I don't want to go alone."

Delwyn looked more like a child again to Alys's eyes. Perhaps it was a trick of the flames, or the sadness in her own heart—her longing for her friend to be what he was. Whatever the reason, the outlines of his face had softened, and Alys saw flashes of the boy he had been. "I will. Right now."

Alys stood, and walked around the fire to him. Then she held out her hand.

When Delwyn placed his hand in hers, it felt cool and dry, like a handful of bones, not flesh. He stood and they walked together, Delwyn as insubstantial next to her as her own shadow. He seemed to know the way better than Alys, unbothered by the darkness or obstructions, and then he stopped.

The hole lay ten feet in front of them, and Alys's feet were buried in ash. She felt in herself the terror of falling in, and she felt the same in the small hand she still held in her own.

"It will be quick, you said. And painless?" Delwyn looked up at her, his face glowing in the moonlight, looking more than ever like her friend now.

Alys felt her eyes stinging. Looked into the face of her friend, remembered the years of searching the horizon for him. She felt the loss of him again. And again and again. She gently squeezed his hand. "Yes, Delwyn. Painless. And then no more pain anymore."

Delwyn looked forward, released Alys's hand. Turned to look up at her again. "Good-bye, Alys."

Ten steps more and he was gone, a flash of white-blond hair descending into black.

Alys sank to her feet and sobbed.

THIRTY-SIX

The next morning broke to a steel gray sky and wind that raked across the rocks.

Benedicta tried once again to convince Alys to take her soul, not to make her lead Alys to Angelica. "Go with you, girl, why?" She stalked around the cave, flying close to Alys, then retreating again. Over and over she'd done it, all the while railing against Alys. "You made me a promise, but you lie. They always lie. People and their lies." She whirled and swirled, leaving a trail of sticks and leaves.

Benedicta maintained her constant arguments as Alys followed her up the mountain. And each time Benedicta accused her of deceit, Alys repeated her promise. "I will do it, Benedicta, I will kill you. But not until you've led me to Angelica. I'm not a liar."

"A liar who lies would say that," Benedicta said.

Alys followed Benedicta through seemingly endless pine forest. The trees grew thick, dark, and close, and all was silent except for the dripping and trickling of springs and the scurrying of small animals through crackling underbrush. After hours of this, when Benedicta had finally wound down her constant complaining, Alys stopped Benedicta with a question that had plagued her. "How do you choose what souls you take, Benedicta? Why attack Defaid but leave the Lakes alone?"

Benedicta was silent for a while, alternately floating and crawling over branches and rocks. Then she paused and looked back over her shoulder at Alys. Alys had avoided looking straight into her black eyes, her wasted face. But now she had to. Alys felt each emotion that crossed Benedicta's features as if they were her own. Hunger. Anger. Bitterness. Also fear. "Sister and I decided long ago to hunt at night. And we hunt the lonely. The solitary. It's safer that way. We slip in, we take, we hide."

Benedicta turned away and moved on, but Alys stopped her again with her voice. "Why Defaid, then?" Alys stared at the back of Benedicta's mud-and-leaf hair. The soul eater had paused midway over a rock, looking less like a woman and more like something that had crawled up from a lake bottom.

Benedicta glanced back at Alys and one side of her mouth curled up. "We could not resist. It brought back memories. Of another time, another village. You remember. You were there."

Alys felt all curiosity drain from her then. That other village had been Gwenith, her home. And now she had no home. She had no more urge to talk to Benedicta. She might have felt anger at her for what she'd done, but instead she felt only vast, aching sadness. It swallowed her whole and it was all she could do to put one foot in front of the other.

An hour or more passed that way, until Alys forced herself to shake the weight from her chest and limbs, to shove the sad thoughts aside. They did not serve her now. Then an unfamiliar sound began growing in Alys's ears, even before she was fully aware of its presence. It had started like a whisper, and then it took on density. It was as if she were stepping through the sound, as if it existed all around her. It was like rolling thunder, but softer at the edges.

And then Alys became aware of the path brightening ahead of her, opening to sky and nothing else.

The sea, when it finally revealed itself to her, was everything that Ren had told her it would be. It went on forever and forever again, and Alys couldn't believe that anything real could be so vast. This wasn't at all like the hideous empty hole. This was full and teeming and Alys felt thrilled by it. She gasped with pleasure, everything else forgotten for a moment. She went straight to the edge, looked down, amazed at the power of so much water. It blasted against the rocks with a whomp and blew up into frothy whiteness. It was beautiful and terrifying.

No wonder Ren had wanted to see it so badly.

Benedicta crouched on the path ahead of her, scowling. "I thought you were in a hurry," she said.

Looking out at the water, an endless expanse that she hadn't even known existed until not so long ago, Alys felt a deep tremble in her chest, then a sudden lightening, as if something heavy had dropped from her shoulders, something she hadn't even been entirely aware she was carrying. She still had no plan for how she could fulfill her promises without destroying herself in the process. But Delwyn's visit last night had given her a thin branch to cling to, the hope that she might not be doomed. She might have some chance to save herself while also saving everyone else. If Delwyn could overcome his fear of the hole and surrender to it, perhaps Alys could convince Angelica and Benedicta to do the same. Perhaps there was still a child hidden within each of them, as there had been in Delwyn.

She climbed on along the cliff edge, behind Benedicta, the sea always beneath them. By the time Benedicta stopped and pointed to a tree shaped like a great ladder, the sky was darkening and weak rays of golden light filtered through the few cracks in the clouds. The tree stood tall and straight and alone, and its branches on both sides were evenly spaced as if intended to be footholds. In the tree, balanced among the branches forty feet above her head, was a shelter that was more nest than house.

"I'll go first," Alys said to Benedicta. She didn't trust the two sisters alone together, not even for a moment.

The sea filled Alys's ears and the wind whipped the loose folds of her trousers. She began to climb, and she didn't stop, not even when the bark ripped into her hands. One hand and foot over another, she kept moving steadily upward and told herself not to rush, since one slip would be the end of her—and of everyone she loved. She looked down occasionally to see Benedicta scuttling up behind her.

Once at the top, Alys pulled herself onto a wooden platform

that supported a tiny hut made of woven branches and a thatched roof. She rose to her feet and looked down, then left and right. The coast stretched on and on. Cliffs and scrub and water. No sign of Angelica anywhere. She reached down a hand to Benedicta. Benedicta's face was cast in shadow. "Don't need your help. Liar."

Once Benedicta had reached the platform, Alys pushed open the door to the hut and they both stepped inside.

The little hut reminded Alys of someplace she'd been before, someplace she struggled to remember. Then it came to her. The shack on the mountain where The Beast had led her. This was different, and yet somehow the same. These wild girls had tried to make a home for themselves here. There were two simple beds made of leaves and moss.

Alys felt a new presence behind her, and she turned. Angelica stood in the doorway, a mirror image of Benedicta. Gone was Angelica's beauty. Could it have been only a short time ago that Alys hadn't seen under its surface? She couldn't imagine that now. Her heart thumped once, twice, so loud in her own ears that she thought Angelica must have heard it as well.

"You should have looked up, girl. That's where I perch. This is my aerie, and you are trespassing." Angelica smiled in the same twisted way that Benedicta had, but Alys felt no despair in Angelica. She was all hardness and meanness and cunning.

The room darkened as if a cloud had passed overhead, and Alys felt coldness squeeze her heart. In a flash of movement unattached to limbs, Angelica was upon Alys, face pressed in close, so close that Alys could smell the nothing on her breath.

Alys tasted the nothing like ash in her own mouth. "I knew you'd come. I've been waiting for you." She turned to look at Benedicta. "I did not expect you would bring her to me, though. Do you love me again?"

"The girl and I made a deal," Benedicta said.

Angelica examined Alys with her big black eyes, the bones in her face twitching and sniffing. Alys felt as if fingertips were spreading open her chest to see what lay inside, and she held herself tight against it. "What does this girl have that you want, Benedicta?"

Alys didn't wait for Benedicta to answer. "An end to her suffering," she said. "She doesn't want to live like you anymore."

Angelica gripped Alys by the throat with one bony hand, pulled her even closer, so close they might have kissed. "Tell me she lies, Sister. Tell me so, and I will kill her now."

"I asked you to come with me to The Beast, Sister," Benedicta said. "I begged you to, but you wouldn't. You still hunger. I do not."

Angelica released Alys, and Alys filled her lungs with air. Then Angelica stepped toward Benedicta, and the two sisters faced each other, reflections of the same dark spirit. Angelica reached for Benedicta's hands, pulled them to her heart. "You would leave me forever, Sister? You would truly leave me? All others left us, Sister. But you and I, we are always. Say it, Sister. *We are always.*"

In that moment Alys saw Angelica and Benedicta as they used to be—in flashes, in sparks, in a glow that seemed to envelop only them when they touched. They were once again

333

the girls she'd seen float through the pasture. Their shining gray owl eyes, their lovely faces framed by rivers of hair as thick and black and rich as soil.

"Come back to me," Angelica said. "We can live here in our aerie forever. Never lonely. Never cold. "

"We do not live, Angelica. Can't you see?" Benedicta pulled one of Angelica's hands from where it pressed into her heart, held it up to Angelica's eyes along with one of her own. Once again the girls had become more skeleton than flesh, and the hands that Benedicta held up for Angelica were hideous and unnatural. "See what we have done to ourselves? We have burned ourselves to ash. There is no more living for us. We are dead already."

Angelica pulled away from her, whirled on Alys. "This is your doing." Then she leapt for Alys once again, gripped her throat in her hand, squeezed and leaned in close, too close. In the suddenness of Angelica's lunge for her, Alys felt nothing but fear, and now she felt that fear inside of her being picked apart by Angelica, being sucked through her and from her. And she thought *No, no, this cannot be,* and she wouldn't let it happen.

So she replaced the fear with darkness. The darkness spread inside of her and filled her veins where blood had been. It turned the breath in her lungs to smoke. It lifted her hair at the roots and picked her toes up off the floor.

Alys spread. She widened. She looked down upon Angelica now—Angelica had been taller than Alys just a moment ago, hadn't she? But Angelica was no longer taller. She was smaller, and shrinking. Puckering and wizening before Alys's eyes. Her skeletal face contracted, her bones squeezed together. And all the while Alys herself grew big, and bigger still. She was filled with dark exhilaration. And now Alys's hand was on Angelica's throat, and Alys squeezed and she heard nothing, not even her own heartbeat anymore.

This was what she had been afraid of. And why, she asked herself, had she been afraid? Why had she resisted this . . . this wonder? This miracle of absence, this obliteration of anything resembling sadness or grief. There was nothing in Alys, and nothing to cause her pain. Nothing to fear, no longer any good or bad to choose between. No conflict or worry or sorrow. No shame. No guilt. Alys needed none of it. She needed only this moment. She needed only the darkness that filled her, that chilled away her pain. That gave her strength she'd never known she had.

Alys's eyes closed, and she gasped with pleasure. Angelica was so small now, so small. And Alys was so large.

Then Alys was falling, and tumbling, and she felt the floor beneath her and it was a shock to her, a surprise to scrape her hands against wood and to have an awareness of her own skin and flesh, and of blood pumping again in her heart and veins.

Benedicta had pushed Alys off Angelica and was lifting her sister. She held her sister, hands under her arms, and at first Angelica looked as small as a child, but ancient and faded. Then as Benedicta held her, Angelica grew larger, until she and her sister once again matched and they looked into each other's faces, hollow black eyes to hollow black eyes.

The moment Angelica had become fully herself again, her

eyes widened and she gripped Benedicta by the shoulders. Benedicta's eyes rounded in response, then her mouth flew open. Benedicta's bony hands clung to her sister—at once resisting and holding on.

Angelica was taking her sister's soul. It was seconds perhaps, moments, and Alys found herself transfixed and unable to move.

Then there was a shift, and Benedicta's grip moved to Angelica's throat. Angelica thrust herself backward, but Benedicta held on, and then it was Angelica whose mouth gaped open. And back and forth it went, the sisters lurching first one way and then another. Alys sensed something else in the room, something unseen, and it lifted the hairs on her arms. Black smoke poured from the sisters' mouths—poured from one sister only to be sucked into the other. One weakened and the other grew strong, and in the next moment the balance shifted again.

Alys wanted it to continue, and she wanted it to end. A stench filled the room, worse than any rot that Alys had ever smelled. The doorway to the aerie stood open and Alys felt an urge to rush past the sisters, to flee downward and never to look back.

Benedicta fell backward through the door, her sister pushing her all the way. It was over, Alys thought. Angelica would kill her sister, throw her into the ocean below, and then it would be just Alys and Angelica. And then it would be just Alys. Dark Alys. Because Alys would destroy Angelica. There was no more doubt in Alys's mind. It would mean Alys's own destruction, too. But hadn't that always been her destiny? Had Alys ever had a choice? No, she had been doomed that first night she met these girls. Doomed to barely live until she died.

The sisters were outlined against the sky, steel gray except for a band of light at the horizon, where the sun lit up the space between cloud and water. Benedicta lurched back, and back again. Alys could see Benedicta had given up, there was no more fight in her. And Angelica could see it, too.

Benedicta's hands fell away from her sister and she fell backward and backward.

Just as Benedicta was about to tumble off the platform, Angelica rushed forward and caught her in her arms. Benedicta looked up at her sister in surprise. "Sister," Benedicta said. "Let me go. I'm so tired." Her voice was like the crackle of dry leaves.

The look that passed over Angelica's skeleton face was no longer black rage. It was pity. And then it was surrender.

The sisters held each other, no space between them, hair mingling, arms and legs tangled, their lips nearly touching, and then they each breathed the other in—and out.

Black smoke curled from their lips, rolling and swirling upward from them, rising in a cloud over them and then spreading out and out. The more smoke that curled out of them, the more the sisters shrank and grayed.

They were turning to ash in front of Alys's eyes. The ocean wind wrapped around them and lifted them in layers. Hair and skin became wind, and then in one last swirl of leaf and twig and dust, Angelica and Benedicta were gone.

THIRTY-SEVEN

Alys stayed in the aerie that night. It was too dark to climb down, and she had no desire to. She needed to bed down in the shelter that Angelica and Benedicta had made for themselves—this nest that held them close in a world where they didn't belong. Alys gathered moss and leaves around her, breathed in the scent of soil. Surrounded by earth and water, held up by a tree, she closed her eyes and went to sleep.

The next morning, she awoke to a pink sky and a specific hunger for food. She longed for oatcake, for the wrapped cheese and apple that were tucked away in the pack she'd left at the foot of Angelica's tree. Mother would have said this was a good sign of health, to want to eat. *Mother.* Alys felt tears form in the corners of her eyes. Thinking of Mother made Alys long for home.

Where was home now? There was no question. Home was

with Cian. Home was with Pawl and Beti, and with all the children of Gwenith. And she knew home was waiting for her.

Alys climbed down from the aerie and retraced her steps along the cliff. The sky brightened and her lungs filled with fresh, salty air. As she walked she ate an apple down to its core, savored sharp cheese and grainy oatcake, and she thought it the most delicious food she'd ever tasted. She licked her fingers, ran her tongue across her teeth. Her mouth tasted of oat, not ash. Her belly felt gloriously full.

The fullness didn't last long. By the time she'd reached Benedicta's cave, Alys was ravenous again. The hole beyond had receded. It seemed to grow smaller even as Alys stood there. At its edges, ash had once again become rock and dirt. It was still barren, but with the possibility that someday, something might grow there again. Alys sat down near the mouth of the hole and she found she no longer feared it. It had become a healing wound, not a gaping tear. She wanted to care for it, not to recoil from it. She reached into her pack and pulled out the last of her dried fruit. She tried to nibble it, to make it last, but she couldn't. It was so good. So good to eat. So good to taste, to feel.

In that moment, she was washed over with something so unfamiliar to her that at first she didn't have a word for it. Then the word came to her.

This was happiness. This was what it felt like to be happy. To be grateful for your own skin and bones. To believe you had a place in the world and you were loved completely—all parts of you, light and dark. And to love someone back—completely.

A shadow crossed the earth in front of her, and Alys looked up to the sky. The Beast flew overhead on Its broad wings. It didn't look down, but she knew It wanted Alys to see It there. That It was there for her. She wondered if she would ever see It again. She surely wanted to, but she thought perhaps she didn't need to. She'd made a nest for The Beast inside of her, in that place that was neither good, nor bad, but was simply Alys.

AND
THIS IS
WHERE
THE
STORY
ENDS.

*S*he'd told the other children of Gwenith all about it. How at first you didn't notice the sound from it, and then it was all around you. How it spread out forever and ever in front of you. But she couldn't tell them what it was like to touch it, because she had never yet done that.

Alys looked back at them all now, their laughter carrying in spurts and sparks on the sea air as it whipped and swirled off the water. Ren was holding Madog's hand and pointing at the water. "See, Dad! See? It's just like you said it would be!"

Enid put the babies down in a sandy spot well away from the water's edge and they chortled and dug in with chubby hands.

Beti clucked over the babies, told Enid and Madog to run

and enjoy the water, and she and Pawl would look after the little ones.

Alys had made Pawl promise that if he came along on this trip to the sea he'd leave the jug at home. And he'd been as good as his word. He always had been, after all. "Go on, lass!" Pawl called to her now. "Dip a toe in!" He waved and smiled at her, and she waved and smiled back.

The other children were spread out all along the ocean's edge. Some sat in the damp sand content enough to take it in with their eyes, shook their heads at going any farther. Others teasingly pushed sisters and brothers toward the waves. For the first time since Alys could remember, they really did look like children. Happy children with the world in front of them.

Alys had taken her socks and boots off, and she looked down at her feet, so white in the bright light of day. Then she looked over at Cian's brown feet, and then up into his brown eyes. "Are you ready?" Alys asked him.

"Ay, fair Alys, I've always been ready." And he had been. He'd received her with open arms the day she returned from the mountain. As if truly he'd never once stopped expecting her. As if she were the one he'd always expected. He took her hand now, and into the sea they walked.

Alys shrieked when the first cold wave lapped up to her knees, shrieked more when it came clean up to her belly, freezing the breath in her chest. But suddenly she warmed from the inside out, and then she felt it—a lift just under her feet. A moment when her feet weren't touching ground at all. She held onto Cian's hand so tight at first, and then it happened again and she was off—off her feet and in the water and she let go of Cian's hand and she looked at him.

And then she laughed.